Metamorphosis

Stephie Walls

Copyright © 2014 by Stephie Walls All rights reserved. No part of this book may be used or reproduced in any form or by any means electronic or mechanical, including photocopying, recording or any information storage and revival systems without prior written permission from the author except where permitted by law.

The characters, places, and events portrayed in this book are fictitious. Any similarity to real persons living or dead is coincidental and not intended by the author.

Contact: stephie@stephiewalls.com or www.facebook.com/stephiewalls2014

ISBN-10: 1501047167

ISBN-13: 978-1501047169

DEDICATION

To my Little Chicken

CHAPTER ONE

I am a dominant female in my every day life. I work as a CEO for Regional Bank, and I'm a no-nonsense woman, driven to succeed. I control every aspect of my life – every single one. What I hadn't figured out was why I was left feeling so empty at the end of the day. Then, the awakening came. I realized my need to be submissive in one area of my life. There is one role in which I don't want to dominate; I don't want to control. I want, no need, for someone to control me. It has been so long since I had it, I didn't remember what an essential part of me it truly is.

My heart burns for a man who can tame my attitude, who can give me one look and heat the pool between my legs, whose glance sends me to my knees in a submissive pose waiting for instructions. I desire with every fiber of my being to have a man take over, for me to trust him to care for me and nourish my soul.

Several years ago, I dated a man who pushed my limits, made me succumb to his needs. I was young and naïve. I considered the things he wanted to do to me taboo and was silently ashamed of how much I loved when he did them. I got off on his pulling my hair, spanking me, taking my ass, binding me, restraining me, but when you have lived in the heart of the Bible Belt, those aren't things people discuss, and they sure don't promote their enjoyment of them. I felt like a freak. When things ended, it left a void I have never been able to fill again, that is, until I met Dax.

Dax Cooper. He walked into my office to make a delivery, and for whatever reason the receptionist didn't stop him; instead, she pointed him directly to me. My office door is open when he lightly raps his knuckles on the wood. Glancing up, my breath catches in my throat as I struggle to acknowledge him, as he looms in the doorway in a brooding way. He exudes power and confidence standing there in his brown uniform with the little yellow logo on the pocket of his shirt, holding my package in one hand and his Diad in the other. The short sleeves of his shirt expose his tan, toned, and tatted forearms. I can see the outline of his broad chest and wonder briefly what it would be like to be caught up in his body. I am soaking in the sight of his form when my eyes reach his face. I'm met with the most haunting green eyes I have ever seen, almost a sage color that screams out in total contrast to his golden skin. His aura engulfs the room. It's intoxicating.

When I neglect to say anything, he clears his throat as the corner of his mouth turns up slightly in an arrogant grin, acknowledging he knows what I am thinking. I struggle to find words before finally spitting out, "Can I help you?"

"I'm looking for Cameron Pierce," he states in a deep tenor that rolls like waves through my body.

I stand to make my way toward him when he starts to approach me. My office is big; he stalks toward me, as if he owns the place, halting my approach. My instincts tell me to hide under my desk before this man reaches me. Instead, I round the front of it, holding out my hand to sign for the package. "I'm Cameron." The feeling of intimidation in my world is so foreign to me, but his presence is overpowering, and what's worse, he can sense it like a shark in bloody waters. Evening out the playing field is a must at this point, although I have no idea why I feel the need to set the delivery guy in his place. Straightening my spine as I finish signing my name, I look him dead in the eyes in raging bitch mode. "In the future, please have the receptionist sign for deliveries. She will get them to the appropriate person."

The son of a bitch erupts in laughter; it is a deep laugh that shakes me. I feel it through my limbs even though he isn't touching me. "Sure thing, Kitten." He shakes his head and turns away without so much as a glance back. I stand stock-still watching him stroll off wondering what the hell has just taken place.

Two days later, same scene. There is a knock on my door, and there he stands package in hand. He doesn't wait for me to respond, just waltzes in when I make eye contact with him. "Cameron Pierce." The way he says my name makes me want to strip for him and get down on my knees. I hate being called Cameron – it's formal, and the only people in my life who use it are my grandmother and the people I work with. But from his lips, it is smooth and melodic. I wonder what it would be like to hear him say my name as he came in my mouth. "Sign here please," once again pushing the Diad in my direction.

"Was I not clear about leaving packages with the receptionist earlier this week?" This man is used to women falling at his feet; you can see it in his cocky demeanor. I refuse to give him the satisfaction of knowing that I want to be one of those women.

"You were clear, Kitten. I just didn't care." He winks at me, but a smile never touches his lips, and then he leaves. Who the hell does this guy think he is and why the fuck is Julie letting him past reception? I make a mental note to ask her that very question the next time I see her. My phone rings, tearing me away from my irritation with the package delivery encounter. My day went from crazy to shit in one phone call. I am kept in meetings the rest of the day and what seems to be half of the night with board members, the CFO, and the rest of the Executive Committee due to a security breach in one of our online divisions. This type of thing is a PR nightmare, not to mention extremely costly to fix.

With all of the security issues my phone is ringing off the hook, and I am being bombarded by emails – I can't get my head above water. Sixteen-hour workdays for weeks at a time have taken a toll on my body. I had completely forgotten about my package delivery guy and never remembered to talk to Julie about allowing people beyond reception who don't have appointments, that is, until the familiar tapping on my door takes me out of my spreadsheet-induced trance. Startled, I look up to find those haunting green eyes boring holes into me. I'm sure he can sense my agitation. Hell, everyone in this office would be retreating for the hills giving me wide girth if they felt what was lingering in the air in my office.

"Sir, I'm not sure what I need to say to get through to you that packages should be left at reception." I hate being ignored, but more than that, I hate being disobeyed, and this guy doesn't give a rip-roaring rat's ass I don't want him in my office.

Completely ignoring me, he hands me the board. "Just sign for the package, Kitten," and with no further ado he is retreating out of my space.

This time I follow him, bound and determined to get Julie to understand. I am a few feet behind him when I see him stop at Julie's desk. He starts to talk to her causing me to hesitate in the hall just outside of his line of vision. Julie gives him a warm smile, but it isn't a come hither smile, it is a familiar one. "Make any headway, Dax?" She beams up at him.

"Nah, I think I'm just irritating the shit out of her."

"Are you going all Dom on her? You know that doesn't work with dominant women, right?" She chuckles at him like he is an idiot.

His face softens talking to her. "She's not dominant, Julie."

At that, Julie bursts out into a fit of roaring laughter. She's a beautiful girl with shoulder-length red hair, highlighted to perfection; she has model-like features with high cheekbones, large, wide-set blue eyes that are such a pale blue sometimes I wonder if there is really any color in them at all; and she's thin. Perfectly proportioned and dressed to kill, not only is she stunning, she's smart as a whip, to boot. She just graduated from Furman University and has been interning here for years. She's finishing the summer in the receptionist role before moving to the Marketing Department.

"I would have to disagree with you there. She's tough as nails. There's never a kink in her armor – she never makes mistakes. She controls this entire company with grace I only wish I had, and she never falters. She's one of those women who can tell you off, and you feel like you won an award when she's done."

"That doesn't make her dominant, at least not where it matters. Anyway, I thought you liked her?" His face shows signs of confusion.

"Oh, I absolutely adore her. I hope to be just like her in ten years. I'm just saying she's not going to put up with anyone's domineering bullshit, not even yours, pretty boy." He softly laughs, and the lull in the conversation greets me with an opening to address the delivery issue.

As I approach them, he straightens, losing the calm demeanor he had when he was talking to Julie. A twinge of jealousy shoots through me; he is carefree and relaxed with her but completely alpha-asshole with me. I swallow the green envy taking me over as I step to the edge of the reception desk. He takes my arrival as his cue to depart, just throwing up a hand to Julie and waving as he pushes through the glass doors.

"Julie, could you please accept the packages that come in going forward? There's no reason for them to be brought directly to me."

"Absolutely, Ms. Pierce. It won't happen again."

"Great. Thank you." I turn to walk off, but she stops me.

"Ms. Pierce?"

"Yes?"

"I know it's none of my business, but Dax Cooper's a great guy."

"I'm sure he is, but he can deliver the packages to you or the mail room." There's the no nonsense woman she was just telling Dax about. Realizing I now have a name for my harasser, I grin. It suits him. It makes me want to say his name out loud, to feel how each letter will glide off my tongue and part my lips. Without another word, I return to my office.

During the heat of the lunch hour the next day, there's a knock on my door again. I am on the phone when I look up to find him looming in front of me. My face flushes red with irritation. Julie's ass is on the line for this one. I hold up my finger indicating he should hold on, which he mistakes for an invitation to sit down in one of the chairs in front of my desk. He watches me intently as I discuss financial issues with our CFO, listening like he cares and understands what I am talking about. His green eyes soften a bit while he soaks me in.

When I finish the call, I just stare at him, baiting him to utter the first words. We sit silently for several minutes. I can play this game all day long; I didn't get where I am at thirty-five by being impatient. I wait for opportunities to present themselves, and then I pounce. I can wait hours if I need to, but this asshat is going to understand that regardless of how he wrinkles my panties, his intrusions on my day have to stop. Sitting back in my chair, I cross my legs resting my hands in my lap. I don't strike a defensive posture; I don't want to give him any thought of having an upper hand. He is on the clock. He will have to leave to go make a delivery or something. He can't outwait me – it just isn't possible. Well over fifteen minutes later, with no sound uttered from either of us, he finally breaks. I start a score tally in my head: Cam one, Dax zero.

"Cameron," his voice is firm and commanding. "We have dinner reservations tonight at seven at Sassafras. Would you like to meet me, or would you prefer I pick you up?"

I'm appalled although slightly turned on by his overconfidence, his assumption I'm available to him on his whim. As much as I would love to spend the evening getting to know the ins and outs of his body, I am not interested in a get-to-know you dinner. I don't have time for men as fixtures in my life. "As thrilling as it is to be told we have a date rather than being asked, I will politely decline."

"No, you won't. I'm not asking if you will go. I'm asking if you want to meet me there, or if you want me to pick you up. Those are your only options, Kitten." His stoic face shows no sign of emotion.

"You're serious? Does this work with all the ladies? You just stroll in their office repeatedly, unannounced after being told not to do so, and they just fall at your feet?"

"I wouldn't know – I've never had to make multiple attempts before." Holy shit, he is dead serious. This guy is blatantly telling me that he doesn't have to encourage women – they just fall for him.

"As enlightening as your past pursuits are, I'm not interested."

"I'm not going to beg. We will have dinner tonight. Since you aren't inclined to answer the question, I will tell you to meet me there. I expect you to be on time." With that he gets up and leaves. He fucking left. Just like that.

Picking up my phone, I call Julie. "Yes, ma'am?" she answers in the same professional voice I've heard for years.

"Julie, how the hell did that man get back to my office?" I am fuming, on the verge of losing my self-control, and it has never happened in the fifteen years I have been working here. Not one time.

"I'm sorry, Ms. Pierce. He wasn't delivering a package. If he had been, I would have accepted it," her voice trembles.

"Julie, come to my office please." I hang up the phone, wishing I had gotten a replacement for my Admin while she is out on maternity leave. Kathryn is a bear as a gatekeeper. No one gets through her by phone or in person. She would have Dax by his balls up against the wall until security removed him from the building, and he would have only made one visit.

Julie comes in looking at the floor thinking she is about to get reprimanded or fired. I sigh, putting my head in my hands on my desk. "Ms. Pierce?" she questions me meekly.

"Julie, first of all, straighten up and stop staring at the floor. Even if you were in trouble, which you are not, never let your fear or trepidation show outwardly. You'll be amazed at what you can get away with if people see confidence." Confusion mars her face momentarily before my words register in her head, and her body language instantly changes. This girl has the makings of a real leader; she just needs someone to mold her and show her how to bring out what's already inside.

"I'm sorry, Ms. Pierce. I shouldn't have let Dax...."

Interrupting her, "Second lesson, never apologize in the business world until someone has told you that you've made a mistake and then be damned sure it isn't a personal apology. You are not here to make people like you; you are here to do a job. You can have both after you have earned the respect of your co-workers. Finally, stop calling me Ms. Pierce. Cameron or Cam will be fine. Now, have a seat."

She complies, keeping her posture erect, confident. Smart girl. "I'm just going to be blunt because I'm too tired to pussyfoot around this situation. Who the hell is Dax Cooper?"

"Well, I've known him since I was a little girl. He's always looked out for me. He works for the package service that delivers here. He's thirty-six." She is listing details like they are items on a grocery list.

"I'm sorry, let me rephrase. Who is Dax Cooper to you?" My patience is waning. It is getting late in the afternoon, and this beast of a man is expecting me at a restaurant downtown in just a couple of hours.

She hesitates. Her eyes drop again. She takes a deep breath, looking back up at me, with tears pooling in her eyes. "He was my oldest brother Jeremy's best friend, lifelong friends. His family has lived across the street from mine before there were any kids in the picture. Our parents seemed to have kids within months of each other, all four years apart, so by the time I was born, Jeremy and Dax were twelve. Anyway, Jeremy was extremely protective of me because I'm the only girl. Dax was always nice but never paid much attention to me. He has three brothers of his own. I was the lone girl in a pool of seven boys. Our families were so tightly knit I didn't know the difference between blood brothers and the neighbors for years.

"When I was fifteen, they were twenty-seven. I went to a party I wasn't supposed to be at; I got drunk and called Jeremy to come pick me up, hoping he could get me in my house without my parents seeing me. When I called him, he was with Dax. It was late, and Dax said he would ride with Jeremy to come get me. They showed up about fifteen minutes later, both giving me the riot act about how immature I was to go to a college party, how someone could have taken advantage of me. I just rolled my eyes at them, ignoring everything they were saying. Jeremy turned to look at me in the backseat, to make sure I was paying attention. When he did, he ran a red light and a truck hit the driver's side of our car. He died at the scene. I was in really bad shape. I had been sitting behind him, and both of my legs were broken, my left arm was broken in multiple places, and I had a head wound. The pressure on my brain put me in a coma for several weeks. Dax never left my side. I've had nightmares for years as the scene replays in my head over and over.

"My parents said he was vigilant – he would shower there, people would bring him clothes, but he never left. Because he refused to leave, he lost his job. When I finally came out of it, he assumed Jeremy's role, and he's been my keeper since then. He's been delivering here for as long as I've been working here, and when I'm in school, he takes the packages to the mailroom. When I'm working, he comes up and delivers anything for our floor just to check in on me."

As Julie tells me her story, I want so badly to tell her I understand every emotion and all the sorrow she has endured. Of course, I don't, doing so I would have to allow myself to relive my own personal grief all over again. She seems to have finished her story. I just stare at her, dumbfounded that the same Dax who broods in my office and ordered me to dinner tonight is the same man Julie just described – the man who has been her protector for the last nine years.

"Cameron, he has been asking about you since I was here last summer. I promise he has a heart of gold."

"Sounds like it." I didn't have anything left to say. She took my silence as dismissal, rising from the chair and going back to her desk.

What the hell does a person do with information like Julie just gave me? I don't know this man from Adam. I had been adamant I wasn't going to meet him tonight, and now I feel like I should give him a chance. Ugh, all I want to do is go home and climb in my bed. The fact is while he is intriguing, we are too different – I can tell that just by looking at him. I don't have time for a relationship and have never been good at meaningless sex.

I glance at the clock at five minutes to seven, knowing I could still make it if I ran, but I resolve to go home and save us both from a pointless charade. I pack up my things and make my way to my car. Pulling out of the garage, I wish I had asked Julie for his phone number so I could at least tell him I wasn't going to show tonight. Instead, I justify my no show by telling myself I never agreed to go in the first place.

CHAPTER TWO

I don't see Dax on Friday. I don't know if he came to see Julie or not. In fact, I don't see him again at all. In fact, I haven't seen him at all for weeks on end. I'm edgy, on high alert, cursing myself every time I look at the door and he doesn't pass through it. I did this to myself; I discarded his advances like he wasn't worth the time of day. Trying to let go of the anxiety I feel toward missing him, I decide to go out with my girlfriends to a bar downtown. It's on a side street off Main Street running through town. Friday nights downtown are usually pretty busy, but when you close the bar down, it's fairly deserted when you leave. My friends head out when I call a cab. They all live in the vicinity while I am out in the suburbs. I told the cab driver I would meet him on Main Street, since it's easier than trying to get near the door to the little hole in the wall dive I was in, and the fresh air would aid in my sobriety.

My first mistake was not going home to change after work before I came out tonight; I am still in a skirt, blouse, and heels. My second mistake was stepping out the side door that my friends had left through that empties into the parking lot for the bar where they had parked. As soon as the door closes, I try to grab the handle to go back in and exit out the front door, but it locked behind me. My third mistake was consuming so much alcohol that I needed a cab to begin with. I feel every drink the moment my heels hit the gravel in the lot. It is pitch black outside. Not a single light shines in the dark alley.

The skin on the back of my neck prickles causing the hair to stand on end. There is someone else in the parking lot with me, but I can't see him or her. There are still a few cars in the lot. I assume they belong to the workers still inside. My heart starts to race. My sole focus becomes getting out onto the street where lights will illuminate the sidewalk. Shuddering with nervous anxiety, I stay close to the building, dragging my hand along the wall effectively blocking off a line of attack. I hear the crunch of the gravel under heavy shoes, a different sound than my own heels create. The pace of the steps picks up, and instinctively mine increase as well. I am only halfway down the wall when I feel an arm around my waist, and my ankle rolls into my heel. The hard grip catches me off guard, and then a hand slips over my mouth. I scream as loud as possible, but it is like a whisper when I try to force sound through my captor's hand.

I struggle against what I assume is a man, throwing my arms in every direction trying to make contact with my attacker, kicking wildly. My body is thrown against the wall, my head bouncing off the brick. The smell of blood permeates my nostrils as I feel it trailing down my neck. The harder I try to fight, the more energy I lose, the more light-headed I become. He keeps restraining me, binding my wrists with some fabric behind my back while he holds my mouth with his enormous hand. His other hand rips at my blouse, tearing it from my chest. Tears start to seep from my eyes. I won't let him win. I will fight with everything I have in me before I allow him to take what he is after. Pleading with him, I beg, "Please – pllleeasse, let me go." Ignoring my muffled cries he tears my bra from my chest. "Please stop. Please." My stifled pleas fall on deaf ears. He hasn't uttered a word, just continues mauling my body with his talons.

Trying to gather my wits, I remember a random Oprah segment about women's self-defense. In the segment, she said if you ever get in a situation you can't get out of, try to lure your captor in close enough to his body to plant a kiss, making him think you are giving in. He had begun to press his body against mine, fumbling with his pants. I attempt to knee him in the crotch, but his thigh blocks it. He holds me closer to the wall, eliminating any freedom I previously had, other than my neck and head. I have to steel my resolve. I sigh deeply into the palm of his hand, silently admitting defeat, and quit fighting. Still holding me tightly against the wall with the brick scraping my skin, he relaxes his grip on my mouth and pulls my skirt passed my hips before it falls to the ground leaving me standing in nothing but my thong. I lean into his shoulder, my forehead resting on his collarbone. His hands take it as an open invitation to grope my body. I am panting in fear, but he seems to think I am aroused. He allows me to nuzzle into his neck. I turn my face into him, smelling the stench that covers his skin. It is an odd, moldy smell that permeates my nose in the most nauseating way. It is a scent I will never forget. Forcing my lips to the vein pulsing in his neck, I kiss him lightly, then an open mouth kiss meets the most sour taste my tongue has ever encountered. I go for it. I open my mouth, exposing my teeth to that vein; I bite down with the intention of continuing until they came back together with a chunk of his flesh in my mouth.

I have no idea how much of his flesh I manage to rip from his neck before he screams like he is on fire. He slams my head into the wall, then his fist in my face, repeating the beating over and over like it is a mantra he is trying to instill in me. With each annihilating blow I lose a little more of my hold on consciousness. I feel his hands all over me; I hear the tear of the only fabric still covering my body; something invades my sex; then darkness consumes me.

There is a lot of yelling, sirens, and arms around me. I struggle to escape but can't get away. I fade in and out but am never coherent enough to make sense of anything going on around me. My eyes flutter open, and I am flat on my back, strapped to what I assume is a gurney in what I presume to be an ambulance. I can't move my head, and my eyes seem to be swelling shut faster than I can blink them. I feel a strong hand gripping my fingers, but I can't see the face attached to the hand. The more I try to move my hand away, the tighter the grip gets. There are tattoos covering the part of the arm attached to the hand holding mine, but there is no voice, there is no body, and there is no face. I feel utterly alone even though there are at least three people in the ambulance with me. I'm scared, and I can't hold onto consciousness.

CHAPTER THREE

I float in and out over what seems to be a short period of time. Each time I try to open my eyes; there's only a small slit that provides any visibility. My throat burns, and I feel like I'm choking. I have the worst migraine I've ever felt, and there isn't a single part of my body that doesn't seem to throb in pain. I'm not lucid. I'm having the most beautifully vivid dreams, and when I do manage to peak out of slumber, it's as if there's an angel next to me, luring me back to unconsciousness with his songs – an acoustic melody softly echoing off the walls of the room. The sound of the guitar is beautiful, and I wish I could hold onto it, hear it forever, and it become part of my spirit.

I finally manage to drag myself into a semi-coherent state, taking note of the stark white walls, the hum of the fluorescent lights above me, and the constant rising and falling of the machine breathing in time with me. I'm alone, and for the first time since my parents died, the solitude scares me. I hear the beep of the heart monitor start to quicken as my anxiety rises. I can't scream for help and can't see through my swollen eyes to find a button to call a nurse. The bathroom door flies open, and a massive form stands there. Or, is it my imagination? A nurse races in, giving me what I assume is a sedative before I can identify the form in my room. Everything darkens, and I hear murmuring voices.

The next time I wake, it's dark. There's a little overhead light behind me, but the sounds are the same. This time, however, I'm not alone. There's a bear of a hand clutching mine. When I turn my head to see whose hand is clutching mine, I get shooting pains in my head, and I whimper with the suffering. My pitiful cries wake him, but I still can't tell who he is.

"Shh, baby. Don't try to move. I'll get the nurse." There's a light kiss on top of my forehead, and though it has a familiar sound, I still can't identify the voice.

The nurse comes in, checking monitors, typing things on her iPad, before acknowledging me. "Ms. Pierce, you gave us quite a scare. Don't try to talk with the tube in your throat. I'll see what we can do to get that taken out soon. Are you in pain?"

I nod my head to communicate.

"Can you hold up your fingers to tell me from one to ten, what your pain level is?" She seems kind. Her voice is patient and warm. I show her eight fingers and point to my head. Then six and point to my arm, which I realize, is in a cast. There's a throb between my legs, and I almost motion a number for that region, but with the memories flooding my brain, I just start to cry instead. Quiet tears stream down my face pooling on my shoulder.

The mammoth of a man stands beside me the moment the waterworks start, wiping them away, caressing my cheek. I try like hell to focus on his face, to recognize him, to hold on to something familiar when the voice I've heard singing to me in my dreams softly whispers in my ear, "Don't cry, Kitten. You're safe." Fucking Dax Cooper. Oddly, I just lean into his voice, my cheek rubbing against the stubble on his face. He kisses me softly on my cheek, sitting back down next to the bed. He picks up a guitar that must have been close by and starts to play, and within minutes, he's lulled me back to sleep.

"Kitten, I need you to wake up. Come on, I know you're tired, but the doctor's here to see you and to take the tube out." I open my eyes wider than it seems I have in years, the light blinding me as I reach up to cover them with my hand. There are cords everywhere; I can't imagine how many machines are monitoring some function of my body. Once my eyes adjust to the light, everything comes into focus. Turning my head is still painful and I'm sporting a massive migraine, but the overall level of pain has definitely dropped since the last time I evaluated it.

The doctor catches my attention in his white lab coat. I just stare at him, waiting for him to speak since I can't. He smiles at me, and I think I just heard Dax growl next to me, but it could have been a machine. "Hi, Ms. Pierce, I'm Dr. Johnson. You seem to be doing much better than the night you came in." I just shrug. I don't know how I felt the night I came in. I look over to Dax for comfort, but he is giving Dr. Johnson the death glare and wringing the life out of my hand in the process. Rounding the room again with my newfound vision, the doctor starts asking about pain levels, but he is more specific in his questions. He tells me that my skull has been fractured in multiple places, hence the reason for the migraine. I rate it at a seven; then change it to a six. My arm has been broken in two spots; it is uncomfortable but not really any pain, so I hold up a one. There are bruises and lacerations all over my back and sides from the brick wall. When questioned about them, I give him a one. Three of the toes on my right foot have been broken, and I show him three fingers. Every time I try to wiggle them, the little bastards shoot pain through my leg. Dr. Johnson hesitates – it doesn't escape my attention that he has gone all around my body but skipped a large section. "Ms. Pierce, would you like us to go over the rest of your injuries privately?"

I look over at Dax; he is the only person in the room that isn't a medical professional. His eyes are swimming with kindness; I'd only seen them so soft when he looked at Julie that day at her desk. "Cameron, if you want to do this privately, I can step outside. I don't mind. Or, I can stay here and hold your hand and try to walk through the heartache with you." If I could reach up and kiss him, I would. His words are soft and sincere; he'd whispered them to me, giving me the choice. "Do you want me to wait in the hall?" I debate, and my guess is he already knows what happened. I don't know how long he's been here, but I'm pretty sure he was in the ambulance with me, how I'm not sure. This is going to be humiliating with or without him, but at least with him I won't be submerged in solitude. I shake my head no and give his hand a small squeeze. When I look back at the doctor, he resumes speaking.

"There is no delicate way to put any of this. You were brutally raped. There was an object used for penetration other than a penis, although that was used as well. There was tearing both inside and out. Your uterine wall was torn as well. There are a lot of stitches, which is the discomfort you still feel. Unfortunately, until those come out and the swelling goes down, we can't evaluate long-term damage. Hopefully, there won't be any other than a few small scars." He keeps talking, but I tune out. It appears Dax is listening intently, so I let my mind wander and block out the voices. At some point, they decide to take out the breathing tube leaving my throat feeling like there is a raging inferno burning through my esophagus. The nurse brings me water but doesn't want me to drink much at one time. She asks if I want pain medication, but I just shake my head no. I want to hold on to a few moments of lucidity, even if I am in pain. The medical posse files out of the room leaving me alone with Dax.

Looking over at him, taking in his overwhelming presence, his beautiful green eyes staring at me, waiting for me to say something. "Dax, why are you here?" My voice is hoarse and comes off harsh, which is unintended.

"I've been with you since the police found you," his voice is smooth and empathetic.

"But how?"

His eyes close slowly as if he is reliving an event he doesn't really want to talk about. "My buddy, Fisher, is on the Greenville PD. I've talked to him a lot about you, so has Julie. When they found you and got your license out of your wallet, he recognized the name, although not the beautiful woman I had spoken so fondly of. He called me." He pauses as if to collect his thoughts, "Geezus, Cameron, he scared the shit out of me. He wouldn't give me any details and just asked if you had any family he could contact. I called Julie, and she said you didn't have any that she was aware of and didn't know how to reach any of your friends. I called Fisher back, found out where you were, and once I got to you, I couldn't leave. I was in the ambulance with you, but I paid hell when we got here because I wasn't a relative. Fisher managed to use his pull to get me in, and once I had been here for a couple of days, the nurses all knew me and left me alone."

Silence fills the room. I don't know what to say to this man. I have been nothing short of a raging bitch to him and stood him up for dinner; yet, here he sits.

"How long have I been here?"

"Today makes the eighth day."

"You've never left?"

"No."

"I kept hearing a guitar and someone singing to me. I thought it was an angel. That was you wasn't it?"

"Yes."

"Why?"

"Why does anyone do anything, Cameron?"

"I don't like that."

Confused, "You don't like what?"

"You calling me Cameron."

"I'm sorry. What would you prefer?"

"No." I can see the pain in his eyes, as if he is about to face rejection after eight days of vigilant watch at my bedside. "My friends call me Cam – but from you…." I hesitate, not sure of what I am about to say. "I prefer Kitten, unless you used that with other women, in which case, you need to stop." I can't make eye contact with him, unsure of how he will take my revelation.

"Kitten is and has been reserved solely for you, Cam. I've never called anyone else Kitten. It just suited you the moment I saw you. You have this sweet look to you, but damn you have some sharp claws." He smiles as he says it, and I know he means it as a compliment. "You look really tired. Are you in pain?"

"Yeah, but I don't want to sleep, and every time they give me pain medication it knocks me out."

"You need to rest. I'll get the nurse to give you something." His voice is back to that no-nonsense alpha I had encountered in my office so many times.

In an attempt to lighten his mood, I say, "Don't go all Dom on me, Dax. I just want to be present for a little while."

He lets out a roaring laugh. "Kitten, you don't know shit about me going Dom, but you will. I'll give you this one since you've been asleep for over a week, but don't test me in the future. I won't be so lenient."

"Can I ask you a question?"

"Anything."

"How bad has this been publicized?"

"You mean what happened to you?" I just nod, dreading what he is about to tell me. "It hasn't. I mean, there were news reports about a woman being raped and beaten but no mention of your name, and baby, even if someone had gotten a picture to release to the press, you weren't recognizable when they found you."

"So no one knows where I am?"

"Well, I do. Julie does. She said she would take care of anyone at work who needed to know and field questions about your absence to anyone who didn't need to know. Your cell phone was pretty much demolished. I guess it got stomped on, so I wasn't able to call any of your friends, and I didn't know of any family to try to find."

I just nod my head. I know I need to reach out to my family, not blood related, but the only family I have. There are five of us girls who are thick as thieves, who have held me up, and me them, since my parents died, my Fishes. "I need you to call my girlfriends. They're the only family I have."

"Okay. Just tell me their names and numbers, and I'll call them." He fumbles around the room looking for a pen and piece of paper to write on. When he turns back to me, tears are streaming down my face. "No, no, no, don't cry. I'll call them. It's okay."

"I don't know any of their phone numbers," I wail. "They've all just been programmed in my phone for so long that I never have to dial them."

He is stifling laughter. "Just give me their names. I'll get Fisher to find their numbers."

"You're laughing at me," I am pouting.

"No, sweetheart, I'm not. I realize that if I lost my phone, I don't think I could even call my parents. Ahh, the age of technology. So let me have it. Give me their names, and I'll call Fisher."

"Piper Pritchard, Charlotte Barton, Sutton Leigh, and Rachel Gordon." I look up at him with hopeful eyes. I need my girls, desperately. "Dax?"

"Yeah, babe?"

"How bad do I look?"

He hesitates, undoubtedly trying to find the least painful words he can. "Umm. Cam, that's kind of an unfair question."

"You said when they found me my face was unrecognizable. Is it still?"

"No, most of the swelling is gone, and the bruises have turned yellowish green. There are a lot of scratches on your face, but they're healing. Your lip was busted open pretty badly, but they sewed it back together. Geez, Cam. You're still fucking beautiful. Do you want a mirror?"

I just nod. He starts looking around the room for one, but other than the one in the bathroom there doesn't seem to be one present. "I'll be right back," he says as he turns out of the room. When he comes back, he says a nurse will bring one up from the maternity ward. As promised, a few minutes later, a huge mirror on wheels strolls through the door. "Kitten, what you look like isn't important. The fact that you're alive is."

He gives me fair warning, but I am not prepared for what I see. My head is enormous, my face sickly shades of green, blue, and yellow. My eye sockets are almost hollow looking, lip busted and swollen covered in stitches, more bruising around my neck and ears. Everywhere I look, there is something wrong, out of place, not the right color. Tears fill my eyes. Dax anticipates my reaction and moves in front of the mirror to block my view. He crouches down in front of me as I sit on the side of the bed. He takes both hands and gently kisses the side of my mouth. When I close my eyes, the tears escape.

"Baby, you're going to look good as new in no time. You're still just as beautiful as you were the day you stood me up." He winks at me eliciting a small grin. I have no idea why he's here or why he's been here. I have no idea why I want him to stay. He feels safe. I feel protected. Tilting his head, he rests his forehead on mine, searching my eyes, for what I don't know. A smile graces his full lips, and he kisses me on the nose.

"I'm sorry, Dax."

"For what?"

"For standing you up that night for dinner, for your spending eight days in this crappy place, for putting you in a position that makes you feel like you need to protect me, for being such a bitch when you came to my office." I can't fathom why he has stayed with me after I dismissed him. He makes me want to tear down the walls I've spent years erecting, yet I know if I let him in, he will have the power to destroy me when he leaves.

"All those things make you endearing, although you will be punished for the dinner incident. I'm going to go call Fisher. Do you want your friends to come see you?" I nod, getting a grin in return.

He returns a few minutes later saying Fisher actually knows Rachel. Figures. She knows everyone in town and has dated most of the men our age. He has her number, so he is going to call her and get her to contact everyone else. Dax doesn't seem to find this odd in the least, so I just went with it. His phone rings about five minutes later. Apparently, it hasn't taken Fisher long to reach Rachel, and my girls are frantic. It makes me smile, not that they are upset, but that they love me enough to be worried.

CHAPTER FOUR

Thirty minutes later, I hear my tribe clicking down the hall toward my room. Dax looks at me, and I laugh. I can see he is trying to decide whether or not to make a break for it. Rachel, she's the loud one in our group, leads the pack. As soon as she walks in the door and catches sight of me, ignoring the huge Dax in our midst, her face goes flat. "Jesus Christ, Cameron Pierce! What the hell happened to you?!"

"Fucking A, Rachel. How about some tact!" Piper, our mother hen, pops up. She is the oldest in the group, although only by a couple of years. I envy her. Everything about her screams perfection, but she's completely immune to it.

"Would you two shut up? Check out the man candy. Who the hell is this, Cam?" Charlotte, better known to us as Charlie, is as lesbian as the day is long, but she appreciates the male form. All four girls turn to Dax, who stands at his acknowledgement.

"Dax Cooper," he says introducing himself to my friends. The only one who hasn't spoken is Sutton. She never takes her eyes off Dax. She's the protective one in the group, and when I say protective, she will take down anyone, male or female, who threatens the happiness of any one of us. She is seriously loyal and the best friend anyone could ask for. I watch her taking in Dax – sizing him up, not just his appearance but his purpose, his intent. She will not let him into the fold easily.

"Sutton," I warn, breaking the intensity that has filled the room, "back down." Dax looks over at me steering all attention in my direction.

"Girls, this is Dax. Remember the delivery guy I told you about who's friends with Julie?"

Rachel, always the imminent flirt, "What the hell were you thinking, Cam? He's sex on a stick. Why on Earth were you a mega bitch to this hot man?"

Dax grins; he is in his element. He's used to women fawning over him. He absorbs their attention although, surprisingly, he doesn't return it. He is polite, but his focus remains on me.

"Thank you, Captain Obvious," Piper rolls her eyes, and Rachel sticks her tongue out at her in return.

Sutton is ignoring the bullshit going on around her, and she is leaning in on her target. "Why are you here?" her glare boring holes in Dax.

He never falters. His confidence can't be shaken. "I've been with her since the police found her. If I had known any of your names, I would have gotten in touch with you sooner."

I could see the storm brewing in Sutton's eyes. She isn't mad at Dax per se; she is scared. Her fear manifests itself in anger. "Sutton…" I warn her.

"You and I are going to talk. Soon." She is threatening Dax. He just gives her a nod of his head and folds his arms across his chest.

Piper tries to rein everyone back in. "What happened, Cam? We've been worried sick. No one could reach you. You haven't been home in days, although I've been by to feed your cats every day. When we called the office, some random girl answering your line told us you were on an unexpected trip. I've called this hospital multiple times to see if you were here and was told they couldn't release patient names."

I don't have the strength to say the words. I can't tell my friends what happened. I can't tell them some random man violated me in every way imaginable. Dax lowers his frame to a crouching position next to the bed, whispering in my ear, asking me if I want him to tell them the clinical version. I just barely nod my head. I can see the shock in my friends' faces when Dax speaks for me.

"Cam was raped and beaten eight days ago. She's been in a medically induced coma until early this morning."

I can't distinguish all of the questions being thrown at Dax and the looks being tossed at me. It is utter chaos, exactly what I can't handle. I squeeze Dax's hand letting him know I am overwhelmed. "Ladies, you're going to have to…."

"We left you that night." Sutton's whisper is somehow more powerful than Dax's domineering voice. "You were waiting on a cab. We left you." She lifts her eyes from the floor to meet mine.

"Oh no, Sutton, don't do that. I told you guys to go. You didn't have anything to do with it." The room is dead silent. I didn't know what else to say; I don't blame my friends. Dax gave them the G-rated version of what took place that night, at least in terms of my injuries and what the police assumed happened based on the shape of my body. I know I will have to give a statement at some point, but no one has mentioned it, and I sure as hell am not interested in rehashing it. After about thirty minutes, my posse unwillingly leaves me with Dax so I can rest. I am surprised by how much relief I feel with their departure. They are everything to me, normally my only comforters, but for whatever reason, as a whole they are too much, exhausting. I just want to lie back and be quiet with Dax, who has proven he will just sit with me.

As I lie back against the comfort of the fluffy pillows, he sits down in the chair next to me; I turn my head to look at him and smile weakly. He reaches out to cup my face, gently stroking my cheek with his thumb.

Then lightly kissing my bruised lips, "Close your eyes, Kitten. I'll be here when you wake up." I think I am asleep before my eyes finish closing.

The next couple of days are more of the same – my friends come to visit although usually separately, not as a clan; nurses and doctors come in and out; and Dax never leaves. Julie brings him clothes; he showers in my bathroom, but only leaves the room to go get food from the cafeteria. We have spent countless hours talking about nothing; he doesn't press or even ask for information about that night. We just get to know each other, and Julie was right – he is an incredible guy. He plays his guitar and sings to me every night to lull me to sleep.

The doctor told us last night that I will be discharged this morning after I give my statement to the police. I didn't sleep worth a damn last night, the thought of reliving that night is more than I can handle. I have managed to avoid any details like the plague because I have been in a protected bubble in the hospital. I worry all night long. I toss and turn, thinking I am crying silently, until I feel the bed move. I have been facing away from Dax to make sure I don't wake him, but he seems to have a sixth sense with my needs. My body stiffens with the dip of the mattress. I feel the heat from his body, and then his arm slides gently under my head, his other across the top of me, pulling me to him. There is nothing sexual about it; it is just comfort that I settle into like a warm bath. He tucks my head into the nook of his shoulder and whispers, "I know you're scared, Kitten, but I've got you. We'll get through tomorrow morning, and then each day after that. You're not alone."

His words open the floodgates, and I sob, body-wracking shudders. I can't catch my breath, and my anxiety level is at an all time high. I relive that night mentally, and every detail seems crystal clear, like I am there again. I began to kick and scream, but Dax never wavers. He just keeps whispering to me, trying to soothe my aching soul. I finally turn into him and just let it all out while he strokes my back in reassuring motions. I fall into a deep sleep locked in his arms, which is how the nurse finds us when she comes in with the officers there to take my statement.

"Cameron, the officers are here to talk to you. Do you want us to step out for a minute so you can get dressed?" The nurse is sweet, and I just nod as Dax starts to come out of his slumber. It is the first time I have noticed what almost two weeks locked in a hospital has done to him physically. The weariness shows on his face, darkness circling his eyes. His looming presence has softened. He wipes the sleep from his eyes and runs his fingers through his hair but doesn't make a move to let me go.

He looks down at me smiling, "Good morning, baby. Do you want me to stay with you while you do this?"

I desperately want him to stay with me, never let go of me. His arms feel like a security blanket, but I also don't want him to know the details of what a stranger did to me. I don't want him to see the weakness that has overcome me. I hadn't given in to it until last night. I want him to think I am stronger than that, just as much as I want him to stay with me. My pride takes over. "I'll be okay, Dax. When we walk out of here today, I have to be able to go back to my life where I'm on my own. This is the first step toward doing that."

He scrunches his face up like I had just slapped him. "What the fuck are you talking about? What life are you going back to on your own?"

"Dax, I can't thank you enough for being here with me through all of this, but you have a job, I have a job, we both have friends and separate lives. I don't expect you to give yours up to nurse me back to reality." I get up and find the bag of clothes Sutton brought me the day before and go to the bathroom. "I'm going to shower. Will you let them in after you change clothes?"

"This conversation is not over, Cameron. You and I are going to talk when they leave." I shrug him off knowing that nothing with Dax Cooper could ever be simple and proceed to take the quickest shower I ever have.

Getting out of the shower, I realize I have nothing to dry my hair with, no styling products, no makeup, nothing but clothes. I twirl my damp, copper-colored hair into a knot on top of my head and put on the jeans and t-shirt Sutton chose. Leave it to her – she always ignores pomp and circumstance. Utilitarian should be her middle name, always going for comfort over fashion. I love that about her, but I feel naked without my armor – putting myself together in my morning routine makes me feel protected. Today, I am bare, but I guess I have been for weeks. Dax hasn't retreated and has seen me exposed to the world. I am momentarily stunned by the thought I care what Dax will think seeing me dressed so casually. Then I hear the voices in the room on the other side of the door and know I have to emerge. Taking a calming breath I open the door to the officers and Dax.

"Baby, come here. I want you to meet Fisher and his partner, Jackson." He smiles a smile that stops me in my tracks. Fisher and Jackson both turn to see what he is looking at. His friends look at me with endearing looks, like they were looking at a long-lost friend of Dax's they have always wanted to meet. My heart skips a beat before he holds his hand out to me walking in my direction. He has somehow managed to pull this together for me, knowing that his friends would put me at ease because he trusts them. My face blushes with his thoughtfulness. When he laces his arm around my waist, he turns to the other men, introducing each. I hadn't heard Jackson's name, but I knew he and Fisher were close and had been since Jeremy's death.

Fisher was the cop on the scene of that accident as well. They had formed an instant bond.

Fisher is beautiful in a rugged, manly, sort of way. He is just as tall as Dax, which I estimate to be around six foot four, with dark, almost black hair. His face is full with the sweetest brown eyes. It is obvious he works out as much as Dax does – he is broad everywhere. Jackson on the other hand is harsh – he has striking, strong features that are severe. He is a couple inches shorter than Dax and Fisher but still really, really good looking. When he opens his mouth to say hello, I soften to him. His voice is like butter, and I don't mean margarine. I mean the lush, calorie-ridden, fattening, robust butter. It fills the room and is all man but in a melt your heart kind of way. I am not going to be able to spend a lot of time around this group of men; they spell disaster for me. They're beautiful, and it would be easy to fall prey to the shield of protection they offer. I refuse to allow myself to become dependent upon anyone again.

I don't extend my hand to either, but neither seems offended. Maybe they know I don't want people touching me. I cringe every time a nurse or doctor reaches for me. I can only stand it if Dax is holding my hand, reassuring me that no one will penetrate his fortress of protection. Even with his arm clutching my waist, I can't offer the simple gesture of a handshake, so I raise my hand in a weak wave. Dax kisses me on the side of the head. "I'll wait outside." I try to give him a smile, but it falls short. He hesitates before retreating to the hall.

Fisher motions for me to sit down. In order to do so, I have to move past him and Jackson. My heart starts racing again as I move further back into the shadows, shaking my head no in response. He looks confused but doesn't argue; instead, he starts talking while Jackson is taking notes. "Cameron, do you remember anything about what happened that night?" I nod but don't respond verbally. "I know this is going to be difficult, but we can't take a statement without words. We will start with yes or no questions, okay?"

"Yes," I croak. My hands are shaking, pulse racing faster and faster with each moment I am left alone with these two men.

"Do you remember anything about that night?" he asks again.

"Yes."

"Were you at CueBalls before the incident?"

"Yes."

"The bartender said you and your friends closed the place down and you called a cab when you left around two in the morning. He said that there were four other women with you. I'm assuming that was Piper, Sutton, Charlie, and Rachel. Is that correct?"

"Yes." So far this isn't that hard. These are basic questions, but I know we will reach a point where I have to utter more than one syllable. It comes faster than I thought it would.

"What happened when you left the building?"

"I went to the bathroom after they left since I had to wait on the cab that was picking me up on Main. I went out the side door. I guess because that was the door my friends had left through. As soon as the door shut, I tried to go back in, but the door had locked behind me. It was really dark in the lot – there was no light. I walked along the wall of the building and could hear heavy footsteps in the gravel that weren't mine…." My voice trails off as I go back in my mind to recall the memory. "I tried to walk faster, but my ankle turned and he was on me. I tried to scream, but he had covered my mouth when he grabbed me. I fought with him; I swear I did." The sobs seem to belong to someone else. I can hear them, but it is as if I am listening to someone else cry. "I kicked, kneed him, elbowed him, everything I could think of, but the harder I fought, the more he punished me."

"What do you mean punished you?" Fisher asks calmly. "Can you give me details?"

"He bound my hands with something behind my back. He kept my mouth covered using it as leverage when he grabbed my hair to slam my head into the brick wall. He punched me in the face so many times, as if he were fighting with another man. He ripped off my bra and blouse. He had discarded my skirt. The only thing I still had on was my heels and my…my panties." I look at Fisher to see anger flooding his face. It frightens me, but I don't know why. He is here to help me, but I start to step backward toward the bathroom door. He steps toward me like he is going to help me, to keep me from falling, and my back hits the door, like that brick wall. My mind goes to the last thing I remember happening that night, the rip of the lace. I squeeze my eyes closed as tightly as possible as a scream rips from my throat. All of the pain from that night comes out as I shriek, "Dax!" I fall to the floor, curling into a ball, crying hysterically, shaking, repeating his name under my breath, calling to him as if he could have been my savior that night, "Dax, Dax, Dax, please help me. Please, Dax. Please help me."

Suddenly, I am off the ground surrounded by his arms, one under my knees the other around my back pushing my head into his neck. His scent is so comforting, and I don't have to open my eyes to know it is him – his smell has become part of me over the last two weeks in this room.

His voice booms, "What the fuck did you say to her, Fisher? You were supposed to be gentle. She hasn't been like this since she woke up!" His anger should make me fear him, but it calms me to know he is on the verge of kicking his friend's ass in my defense even as I continue to shake in his arms as he sits down.

Fisher comes back at him much calmer than I anticipated he would. "Dax, calm down. Your being hysterical isn't going to help. She's been through a traumatic situation, and she's not going to come out of it unscathed."

"Goddammit, Fisher, what did you say to her that triggered this?" He is just rocking me slowly in his lap on the bed, as if I can't hear them talking.

"I have to ask what happened, and she has to attempt to give us her side. I can't keep him forever without her statement. You know this. We have talked about it repeatedly over the last two weeks."

"I knew I shouldn't have left the fucking room. Fuck, Fisher...."

I interrupt him, looking at Dax, "You...you know who did this to me?"

Dax looks to Fisher as if seeking permission to tell me something he knows. Fisher nods in agreement. "The bartender was going to his car in the parking lot and found him on top of you. He ripped the guy off and started pummeling his face. He screamed for help to another worker coming out the same door. They called 9-1-1 while the bartender beat the guy enough that he wasn't going to move. The waitress who called 9-1-1 brought towels out from the bar to cover you up until the police arrived. She stayed with you until I got there. I never saw the guy who attacked you, Kitten. I still haven't seen him. He would be dead if I had reached him." There is no doubt in my mind that Dax would have killed the man with his bear hands, not just for me, but for any woman who endured what I went through. That's just the man he is.

I had calmed in his arms listening to him when Fisher asks me, "Cameron, did you try to hurt him?"

"Of course. I kicked, punched, anything I could do."

"Did you use your teeth?" He is hesitant in his question, and Dax looks thoroughly confused. It hit me like a ton of bricks.

"Oprah," I say more to myself than anyone listening.

"Excuse me?" Fisher asks.

"Yes. I used my teeth. His neck. I bit down on his neck…the left side."

"Bingo," Fisher smiles.

"What are you grinning for?" Dax asks in a pissed off alpha tone.

"She bit the shit out of him, Dax. When I say bit him, she took an enormous chunk of flesh from the left side of his neck. Like she bit down on him until her teeth met." Fisher looks toward me, "You've got fight, girl. You're gonna make it through this. Let Dax help you." He asks me a few more questions before telling me that I will need to come to the police department to identify the guy. I tell him that I never really saw his face, but Fisher assures me that it will be easy enough to pick out the guy who has a large bandage on the side of his neck. Most of his face isn't all that recognizable anyhow; the bartender did a number on him, breaking several bones in his cheeks, including his jaw. "Don't worry, Cameron. Between what you are able to tell us, your saliva around the wound connecting you via DNA, and his sperm that was recovered from you in the ER, he's not going to see freedom for a long time."

"Wait, no, Fisher, I don't want to press charges!" I become hysterical again.

"What are you talking about, Cam?" Dax, bless his heart, he just doesn't know the *me* outside of these walls.

"If I press charges, there will be a court case, and it will make the media. My reputation in the business world will be destroyed. I'll lose my job, the confidence my colleagues have in me, the respect of my employees. Absolutely not. No charges."

"You have got to be shitting me, Cameron!" Dax's voice booms in my ear.

Pulling myself out of his lap, I retreat away from the three men. "No! No charges."

Fisher steps up, but I hold my hand up telling him not to come closer. He stops moving but starts talking. "Cameron, I urge you not do to this. This man will do this to another woman."

"Cam! You. Will. Press. Charges." He enunciates each word, making them individual sentences to emphasize he isn't playing with me. This is not a request – this is a demand. Dax is going Dom on me, or so he thinks.

"No, Dax, I will not. Fisher, if there's anything else you need from me, I will get a new phone today, and you should be able to reach me at the number I gave you. Now, if you all will excuse me, I would like to get my stuff together, call my friends, and go home." Fisher and Jackson say goodbye after telling me that if they don't hear from me in twenty-four hours, they will have to release my attacker. They both walk out. Dax, however, does not.

"You are not calling your friends. They are not taking you home. You are coming home with me."

I laugh. I can't control it. I clutch my stomach, doubled over. I fall to my knees laughing until I am crying. The crying from tears turns into sobbing. The emotional roller coaster doesn't seem to want to pull back into the corral and let me off.

Once again, Dax scoops me off the floor. "This is why you are not going home." He holds me to his massive chest stroking my head, careful to avoid the land mines of injuries. When I have let all of the emotion out that I can possibly release in one sitting, he looks down at me. "You ready to get out of here?" I just nod at him. He is the only person I feel safe with right now, and I don't have the strength to argue about this.

With the discharge instructions and paperwork from the nurse on duty, Dax takes my hand and leads me out the hospital doors. The sun is blinding, but I have never seen something as beautiful in my life. The sky is a crystalline blue dotted with a few white whiffs of clouds, and the sunshine a powerful white, taunting me to look at it but forcing me to turn my eyes away from its agonizing beauty. Dax lets me enjoy the sting of the light for a moment before capturing my face in his hands, kissing me, a slow and unobtrusive kiss – just Dax being Dax. It lasts just long enough for me to realize there is an attraction for him that now frightens me, where as before, it simply irritated me.

CHAPTER FIVE

Dax lives in an old farmhouse on fifty acres of land in Fountain Inn. I didn't realize you could find this sort of solitude less than ten miles from my own house. It is nothing like I would have expected from him. Scarlett O'Hara, yes, Dax Cooper, nope. It's a huge two-story, white house, with a dream porch wrapping around the entire perimeter of the lower floor. Rocking chairs are on the porch, along with huge fans in the shapes of leaves. The landscaping in front of the house is painstakingly cared for. He has a circular driveway, and on the side closest to the house are gobs and gobs of gorgeous flowers in every color, shape, and size imaginable, their smell permeating the air in a sweet way that you can only find in the South. There is lush green grass on the other side of the driveway with a fountain in the middle of the circle. The fountain is a male angel standing in a pool of water holding the hand of a little girl in a dress. There are little brown birds flitting in the water. Dax catches me staring, taking it in. "It reminded me of Jeremy and Julie." My heart breaks for him. I turn to him, locking my arms around his waist, squeezing him, knowing the loss of his friend, his surrogate brother, would have been life altering. "It was a long time ago, baby," all he says before prying me off his mid-section to pull me inside.

The house is in perfect condition inside. Everything has been painstakingly restored to what it would have been a hundred years ago, but modernized with running water, plumbing, electricity. The house is warm and inviting. He shows me the front room where a grand piano sits on display, and there are several guitars lining the wall, but we don't stop long enough for me to ask questions. We continue the tour through the dining room, kitchen, breakfast room, formal living room, bathroom, a large family room, the laundry room, and what he refers to as the mudroom before he takes me upstairs. There are four spacious bedrooms, two of which have their own bathrooms, while two share a bathroom, and then the master bedroom. The master bedroom has a library off of it stuffed with books, a comfortable looking couch, and a desk. The master has a huge wooden bed in it, a matching dresser, two nightstands, and a tall chest of drawers. The walls are a golden color, and there is a blue plaid comforter on the bed. There is a large dark blue rug on the floor covering the majority of the hardwood in the room. It dawns on me there is no carpet in the entire house, all hardwoods. Every room is perfectly decorated in a masculine, country, but also modern, chic look – if that even exists. I love every inch of this house, but none of it, not one room, is what I would have picked out for Dax. He is obviously proud of it.

"Your house is beautiful," I say as I admire the high ceilings and what appears to be hand carved moldings.

"Thank you. It took me years to restore. Jeremy helped me with a lot of it; we had pretty much finished the downstairs when he died. Since then, I've done most everything myself. It's taken a lot longer but been worth it. I got the house for a steal and paid it off in a few years, and I forced myself to pay for all of the renovations in cash as I went along, so I don't have a mortgage payment. Jeremy thought I was crazy when I bought this place at age nineteen."

"You bought this house at nineteen?" I am incredulous. He's a delivery driver, for the love of God.

"When my grandfather passed away, he left all of the grandkids large sums of money. I paid for college and bought this house. I invested in my future." He is succinct in his answer.

I, on the other hand, now only have more questions. "Where did you go to college?"

He is making his way toward the kitchen. "Juilliard," he calls casually over his shoulder.

"You went to Juilliard? Like the Juilliard in New York?"

"Yes. Are you surprised?" I can't tell if he is playing with me or hurt by my shock.

"A little. Did you graduate?" I ask as I take a sip of the drink he hands me.

"Cameron, I'm starting to think you believe I'm an idiot. Yes, I graduated with a B.A. and a Ph.D."

Spitting my tea all over his chest, I wipe my mouth. "You graduated from Juilliard in New York, with a Ph.D.? In what?" I sound like an idiot, even to myself.

He just laughs at me. "A Doctorate in Musical Arts."

"The guitar."

"No baby, the guitar is something I play with. I went to Juilliard for piano on full scholarship. I paid for my living expenses in New York while I was there."

"So why do you deliver packages now?"

"Actually, I don't anymore." He walks off leaving me with that answer hanging in the air.

I take off after him. "What do you mean you don't deliver packages anymore?" I grab his arm to try to force him to turn around and look at me.

"It's not a big deal, Cam."

"It is to me. Tell me why," demanding answers but my tone tells him I am weak.

"I was let go. It really doesn't matter."

"Because of me?" It's rhetorical really.

"I ran out of vacation time. I took a leave of absence, but when they found out you weren't an immediate family member, the Union encouraged me to resume my route or risk being replaced by a driver who was working splits while waiting to get one. I didn't go back on the route, so I lost it."

"Why didn't you go back?" My brow furrows looking up at him in utter confusion.

"I told you I would be there. For days, I told you if you would wake up I wouldn't leave your side. I promised you I would take care of you; never let anyone else hurt you. When I make a promise, I keep it."

I am talking to myself when I mutter, "He did the same with Julie."

"What? I didn't hear you."

"Nothing. I was just thinking that you did the same thing for Julie."

"Julie's like a sister to me and has been since the day she was born. I will always look after her because that's what Jeremy did."

I let it go. I don't want to think that he thought of me like a sister and did this out of obligation. I don't have any business thinking about any kind of relationship with a man after what I have just endured.

"So why on Earth did you ever come back to Greenville after graduating from Juilliard?"

"This is my home, Cameron. My family is here. My friends are here. My entire life resides in this county. Everything I love is here. I never had any intention of staying in New York, but I wanted the best education I could get. That was at Juilliard."

"What did you do when you came home?"

"You mean after college?" I nod my head yes. "I taught music at Furman."

How could I not have known this, how could it never have come up in all the time we spent talking in the hospital?

"Will you play for me?"

"Maybe later. I need to go get the bags out of the truck. Make yourself at home." I am hurt by his rejection. For whatever reason, he made it obvious this part of his life is off limits to me. When he comes back in, I ask him which room he prefers I use. He said any of them were fine. I take my bag from him telling him I am going to take a nap and make my way to the top of the stairs to the first room on the right.

CHAPTER SIX

Stepping in, I realize this room is as masculine as Dax's, but it has a lot more personal touches to it. There are pictures of Dax at a much younger age with another guy. As I get to the end of the dresser, there is one larger picture with Dax and another guy, who must be Jeremy, because this is a picture of both families at what appears to be a backyard cookout. I even recognize a little bitty Julie being held by Jeremy with a huge smile on his face. When I open the closet door, there is lots of male activity equipment, like rollerblades, body board, water skis, life jackets, etc. I reach out to touch the life jacket, but something pulls me back. Dax's hand is securely attached to my elbow. "Don't touch it."

    I keep waiting for him to say something else, but he just picks my bag up off the bed with his free hand and escorts me out of the room by my arm like I am a child who's been caught with her hand in the cookie jar. The force in his grasp scares me, and I need to get away from him. He continues to pull me across the hall where he drops my bag on another bed. He lets me go without saying a single word, walks out of the room, closing the door behind him. I don't know what the hell I have done, but obviously I screwed up. I want to go home, home to the comfort of my things surrounding me, my bed, my music, my life. I still don't have a damn cell phone, but I had made all of my girls write down their numbers for me in case I needed them, which I had tucked neatly in my bag at the hospital. I had seen a landline in Dax's bedroom when we toured the house, so I sneak out of the room as quietly as possible to get to it. When I reach Dax's room, I hear the sound of his shower running. He can't have been in there long, so I figure it is safe to call Sutton. She is the best bet – uber protective and would die trying to kick Dax's ass if she thinks he is hurting me in anyway.

Thank God, she answers when I call. "Sutton, I don't have time to talk, get a piece of paper and listen to me."

"Geez, okay Cam. What's going on?"

"I'm at Dax's house, I have no idea where my car is, I don't have a cell phone, and I want to go home. Will you please come pick me up?"

"Yeah, sure. What's the address?"

"Fuck, I don't know Sutton."

"How the hell am I supposed to pick you up if you don't tell me where you are, Cam?"

I give her directions the best I can remember. Luckily, I've lived in this area my entire life, so I can give round about directions to just about anywhere. Sutton knows where I am talking about and says she'll be here in twenty minutes. I hang up and scurry out of his room right as the shower turns off.

The room he placed me in is on the front of the house. I told Sutton not to pull into the driveway and not to honk but that I would watch for her and would come out as soon as I saw her. She thought I was acting strange but didn't say anything. When she pulls up, I creep down the stairs and hear the TV in the family room. When I open the front door, all of a sudden I hear, "Front door ajar" in an electronic voice. Fucking hell, why hadn't I noticed that when we came in the damn house? I close the door quickly behind me and run like hell for Sutton's car.

I hear the door open behind me when I am close to the fountain. I don't have to look back to know who it is. Then I hear the hammering of his footsteps behind me, calling my name, "Cameron! Fucking wait!"

Great, Sutton is now out of the car ready to step between Dax and me. He catches me with an arm around the waist from behind, suddenly shooting me back to the night I was raped. All sense of reality escapes me, and I am in fight mode, trying to escape, when we hit the ground. It is as if I am on the ground minus my panties again, sobbing for Dax. "Dax, please help me. Dax! Please! Dax." I plead between cries. I need him, need him to stop this man from hurting me.

"Baby, I'm right here."

"Please let me go. I need Dax, please." I weep, begging my attacker to leave me alone, repeating Dax's name over and over.

"Cameron, look at me." With no acknowledgement from me, he repeats himself, in a firmer, more authoritative voice, "Cameron. Look. At. Me." I open my eyes blurred by tears, but I can see the green of his eyes. My comfort. I relax in his arms although the tears don't stop.

Then I hear Sutton, "What the hell just happened?" I don't know if she is talking to Dax or me, and since I can't answer her, I let him respond.

"She has triggers, although I don't know what caused this one. They send her back to that night."

"Geezus, has this happened before?"

"This morning with the policemen who were trying to take her statement. I don't know what happened then either because I wasn't in the room, just that she did the same thing. She screamed my name, then kept repeating it like a chant that would end her nightmare."

"Cam, sweetie, you don't need to be alone. Why don't you come to my house tonight? I'll get the rest of the girls to come over." Sutton is overwhelmed and thinks she would be wise to have backup. God, even my friends don't want to deal with this shit.

"She's not leaving my house, Sutton." He stands with me still in his arms turning back toward the house.

"What the hell do you think you're doing Dax? You can't hold her hostage!" Sutton has now launched into angry, protective friend mode, having snapped out of overwhelmed like the flick of a light switch.

"I'm not holding her hostage. This is where she needs to be." He is firm in his response, and I already know he isn't going to give in to her, no matter what she says.

"She *needs* to be with people who love her, not some barbaric ass out to prove himself." She just issued a challenge, and she doesn't back down from one.

"Was she crying your name, pleading for you to save her, Sutton? No. She wasn't. She was sobbing mine, begging me. You and your friends are welcome in my home anytime, but do not come here thinking you are going to take Cam away because you *love* her." I don't say anything; I just cling to his neck as he starts walking.

"Dax! Stop this shit. She needs *us!*" Sutton is wailing and following him into the house.

He makes his way, with me in tow, to the family room, sitting down in a massive chair that encompasses both of us, before turning off the television. Sutton stands motionless in the doorway. My eyes have become so heavy I am struggling to keep them open. As if he can sense my needs, he tips his mouth to my ear, "Sleep, baby. I've got you." I allow my eyes to close promising myself I can listen to their conversation behind closed lids as he strokes my hair.

"She's my responsibility, Sutton. I'm not going to argue with you. You're upsetting her."

"I'm upsetting her? She called *me* to come pick her up! Where the hell were you when that conversation took place?" I didn't hear his response as I faded into sleep.

I wake, what I assume to be several hours later seeing darkness in the windows, with all four of my girls sitting around the family room. When I try to stretch, I am locked up tight in two huge arms that are unrelenting. Dax relaxes his clutch on me when he realizes I was trying to stretch not fight him.

"Hey, Kitten, did you sleep well?" I look at him and then around the room.

"What are you guys doing here?"

Rachel being the loud mouth pipes up first. "Apparently, Dax there went all barbaric on Sutton. She called us refusing to leave and wanting reinforcements. By the time we all got here, everyone calmed down, and you were out like the damn dead in his arms." I know she isn't done when she takes in a deep breath before continuing. "We've all agreed that this is the best place for you to be for now, Cammy." Ahh, fuck. She is using a childhood nickname to try to coddle me. "Fisher gave Dax the name of a psychiatrist, who is supposed to be the best in Greenville in dealing with sexual trauma. We think you should stay with him while you go to counseling."

"Are you guys fucking crazy? I'm not staying here! I want to go home. I want to be in my house, with my things, where life is familiar. I don't even know Dax." My choice of words are ironic since he's the person I plead for when a trigger sends me back. I feel him tense at my words knowing they hurt him.

"Sorry, Cammy. Dax made good points that we couldn't argue with. He isn't working, so he has the freedom to be with you all the time and can take you to and from appointments. He can deal with your triggers as you encounter them, and let's be honest, his voice seems to be the only thing that pulls you out of them." Piper, ever the voice of reason, she's supposed to be the mother hen of the group. I can't believe she's selling me out to Dax.

I try to pull away from him. I'm hurt. My friends don't want me. Dax sees me as a responsibility. Standing up, "I'm sorry I'm such a burden for you guys," I say looking at each of my friends, "and a responsibility to you," scorching Dax with a heated glare. Walking out of the room, I make my way upstairs to the bedroom that I have somehow been relegated to. Locking the door behind me, I throw myself on the bed. I can hear them talking in the family room through the vent.

"We knew she wouldn't take it well. Dax, you have to understand how independent she is. She hasn't relied on anyone since her parents died. She's going to want to go back to work. She's going to fight you on pressing charges. Hell, she's going to fight you on everything you try to make her do. I hope you know what you are in for because your life is about to be all kinds of complicated." Leave it to Charlie to send fair warning.

"I can handle it," is his only response.

"So help me God, Dax, if you hurt her, I will kill you. I don't mean I will be a little bitch who annoys the shit out of you. I mean I will take a forty-five to your goddamn head and blow it off." Sutton spent years in the Army, and she doesn't sugar coat shit for anyone, and if she says she will kill him, she will kill him.

I hear the front door close, and the house goes silent except for the footsteps on the stairs. Then, there is the tap on my door.

CHAPTER SEVEN

"What?" I feel childish. I had just thrown a massive hissy fit in front of my friends and a guy that I have all kinds of crazy, mixed up emotions for. I am embarrassed and just want to be left alone.

"Open the door, Kitten."

"No."

"Open the fucking door, or I will kick it in." It's amazing how threatening his words are, but his tone isn't the slightest bit intimidating.

Without a word, I stand and unlock it but don't open it. I go back to the bed stomach down burying my face in a pillow. I hear the creak of the door as it opens and feel the bed dip when he sits down next to my head, but I refuse to acknowledge him.

"When I came back from Juilliard, Jeremy moved in with me. He was my best friend, my brother. Our families are so intertwined most people don't know where one ends and the other one begins. Neither one of us dated much. He didn't want to live at home, I had the house, and he was here so much working on it, it just made sense for him to live here. When he died, I never touched a thing in his room. I left everything exactly where it was. I had the maid go through it a year or so after he died to get his clothes and donate them to Goodwill, but everything else in there is exactly as he left it ten years ago. It was the only room on this floor that was completed while we worked on the downstairs. I never stepped foot in it again. I should have explained when I found you in there, but I wasn't thinking. I told you any room because in my mind that meant any room but that one because that's Jeremy's. I'm sorry."

I don't say anything. I am heart broken for this man, who outwardly is authoritative, controlling, demanding, domineering, and completely alpha, but there are signs of his weakness, each of them pointing to Jeremy, a heartache that has never healed. The fountain, the bedroom, the things in it – they are all memories of a man he will never see again on this side of eternity.

"So, whose room is this? Are you going to throw me out of it next? Since you won't allow me to go home, I need to know what I am and am not permitted to touch and do in your home." It is a cheap, petty shot, but I take it anyway because I have lost the element of control.

"It's your room, Cam. You can do whatever you'd like to in it. If you want to decorate it, paint it, color on the walls, I don't care. But, while you are in my home, you will treat me with respect. You will not act like a child."

"Respect? Are you kidding me? You want me to respect someone who is holding me captive? Who convinced the only family I know that this is where I should be, against my will?" I am fuming mad, my face a hundred shades of red.

"It's late Cameron. I'm not going to debate respect with you. I do believe this is where you should be. This is where I can provide for you best. If you consider that being held captive, you can leave after you meet with the psychiatrist if she agrees you shouldn't be here. Your appointment is tomorrow at ten. Surely you can suffer through one night." He gets up to leave.

"Why do you feel responsible for me Dax? You didn't create this problem. You weren't even there. It's not like you failed me in some way. I didn't really even know you."

"Because you're mine, Cam." With that he closes the door behind him. I listen for his footsteps as he retreats to his bedroom. His proclamation is asinine. I don't belong to anyone and haven't since my parents' death. I want to believe I control my destiny. I don't need anyone else to claim me nor do I want it.

I change clothes, putting on the nightshirt that Sutton had brought to the hospital. I hate wearing it because it smells all kinds of medicinal, but I don't have any other options. A moment later, there is another light knock on the door, but when I open it the hallway is empty, except for the neatly folded men's t-shirt and boxers that sit on the floor. There is a note on top of them that says there is food in the kitchen if I am hungry. I'm not. I feel sick to my stomach.

I pull on the shorts and shirt which smell of Dax's woodsy scent and turn the bed down to crawl in. Lying back on the pillows, sleep takes over.

His hands are tearing my blouse; my bra is gone soon thereafter. I fight, as hard as I can I fight, but I can't escape him. When my panties tear, I see the metal pipe the man pulls out of his pocket. It has ragged edges on the ends although the pipe itself is smooth. It is cold when it hits between my legs, but the cold does nothing to dull the pain when it slices through me. I scream in agony.

"Cameron! Wake up!" I jolt to a sitting position drawing my knees to my chest in an attempt to shield my body from the onslaught. I have no idea where I am other than in the dark, not in the hospital and not in my house. "Cameron," the voice says again. I look toward the figure kneeling half on and half off the bed. Dax. "Look at me, Cam." I can see his face, but I can't see his eyes. I need to see them. Sage green.

"Light. Please. Light," He understands what I am trying to say as he reaches up and pulls the string on the ceiling fan. I grab his face in my hands staring deep into the depths of green, finding my solace there. He knows they ground me, even though I haven't told him. He never looks away. He just stares straight into my soul. I am panicked, but he takes control until he sees my shoulders visibly relax. Picking me up, he takes me down the hall to his room. Lying me down on the bed, he crawls in behind me. Pulling the covers up, he slides an arm under my neck and hooks one around my waist drawing me impossibly close to him.

"You shouldn't have been in there to begin with." I know he is referring to the bedroom, but I don't understand why.

"But you told me to use that room." I am completely muddled. He told me that was my room. I could do anything I wanted to it.

"It is yours to do what you want in it, love, but it's not where you will be sleeping any more."

"I don't understand, Dax. You're confusing the hell out of me."

He turns me over to face him. "Did I make my intensions clear in your office weeks ago when I asked you to dinner?"

"You didn't ask me. You ordered me."

"That's not my point. Did you understand my intensions?"

"That you wanted to get me in your bed? Yeah, I got that loud and clear. Oh and look, here I am. Guess that worked out for you, huh?"

"Good God, Cam. First of all, I never said I wanted you in my bed. I told you to meet me for dinner, and we would discuss the rest then. Was there any doubt in your mind what I wanted to discuss?"

"No, I figured you were looking for a fuck buddy and assumed I would be quiet about it because of my job. Hence the reason I didn't show."

He laughs. I mean, genuinely laughs, at me. My brows come together to show my disapproval. "Bullshit, you didn't show because you were afraid and unwilling to give up control, which, Kitten, you will give up. I know you heard my conversation with Julie that day at her desk. I know you heard her ask me if I had gone all Dom on you. I also know you heard me say that I didn't believe a word of what she said – you *are* submissive. So you knew my intentions on some level. You further knew I was serious regarding my intentions when I never left your side in the hospital. Did you not?"

"Yes. No. God, Dax. I don't know." I can't explain my confusion when I don't understand it myself – the attraction to him, the way he makes me question who I am, everything I have believed about myself suddenly turned upside down every time he's in my presence.

"Then let me make this clear for you. I've watched you for well over a year. I could have had any number of women during that time, but I haven't, haven't wanted to and still don't. I want you. I will have you in every sense of the word but not until you're ready. You will however sleep in my bed. You will let me hold you. You will allow me to comfort you. You will allow me to take care of you. None of those things are optional, Cam. You don't belong in another room; you belong with me, here. You don't have nightmares with me. You don't fall prey to triggers with me. You cry for me when they hit you. Subconsciously, you know you need me in the way I need you. The rest of it will come in time, but understand, in no uncertain terms – from the top of your head, to the tips of your toes – You. Belong. To. Me."

"I don't belong to anyone, Dax."

"Oh you do. You're mine. You know it, and that's what scares the shit out of you most." Tucking my head into the nook of his shoulder, he kisses the top of my head, "Good night, Kitten."

CHAPTER EIGHT

Dax wakes me in the morning having obviously been up for some time. He has fixed breakfast, which is waiting for me on the table. "Once your done eating, you need to get dressed so we can head into town for your appointment."

I just pull the covers up over my head, wishing the day away. Dax laughs, pulling them back down. "Ugh, Dax, can't we do this another day?"

"No, baby, you can't. I know you aren't looking forward to it, but it's a necessary evil."

An hour later we are in his truck, driving up I-385 toward Downtown Greenville. We pull up to an office building, parking in the garage. I follow Dax silently to the elevator up to the fifth floor. When we get to the receptionist desk, he gives the girl my name and takes a seat. He squeezes my hand, reassuring me it is going to be okay. When the door opens to the waiting room, an older woman, probably in her late sixties, calls my name. I stand looking down at Dax wondering why he is still seated. "I'll be right here," he smiles gently at me.

"You're not coming back with me?" I am dumbfounded. I need him with me. He knows I need him. He shakes his head in answer to my first question. "Why not?" I howl a little too loudly.

The lady, whose name I still didn't know, says, "Mr. Cooper, you are welcome to join us if it makes Ms. Pierce more comfortable."

He looks at me when he speaks to her, "She'll be ok. I'm out here if she needs me." He squeezes my hand again before dropping it. I want to argue, but Dax has already proven to me when he sets his mind to something there's no deterring him. I follow her back to her office, looking over my shoulder. He never looks up. It stings a little to think he can be so callous toward me.

The woman motions for me to sit anywhere I want. Just to be a smart ass, I almost sit in what is obviously her chair, but I figure the more I play nice, the faster I can get her to tell Dax I should go home and back to work.

She finally introduces herself as Dr. Wright. How apropos. "Cameron, why did you want Dax to come back with you?"

"Umm, I don't know. He's been with me since I woke up."

"Were you two close before then?" she asks.

I snort in a very unladylike fashion. "No, we weren't."

"Why is that funny?"

"When you look at Dax, what type of person do you immediately see?"

"I try not to judge a book by its cover, Cameron. People are rarely what they portray on the outside." Oh lawd, psycho babble.

"Humor me here." I roll my eyes as I say it, and her lip turns up slightly in her attempt to keep from smiling. She knows what I am getting at.

"Okay, I would say he looks like a bad boy with all of the tattoos."

"And?"

"I'm not sure what you're getting at, Cameron."

"First of all, call me Cam. Secondly, I'll just tell you what I thought when I first met him. Beyond just looking like a bad boy, a really, really good looking one, he was a delivery driver for a package company; he had an attitude a mile high; and thought he was God's gift to women. I assumed his lack of education but generous gift in the body department probably got him everything he wanted with little regard for anyone else."

"That's a lot to gather from a first meeting."

"No, that wasn't the first meeting, that was the culmination of several brief encounters where he refused to do as I asked him to with regard to packages being delivered on my floor. Anyway, the last time I saw him before the…incident…he came into my office and told me I would have dinner with him that night. He told me where to meet him and what time. He didn't ask, he didn't suggest, he told. Needless to say, I didn't show up. I figured if I stood him up he would get the hint and leave me alone at work, which presumably he did."

"I'm assuming somewhere along the way your opinion has changed?" She isn't really asking a question; she is simply leading my story to ensure I know she is still following me.

"The whole time I was in a coma, I had these beautiful, vivid dreams. They weren't really about anything that I can recall other than color. The colors changed with the music creating the most radiant kaleidoscope I had ever seen. Although I can't be sure, I think I have always dreamed in black and white prior. Maybe it was the drugs; hell, I don't know. What I do know is I had an angel with me in my subconscious – one guiding me through the cascade of hues, through the rhythm of the music, and the lyrics – wow. That voice was heavenly. That voice provided calm, serenity, a peace I've never known. When I woke up, that voice was still sitting beside my bed, tatted up both arms, the arrogance gone, the hardness normally in his eyes dissipated. What remained was this stunning man, with the softest green eyes, who had a gentle touch. One who never left my side. I still don't know the why behind that question. But he didn't. We became surprisingly close over the next several days in the hospital, but it wasn't until he took me to his house that my entire image of him was shattered."

"How so?"

"That man sitting out there is *Dr.* Dax Cooper. He graduated with honors from Julliard. He completely renovated a hundred year old farmhouse he owns out right. His best friend died ten years ago, and he checks on his friend's little sister every single day as if she were his own. He's protective, kind, and loyal. Nothing like the original package he presented to me."

"Does that bother you?"

"Do you mean does it bother me he isn't what I thought he was?" She nods in answer. "No, not at all. I'm not usually surprised by people, but he surprised me."

"Then what about it bothers you?"

"Nothing."

"Are you being honest with yourself?"

I hesitate, knowing this is going to prolong getting out of her care, but it does bother me. I might as well let a professional tell me how to fix it. "Nothing about the revelation that Dax is completely different than I assumed him to be bothers me. What bothers me is my desire for him." I swallow hard before continuing. "I was raped two weeks ago. Violently raped. How on Earth can I have feelings for a man I really didn't know prior to that? Isn't it off kilter to be drawn to a man after one has so painfully marked you? Damaged you?"

"Well, I think there is a lot tied up in those questions. I'm glad to hear you can acknowledge what happened to you. That is a huge step in the right direction. It's possible Dax has played a part in your healing process. It's also possible he is allowing you to become dependent upon him. The mind reacts to rape in very different ways for different women but almost always leaves them feeling just as you described – off kilter, marked, and damaged. Our time today is almost up, but I'd like to see you back this week. In the meantime, I'm a big believer in journaling. I want you to get a journal and start writing every day about anything that happens to you – good, bad, indifferent. If something sticks out in your day, try to think about why it stuck out to you. Bring it back with you on Thursday, and we will talk about what you wrote. We will also continue to explore your relationship with Dax and eventually your trauma."

That's it? This was painless. It doesn't seem like I told her anything, and I couldn't have been in there for an hour. I join Dax in the waiting room. He stands, taking my hand, and utters a goodbye to my shrink. "Bye, Shelly. It was good to see you."

Once we reach the elevator and I am sure no one is within earshot I ask him, "How do you know her? I thought Fisher recommended her."

"He did recommend her. I also happen to know her."

"How?"

"That's Jeremy's mom, sweetheart."

I clamp my mouth shut. This has to be some sort of conflict of interest. My God, I just told that woman how shallow my thoughts of Dax were when I met him, then how wonderful he was, while admitting that I am having racy thoughts about him two weeks after I have been raped. Fucking kill me now.

CHAPTER NINE

"Kitten, I know you don't want to talk about this, but we are quickly running out of time. Since we are downtown, it would make more sense to handle it now than to go back home and come back."

"What are you talking about?"

"I want you to go by the PD and press charges."

"No." My position on this is firm. It will destroy who I am.

"Cameron," he draws my name out like my father used to do when I was in trouble. Ugh, I hated that then and just as much now.

"No, Dax. Absolutely not. I need to go back to work, not be defending myself in public, or pushing away unwanted sympathy or accusing glances."

"Well you aren't going back to work any time soon, so you won't be defending yourself in public or shaking anything off – accusatory or sympathetic."

"I'm going back to work tomorrow. I have been out for over two weeks. I have a job to do." This is another point I won't budge on.

"I'll let you go back to work tomorrow if you press charges." He gives me a smug look.

"I'm not bargaining with you. I'm not pressing charges, and I'm still going back to work tomorrow."

"Okay, let me make a deal with you that meets both of our needs."

I sigh. He obviously didn't hear my last sentence where I said I'm not bargaining.

"I'll take you to the PD. Fisher is there and can arrange the line up. If you can go in and identify the man and not want to charge him, I'll let it go. If you can do that and come back out without breaking down, I'll drive you to work myself tomorrow morning."

"Really? That's all it takes to appease you? Just walk in, identify him, and walk back out?" This is too easy.

"Without breaking down. Yes, that's it."

"Deal."

"Don't be so quick to sell your soul, Cameron. If you break down, you press charges while we are there, and you don't go back to work until I think you're ready." His eyes have turned a steely green, his resolve showing through them. He is serious.

"Dax, you haven't met Board Room Cameron. I can put on a show for anyone. All you said I had to do was get out without breaking down. You didn't say I couldn't do it in the truck."

"Fair enough. Let the show begin." That smug smile is back on his face, but I am determined to get my way in this.

Fisher meets us at the front of the police department before taking us back to an interrogation room. He indicates that they are lining men up across the hall and I will view them through one-way glass. There is a knock on the door causing Fisher to lean back in his chair to turn the knob while he keeps shooting the shit with Dax. When the door opens, his chair hit four legs again. "They're ready. Come on, guys."

Once again, I stand, and Dax sits in his seat. "Come on, Dax."

"I'll wait here for you, Kitten. It's just right across the hall."

"You're not coming with me?"

"No. You said you could handle it."

"I didn't know you weren't going to be with me!" I am hollering at him, but his face never changes.

"I told you not to sell your soul too quickly, Cam. You didn't ask any questions, just told me you were good – that you could put on any act. If you truly don't want to press charges, you will need to be comfortable walking the streets without me because I can't be with you every second of the day. If you want to go back to work, you will have to defend yourself from eight to five while you're there. I'm not trying to be mean baby, but this is what you said you want. I need you to prove it to me."

"Fine. Once I do, I want to go home."

"That, my dear, was not part of the negotiations. Let's get past this, then we will talk about your living arrangements."

With that I walk across the hall, minus Dax, determined to get through this and back to work tomorrow. Fisher is here with me. I will be fine. He closes the door, and I sit in darkness near a pane of glass that shows an illuminated, dingy room, with measurements painted on the wall to illustrate each prisoner's height. I don't know what the man looked like. I never had enough light to see his face. I think I could identify him by smell though, but I doubt they would allow me to positively ID someone by scent. There is still no one in the light, but that pungent scent hits my nostrils with a force I don't recognize. Blackness starts to encroach my vision. I look into the light trying to keep the demons at bay. I am choking on the aroma that is permeating my nostrils, mouth, and lungs. The men file in, standing in a row, not facing me, instead with their right shoulders to me. The second from the right, I can see the damage I did to his neck, and suddenly I am there again, nuzzling into his neck, waiting for my opportunity to present itself. I start to choke on every breath I take. The air is rancid, but I can't retreat from the scene playing in my mind. As I bite down in memory, my head slams against the brick wall, and I am pleading for my life again. "Please… God, please don't hurt me. Dax, Dax, don't let him…"

"Dax!" Fisher is screaming, opening the door at the same time, "Daxxxx!"

"Dax. Dax. Please Dax. Please keep him off of me." I am still standing, but my head is beating against the glass behind me.

"Geezus, Fisher!" Dax screams. Turning his attention toward me, he pulls me from the window, grabbing my face with both hands, but I keep trying to fight him off. Kicking. Punching. Begging him to let me go. Calling for Dax to save me. "Cameron. Open your eyes." I know someone is talking to me, but I can't get to the voice. I give in to the blackness that drowns out the memory.

"Cameron. Open your eyes and look at me." Dax's controlling voice is out in full force, but I don't know why he is using it with me. "Cameron, baby, open your eyes and talk to me." I open my eyes in a dark room wondering why the hell I am lying on the floor with Dax looming over me. "It's just me. Can I pick you up?" Still marred by confusion, I simply nod. When he lifts me from the floor, Fisher's face looks like he has seen a ghost. I have no idea what happened in this room, but for a police officer, Fisher doesn't seem to be able to handle much. Dax makes his way to a plastic chair, sitting down with me in his lap. Stroking my hair, "Cam, baby, what happened?"

"What do you mean? I thought you wanted me to identify that guy."

Fisher speaks this time, presumably because Dax wasn't in the room when we started this. "Cameron, you were complaining about the stench in the room, the moment the men walked in you locked eyes on the one who hurt you and started gagging and choking, then screaming. When the screaming started, you were pounding your head against the glass wall. You begged for Dax to make it stop, pleaded for him. When I got him in the room, he tried to get you to come back from where ever you went, but you blacked out."

I look up at Dax to find an unsettled look on his beautiful face, but those grassy green eyes always comfort me. "I could smell him. As soon as they walked in the room, the odor was overwhelming, suffocating. I was choking on him. When I saw him, my mind went back to that smell, where I knew it from; it was all over his neck. I waited for him to get close enough to my mouth to bite him, the entire time, wanting to throw up from that scent. I smelled it again. It was the second guy from the end on the right." Looking back through the glass to the lighted room, I glance at the numbers, "Number six."

Dax doesn't give me a ration of shit. He doesn't say I told you so. He doesn't gloat at all. I can't be sure, but I'd be willing to bet he knew something would trigger an episode, reminding me I need to be with him. He just holds me, tracing circles on my back while my pulse returns to normal and my breathing slows. I love how he is able to calm me like this but hate it in the same regard. I've always been my own calming presence. I feel like a fish out of water at this point; my entire life seems to be up in the air. Dax is right. If I can't do *this* without going into hysteria, how will I go back to work where I'm on my own for eight plus hours a day? Pushing those thoughts aside, I decide to deal with one situation at a time. Right now, I needed to give Fisher a statement. Then I will need to contact an attorney and try to get a meeting with the Executive Committee at the bank to discuss my immediate future. My dad used to tell me that when faced with consuming an elephant, you do it one bite at a time. My statement to the police was the first bite in a multi-course meal.

Finishing up at the police department, we climb in the truck. "Hey, Dax?"

"Yeah?"

"I have a few things I need to do. Do you want to go with me or take me to get my car?"

"I'll take you. Where do you need to go?"

"I need to go by the bank to set up meeting with the Executive Committee to talk about my job. I need to call an attorney. Then I need to get a new cell phone and go to my house. Oh, and I'm supposed to get a journal to start writing about my days."

"Send the Executive Committee an email letting them know you are taking a leave of absence. I'll arrange an attorney. We can get you a new phone and a journal and then stop by your house. You're right, you need to get some of your things."

"Dax, I need to go in and talk to my colleagues."

"No, Cameron, you don't. You have been through a traumatic ordeal, and you haven't been released medically. If anything, you need to contact HR about taking a leave of absence."

"Ugh. You are so infuriating. This is my *life*. Do you get that? Do you understand how hard I worked to get where I am? This one incident could destroy everything I've accomplished until now."

"Or, it could close that door and open another. Don't make life's path such a narrow one. It's a broad road with lots of side trails; enjoy walking off the path sometimes. You'll be amazed at the beauty you might find."

I am gawking at him in utter disbelief. He sees the shock on my face at how flippantly he regards my livelihood.

"Cam, you're job doesn't define you. The public opinion of you doesn't either. What matters is how you feel about yourself and the people who love you. Your life has forever been changed in the last two weeks. I'm not downplaying the things that are important to you, but I'm trying to make you see that you are more important than those things."

He starts the truck without any further discussion. We go get a new phone, pick up a journal, which I admit I am less than interested in keeping, then to my house. I don't see the point in arguing with Dax about staying at his house because in all honesty, after last night and today, I don't want to be away from him, but I have certain stipulations. Before I get into them, I pull up my email on my laptop and compose an email to the EC at the bank, describing in as few details as possible what happened over the last two weeks, that I hadn't been cleared to return to work (although I don't think a broken arm and a few broken toes were reason to stay home from a desk job, but Dax thinks the head injury is). I ask for an undetermined leave of absence since I don't know when I will be released to work, offering to work from home, etc. I copy HR on my email to ask them to send me whatever forms are necessary to file. I cringe when I hit send, knowing that an era of my life ended with the click of the mouse. I try to put the thoughts aside because in reality it doesn't matter what their decision is; mentally I'm not ready to go back to work, and I just don't want to admit that to myself.

Dax is sitting on my bed petting Mr. Whiskers, one of my two Persians, the other being Sassy Sultenpuss, who is watching him from the corner of my desk. He looks up at me and smiles when he realizes I did what he asked me to do. The next task is determining what to bring with me.

"How long are you making me stay at your house?" I ask him in a baiting tone.

"Indefinitely."

"Dax, I'm not staying indefinitely. Be serious. How much do I need to pack?"

"I'm being serious, Kitten. I'm not putting a timeframe on it."

"I don't know why I bother talking to you sometimes," I huff at him.

"That makes two of us. Just do what you're told, and things will go a lot smoother. Are you bringing the flea bags with you?"

"If you are referring to Mr. Whiskers and Sassy Sultenpuss, then yes. I can't keep expecting my friends to come take care of them. And you will find I don't follow instructions well Mr. Cooper."

"That is not a new revelation, love. You fight even when you're wrong just for the pleasure of arguing." There is a smile in his eyes, he likes my spunk, even if it tends to drive him a little nuts. "Seriously, pack what you need for a while. I think you should bring your car with you too."

I throw my bags in my SUV and load my kitties and their supplies in the backseat after locking up my house. I proceed to follow Dax to what will be my new home for the time being. I am still not sure why I'm not fighting harder against this but I need him. I don't want to be without him around.

Arriving at his house, he takes my bags and I got the fur balls settled in. I assume he took my bags to my room but am surprised when I go up there to find they aren't there. Hollering down the stairs, "Dax, where are my bags?"

"In our room."

My heart skips a beat and swoons all at once. For years, I have wanted a man who would take charge, who would take the burden of decision making at home off my plate, not just sexually but in every way possible. A man who is strong enough to take me head on but will always have my best interest at heart. Who the hell would have thought Dax Cooper could be that man? When I get to his room, I dig through my bags until I find comfy clothes to lounge around in. I still have this stupid journaling assignment to complete and I am already tired.

I trudge down the stairs to the family room with my journal and a pen in hand to find Dax in his chair holding a hand out to me. I take it as he pulls me into his lap. I drop my stuff on the floor next to it not sure how to react to this sudden affection that hasn't been brought on by a panic attack.

CHAPTER TEN

I haven't dated in a long time, minimum three years. When I landed the promotion at Regional Bank, I dove into my work, determined no one would regret giving me the opportunity of CEO at such a young age. I have been with them since I graduated from the University of North Carolina and then completed my MBA at the University of South Carolina while working. Needless to say, I have spent over fifteen years of my life with them. Men, other than those who held clout in the banking industry, weren't on my radar – they were just a distraction. I never longed for the white picket fence or the family with a dog. My goal has always been to be successful in my career.

My head is all over the place these days. I feel like I need to be at work because that's what I'm good at. That's what I'm programmed to do. But for the first time in my life, I'm wondering what I'm missing by living and breathing the business world. I haven't been in a serious relationship in over a decade, and until now that hasn't bothered me; yet sitting here in his lap, I feel like a teenager who doesn't have a clue how to act, suddenly timid.

"Relax, Kitten." He pulls me into his chest, but I am still stiff. I can accept comfort from him when there is trauma involved or panic, but I am struggling with it on a normal basis. "What's wrong?"

"Nothing." The infamous lie from a woman.

He pulls back to look in my eyes. "Cam," he draws out my name again, warning me to be honest with him.

"I don't know, Dax. I don't know how to do this."

"Don't know how to do what?"

"Be with someone. I mean I don't even know if that's what you want. I know you said I'm yours, but what does that mean? You said I was your responsibility – that's not a ringing endorsement, more like a liability. I don't know what to do when I'm not calling the shots." I am rambling, and he is smirking at me, apparently enjoying my discomfort.

"You are my responsibility because you are mine. That is not a burden; it is a privilege. When you trust me and put your faith in me to provide for you in every way, it becomes an honor. I want all of you. I know you aren't there yet, I know you aren't ready to trust, and you aren't ready for anything physical, but I'm patient. I will wait, but once you submit there won't be any turning back from me."

"I do trust you!"

"No you don't, and you shouldn't after what you've been through."

"That's not true. You are the only person I can let near me, the only person who doesn't freak me out when touching me. I'm living in your house."

"Right now, you need a comfort I give you that no one else does, but you don't trust me, not one hundred percent – but I promise you love, you will."

"You said you want me to submit to you. Are you into that?"

"Do you mean am I into BDSM? The lifestyle?" I nod my head, almost afraid of his answer yet craving a yes, "Not the one commercialized in the last couple of years, at least not anymore. But yes, I'm very dominant and you are very submissive."

"What do you mean anymore? And why do you keep saying I'm submissive? You know I'm a control freak."

"I was into the BDSM club scene in college; it was big in New York, in the South, not so much. When I came home, I realized it wasn't the bondage, the spanking, or the toys that drew me to the lifestyle, but the need for a woman to submit to me. Submission is not about being weak, Cam. It is the ultimate position of power in this type of relationship. The submissive has all of the control. I want you to trust me to always push your boundaries but never take you further than you can go."

"So, you just mean sexually?"

"No, not just sexually, and for us I don't think that will come for a while. I want you to be free to be whoever you are outside of our home, but inside of it, inside the boundaries of our relationship, I want you to submit to me in every way – not question my judgment, to know everything I say or do will be to make you a better you."

"I'm sure I sound daft, but I really don't understand. What do you want from me? Is this a relationship of convenience? Would you expect me to call you Sir or Master?"

"When we are together sexually, yes, I would insist you call me Sir, but I don't have any desire to be your master. Surely you know how deep my feelings are for you."

"But why? You don't even know me."

"I know enough. I know I've waited a long time to meet you, to have an opportunity with you, for you to see past what you thought I was. I know you want this as much as I do, but you're afraid to give up the illusion of control. But if you're honest with yourself, it's the only area of your life you haven't had any control over."

He watches me, presumably looking for a response, but I can't give him one that won't sound lame. So instead, I get as far away from him as I can physically. Picking up my journal, I hit the couch where I proceed to stare at a blank page for what seems to be an hour when it dawns on me, this is my opportunity to write down what I'm thinking, to ask all the stupid questions I want to in order to purge myself of the feelings I'm having.

My journal has become my saving grace. Initially, I thought it would be stupid – I would never be able to write about things that happened to me during the day or my inner thoughts, but the words just seem to pour onto the page, and each time I take them with me to see Dr. Wright, she reads them with a smile. She thinks I am progressing well through my feelings about Dax, and she's proud of me for not having rushed into anything physical. Besides sleeping beside him at night, he holds me, but he has never made any sexual advances. I have been meeting with her twice a week for the last few weeks and have almost filled the entire notebook in that time.

I heard back from both HR and the EC at the bank the day after I sent the email, granting me three months leave of absence, but they didn't think I needed to be working from home but should be focused on my recovery. They also said they would field all inquiries and there would be no public acknowledgment of the incident. When I first got the email, I was distraught that they were doing so well without me, hadn't begged me to come back, or acted like the world was crumbling without my presence. But after meeting with Dr. Wright, I concede they are all right, even Dax. I'm not ready to be in a position of responsibility when I still have a hard time leaving the house without Dax by my side.

I tried to go to the grocery store to get cat food by myself the first week. I was fine until I reached for the bag on the top shelf and bumped into a man grabbing for the same bag. It sent me into a panic attack, and the store manager had to call Dax to come pick me up. I haven't tried again since then. I'm worried that my constant presence will cause Dax to retreat, needing space. He always seems to take it in stride, and he seems to feed off my need for his support. Oddly, I'm growing more and more comfortable with him and our relationship, although I would call it more of a friendship since a relationship would imply that one or both of us is admitting to growing emotions. And although mine were, I'm not admitting it, and there is zero intimate contact.

He knows I haven't even begun to scratch the surface with Dr. Wright. I've told him in a roundabout way what we have discussed in my sessions, although I certainly haven't admitted the feelings I'm harboring for him. He hasn't said the words, but I know, until I deal with the rape, he won't pursue anything beyond what we are currently doing – which consists of kisses to my forehead or hands, hugs, and holding me at night. As much as I want to try to move beyond those things, I don't want to deal with what happened. I don't want to think about it, much less process it, but I do want more from him.

Looking down at the pad in my lap, I realize that I have written down every detailed thought I was feeling for him, from worrying that I am falling in love with him to craving an intimate touch from him, knowing I was going to have to show this to Dr. Wright, I proceed to rip the pages from the journal. The noise from tearing the pages catches Dax's attention.

"What are you doing, love?"

"Nothing, just going to throw these away and start over for today." My attempt to act nonchalant is destroyed by my need to reach the trashcan at light speed. He follows behind me as I pick up my pace until I am in a full-blown run, tearing the pages into pieces as I storm the kitchen.

"Cameron!" His voice booms through the house stopping me dead in my tracks holding wads of paper.

I just stand there waiting for him to give me instructions I know I will follow, hoping they don't include handing over my tattered shreds. But sure as shit, if I think it, he senses it and calls me out on it. I hear him take the remaining steps to me, circling his arms around my waist with a reassuring squeeze. I am a step away from the trashcan, I might be able to lean into it and toss the paper. As I lean, he catches my hands, and I slump my shoulders in defeat.

"Explain," is all he says.

"Explain what?" I ask as if I am not aware of exactly what he wants.

Taking the remains of the pages in his hands, he releases me, holding them up in front of me. "This."

I could keep this going, but in the end, he will get what he wants because I will give it to him, wanting to please him. I have no idea when I became compliant, but at times like these it is a trait I don't find endearing in myself. "I just want to start over." He waits for me to continue. "I wasn't thinking about what I was writing. It was just stream of consciousness; I don't think it even makes sense. Anyway, I don't want Dr. Wright reading them. I'd rather start over."

"What were you writing about that you don't want to share it with Shelly?"

"Can't you let this go, Dax? Please?" I don't know why I bother since he never gives in to my pleading.

"Not until you tell me why you don't want her reading this, but you haven't had any issues with her reading every other word you've written."

Frustrated and verging on angry at my stupidity for reacting the way I did, I just blurt it out, "Because I don't want her to know how I feel about you!" I cringe as soon as the words leave my lips.

"How do you feel about me, Kitten?"

"Ugh…I don't know." I drop my head staring at the floor.

"You don't want me to know either?"

I just shake my head, still not making eye contact. I want to run to my room, not the room I share at night with Dax, but mine.

"I'd like to read what you wrote." His voice commands me, and there's reverence in it but utter control as well. I want to make him happy even if it makes me uncomfortable; I love to see him smile, especially if I am able to put that smile on his face.

"I'm going to my room." I leave him with the remains of my journal, silently giving him permission to try to piece them back together. I reach my room at the top of the stairs, although I spend little time in there, I have put in some personal effects, primarily pictures of my friends and some of my favorite books I can't bear to be without. My computer hangs out in there as well, but I have little need for it these days. I close the door behind me. Making myself comfortable on the bed, I drift off to sleep.

Other than the first night I came home from the hospital, this is the first time I have slept without being connected to Dax in someway. If I nap, it is usually on the couch with him while he watches TV, and I sleep in his bed at night. I have been afraid to attempt sleeping without him to ward my demons away. When I wake up, I am staring out the window, amazed that I had napped peacefully on my own. Rolling on to my back, I about jump out of my skin when I see him sitting in the chair close to the door, holding what I assume are the reassembled pieces of my journal. "How long have you been sitting there?"

"I came up as soon as I put the puzzle back together and read it. You were already asleep. I didn't want you to have any nightmares, so I kissed you on the cheek and sat down to wait."

"You read it?" My voice trembles. He now knows my most inner thoughts that I haven't shared with anyone, for fear that speaking them would make them reality, making me vulnerable.

"Wasn't that the intention when you left them with me?"

He came in here to say something, and I know I'm not going to like whatever it is. "Dax, we don't have to do this, okay? Let's just pretend you never read them and keep things the way they are."

"Are you fucking kidding me?" He leans forward with his elbows on his knees. "You want me to pretend I didn't read this?"

I just shrug my shoulders. It seems logical to me.

"Cam, baby, I can't come back from this. I don't want to. What I want is to talk to you about what we need to do to get you to a point where we can move forward together."

"Dax, you don't have to do this. You don't have to pretend you feel the same things to protect me or keep from hurting my feelings."

He stands, dropping the papers on the chair, coming to the bed. Sitting down next to me, he pulls me across his lap, stiff as a board because I don't know what is coming. He wraps his arms around me using one hand to tilt my head towards him. He watches my eyes for warning signs and proceeds cautiously, but when his lips meet mine, my eyes close. He holds one side of my face with his hand while softly invading my space. He doesn't part my lips, but the closed mouth kisses are full of emotion. When he kisses my forehead, I open my eyes, unsure of why he stopped but grateful that he has. "We need to talk about this, Cam."

"I don't want to."

"Okay, then you listen and I'll talk. I can't tell you how many times I have reread the words you wrote, memorizing them, etching them into my brain. Baby, I want all of you. I want to be buried balls-deep in you both mentally and physically. I want to taste every inch of your body. I don't want there to be a single spot I'm not intimately familiar with. I want to please you and for you to please me. I want to hold you, to share my day with you, to love you, but I need you to be whole again to do that. I know you don't want to face what happened, but you have to. I don't want my touch to ever be a trigger for you. No one has touched you intimately since then. I want to move through this slowly with someone guiding you, helping you reach the other side of it without torturing you in the process. You and I can deal with our feelings for each other, and let me assure you Cameron, I do love you, the same way you love me, and I will still love you on the other side of this. We can navigate our relationship at whatever pace you're comfortable with, but I will not touch you in any intimate way until you can honestly tell me that you have talked to Shelly about what happened that night."

I start to cry. I don't think anyone, other than my girlfriends, has told me they love me since my parents died, and while he didn't say the three little words in the magical sense, he admitted them. But if I'm being honest with myself, I don't know which will be more painful – not having him because I won't face the issue at hand or facing the issue and it destroying me.

"Sweetheart, why are you crying?"

"I can't do it, Dax. I can't talk about it. I don't want to talk about it. I don't want to think about it. I want to pretend it never happened and just be happy in my little bubble in your world."

"You can still be happy in your bubble in my world, although I must say, your world has collided with mine. Your friends might as well move in with us. Were you guys together this much before all of this?" I nod yes. We are always together. We are all single, in our thirties, with no kids. We had no reason not to be together. "This isn't something I'm going to give in on, Cam. You either talk to Dr. Wright about it and start to heal the wound, or nothing moves forward with us. Don't get me wrong – I won't let you go, but this is going to get more and more painful for both of us." He winks at me, and it dawns on me that he's as sexually frustrated as I am; he's just good at hiding it.

"Will you come with me?"

"If that'll help you get started, yes."

I call Dr. Wright and tell her what happened and ask if Dax could join our next session. She happily agrees, saying he is like one of her own.

CHAPTER ELEVEN

The next morning, he holds my hand as we walk into Dr. Wright's office, giving her a one-armed side hug as we enter. He leads me to the couch, and once again, I want her chair, the position of authority, control, but instead I let Dax lead. When we sit down, he releases my hand putting his arm around the top of the couch behind me leaving me feeling alone. When I look at him, he knows instantly what I'm craving and lets his fingers dance lazily on the back of my neck, reassuring me he is still there.

    Dr. Wright just jumps right in. "Cam, you said you want to talk about the rape today and asked that Dax join you. Can you tell me what spurred this sudden interest in pursuing this path?"

I want to look to Dax and have him answer the question, but I refuse to be that weak; I just need to get through the incident – talk about it, get it over with, and move on to a normal life, or at least try to piece together some semblance of what my life was a few months ago. "This is why I came to see you to begin with. It's time to get the show on the road. So tell me, Doc, what do you want to know?"

She goes with it, surprisingly, although I could see the questions in her eyes and don't dare look at Dax. "Okay. Let's start with what you remember about that night."

I am able to tell her the story as if it happened to someone else. Putting my mask on, the mask I have worn for years, I begin telling the events of that night like I am repeating a story of random violence. The bruises have faded. The cast has been removed from my arm. There are no longer any visible signs of my struggle. It is easy to pretend it didn't happen to me. So I give her a textbook-like recount. It is factual, but superficial. She knows it, I know it, and I'm sure Dax knows it, too.

"Cam, why are you giving such a clinical account of that night?" Dr. Wright asks.

"Most of what happened was painful. I was beaten up, but while I know it hurt, I can't recall the physical pain. It's like I'm telling you a story about something that happened to someone I knew because that's how it replays in my mind. I didn't know the extent of the damage caused by the rape until they told me in the hospital."

"Are you afraid of him?"

"No, he's in jail."

"Are you afraid of another someone like him?"

"No." It is a bold faced lie, but the mission here is to move through this as quickly as possible. Dax's fingers stop moving on my neck, and I make the mistake of looking at him. Fuck. "Yes."

"What makes you afraid of another man?"

"I'm not afraid of other men. I don't know; I haven't been around any other men. I just don't want anyone to touch me or get in my space. It makes me want to fade into the darkness to escape."

"What about Dax? He definitely seems to be in your space, and you seem fine with him touching you." I just shrug. I don't have an answer for that. I have asked myself the same question a hundred times in the last couple of months and never come up with an answer. I finally quit asking and just accepted it.

"Have you two had any type of intimate relationship since the incident?" She is as cool as a cucumber, totally professional, but I am every shade of red – I can feel the embarrassment burning my cheeks.

"No." Succinct.

"So is it intimate contact you are afraid of?"

"I don't know. There hasn't been any intimate contact with anyone else. I haven't really gone out without Dax since that first week out of the hospital. I'm fine if he's with me, but men don't approach me either, so I don't have to worry about contact."

We talk superficially about my previous relationships with men. I think Dax is shocked to hear I haven't been in a sexual relationship in three years but really haven't been in a serious relationship in longer than that. Dr. Wright thinks there is a connection between my distance from men in general prior to the incident and my distain for them now.

"Your assignment for our next visit is to take a trip to a public place where there will be men, like a grocery store, and without Dax. He can be in the parking lot, but I'd like for you to attempt to go in on your own. I want you to interact with a male, even if you just buy a pack of gum at the register from a male cashier and come right back out. When you're done, I want you to write about what you feel when you interact with a male you don't know. Dax, I would like for you to continue joining us until Cam is comfortable enough to dig into the reality of what happened."

The ride home is quiet. Dax keeps his hand on my knee but doesn't speak. When we get to his house, I am borderline angry and mentally exhausted. I want to tell Dax what utter bullshit I think all of this is, but I know it's futile. He thinks it's important, and Dr.

Wright, who I am now going to refer to as Dr. Right, agrees with him. They didn't go through this. What the hell do they know? Lots of people suppress memories and live perfectly happy lives, and I want to be that person. "Cam, come sit and talk to me."

"Dax, I don't want to talk right now."

"I didn't ask you if you wanted to." He makes his way to his chair while my mind screams at my feet for following him.

I want to sit on the couch but am quickly corrected when I am ushered backward by two strong arms pulling me down into his lap.

"Tell me why you're mad, Kitten."

I open my mouth to deny my anger when he interrupts me. "Be honest with me. I know when you're lying, and it doesn't do either of us any good."

"Neither does telling the truth," I retort bitterly.

"It may not seem like it now, but in the future you will appreciate that we can talk openly. Why are you angry?"

"I don't understand why you guys are making such a big deal out of this. I've been doing fine. I haven't had any episodes. Nothing has triggered a panic attack. I think it's stupid that she wants me to go to a grocery store alone and purposely interact with someone I don't know. You said you would protect me, Dax. Why are you making me do this?"

"Do you feel like you are really living, Cameron? Don't get me wrong; I love spending all of my time with you. I don't have to work and don't care if I do, but you enjoy work, you crave it, you fought me over it. What changed?"

"My life isn't that different, Dax, other than your being in it all the time and not working. Okay, I guess it's completely changed, but like you said, life has broad paths, why stick to the middle, why not venture out on the trails?"

"Baby, I don't care if you ever work again. You can put your house on the market tomorrow and never leave here, and I'll be a happy man, but that's not how you're geared. You're living in a bubble, as you put it, where your friends come here to your new world, and you never venture outside. I wouldn't be as worried about your interaction in public if you ever went in public without me. You don't even go out with your friends anymore."

The wall cracks. The one I had so carefully built since I woke in the hospital room. "They left me, Dax! I was there alone. If one of them, any of them had stayed, I wouldn't have been there to fend for myself. One of them could have called for help but they didn't. They left me. I'm angry with my friends, I'm afraid of men, I'm scared of the dark, I don't like musky smells, I can't stand to see a metal pipe, and I'm fucking terrified of my own damn shadow. I don't think I'll ever be able to go back to the person I was, and the sooner you see that the faster you are going to leave me!" I can't stop the choking sobs, the tears streaming down my face onto his neck, the ugly crying that leaves me hiccupping and unable to speak clearly, face puffy, eyes red.

"Kitten, why do metal pipes bother you?"

Damn it. Part of the reason I never lose my composure, don't give into emotional outbursts, is because I don't say things that I don't want known. I shrug hoping he will take it as a hysterical explosion of the mouth.

With my chin firmly in hand, he forces me to look him in the eyes. The sage green is on fire; there is rage behind them. "Why. Do. Metal. Pipes. Bother. You?"

Struggling to get free from his grasp, my entire body is wracked with emotion. Unable to control it or hold it back, I collapse into him. "Because I remember what he did to me with it," my words barely audible. I haven't admitted this to anyone. Bits and pieces are starting to come back to me, but they are jagged clips, a lot of the scene still cut out by blackness.

"Please don't push me away, Dax. Please don't leave me to deal with this on my own. The demon is stronger than I am, and I can't hold it at bay much longer." I can tell by the way he is looking at me he can see the pain and torment in my eyes. My pleading doesn't fall on deaf ears. Part of what draws me to him is his willingness to shoulder my burden allowing me to be weak.

"I'm not leaving you. I promised you we would get through this one day at a time. We will, but you have to let people help you. I'm going to call Shelly and see if she can meet with us again tomorrow." I nod. I hate to agree I needed to divulge the truth, but keeping it inside is eating me alive.

Dr. Right must either love her job or adore Dax, although I guess it's a bit of both, because she agrees to come by after her last appointment tonight. I make Dax call off my posse for the evening so I can do this. He knows I don't ever want them to know the depths of what happened that night. They have the basic details; they don't need the intimate ones, and they don't need to know how much psychological damage has been done if I can keep them from finding out. The truth is, rationally, I know it's not their fault, but I can't escape the resentment I feel, the abandonment; maybe if one of them had stayed, it wouldn't have happened.

Piper is fine. She wants us all to go out for dinner tomorrow night. I'm not keen on the idea, but Dax accepted her invitation telling her to let us know when and where. Charlie just wants Dax to give me a hug for her, ever the sweet one of the group. Rachel gives him a bunch of lip about controlling the people I see and when but concedes when he tells her that my psychiatrist is making a house call. He hasn't said it, but I'm not sure Rachel is his favorite person. Sutton refuses to talk to him, insisting on talking to me herself to make sure I am all right.

"Hey Sutt," I try to sound cheerful, but she sees through my bullshit. She always has. I don't have to say a word and the girl can tell you exactly what I'm thinking.

"Cam, you okay?"

"Not really, but I'm getting there." There is no point in lying to her. If I try, she'll show up here, and all hell will break lose until she breaks me down.

"Didn't you have a counseling appointment today?"

"I haven't been completely honest with my shrink." I am ashamed I've been hiding, but I knew Sutton would understand. When she came back stateside from Afghanistan, she had changed. It took her a long time to work through what she had seen and done.

"You know counseling is pointless if you don't give them the truth to work with, right Cam?" It is a rhetorical question. "What happened that made you need to talk to her after hours?"

"I let a detail slip to Dax, and it broke me. Admitting it out loud made it more real. He called Dr. Right."

"I know you need this, Cam. I also know you don't want to do it. I know what it feels like to always be strong and then someone break your will. I wish I was the one you were leaning on, but I understand why it's him. Don't tell him this, but I love him for being there when we weren't. He's the opposite of anything I would have ever picked for you, but when I watch the way he interacts with you, see the way he looks at you, how he can calm you, he's it, Cam. You better make his pushy ass call me tonight to let me know you're surviving."

"I'm not sure about all of that, but I will definitely make sure he calls you. Will you update everyone else after that?" I finish the sentence with a nervous laugh. Sutton knows I'm scared.

"Yep. Love you, Fish."

"Love you too, Fish!" With that I hang up to find Dax staring at me.

"Fish," he questions?

I laugh, knowing how silly it sounds to outsiders. "Yeah, Fish. We all call each other Fish. Sutton and I were always posting stuff on Facebook or saying stuff out in public and realized we called each other bitch a lot. It was kind of inappropriate in both settings, so we started to use animal names for cuss words, fish for bitch, duck for fuck, et cetera. It just kind of stuck because we called each other bitch like it was a nickname. So, now the five of us are all Fishes. It's dumb, but it's our thing."

"Women," he says shaking his head but has a huge grin on his face.

CHAPTER TWELVE

The knock on the door sends me into a dizzying array of fear. I knew Dr. Right was coming, but when she announces her arrival, it sends me straight into Dax's chest. His robust arms enfold me, hugging me tightly, reassuring me. Kissing me softly on the temple, he attempts to separate from me, but I won't let go. I am desperate to stay close to him. If there is no space between us, no one can hurt me. "Kitten, I need to answer the door." I stand firmly planted, unwilling to let go. He tries to pry me from him. When he makes no progress, he murmurs something I can't hear just before he hefts me into his arms. I quickly move my grasp from his middle to his neck, tucking myself into his frame.

Nuzzling into his neck, I whisper, "I'm sorry Dax." The doorbell rings again, but he stops and tries to look at me.

When he can't find my eyes, he speaks into my hair, lips touching my scalp. I can feel his words through the vibrations. "Don't be scared, baby. I've got you."

Somehow, I know he does. I don't know why he wants me, but I know he has me. I would do anything to make this man pleased with me, happy he chose me. Maybe someday he can even love me in my brokenness. I have never aimed to please a man, but something in Dax draws that out of me. That night changed me more than I can comprehend, or maybe it was just more than I am ready to admit.

He manages to let Dr. Right in the door, and she greets him with a warm hug, embracing me at the same time. I flinch. Her touch is not threatening, but it's invading the protection Dax offers. It bothers me. Dax motions her into the family room without ever losing his grip on me. Sitting down with me in his chair, this is the safest place I could be; yet I feel exposed.

"Cam, can you look at me?" she asks me.

I cling tighter to Dax causing him to stroke my hair. Whispering in my ear, "Baby, this is going to be tough, but you have to start somewhere."

I know he is right, but it takes every ounce of willpower I can summon to pick my head up off his shoulder to make eye contact with her.

"Dax told me on the phone you remembered some details that went beyond what you have told the police, or anyone else for that matter. Can you share those with me?"

The silence lingers in the air like a putrid smell. It is heavy, and I can taste it on my tongue. I pry myself free just in time to make it to the bathroom before my stomach empties itself. Violent retching, stomach acid burning my throat and mouth, I can't shake the stench that is *his* smell. They had followed me into the bathroom, which seems overly crowed at this point. Sobbing overtakes the purging until words are flowing from my mouth. Vivid details of an incident that never should have happened, and I never want to relive. Dax hears every word of what that man did to my body. I know there will never be a way he can love someone as abused and broken as I was left that night. What man would want a woman who had been savagely claimed by another, brutally taken against her will, treated as debris? All of my insecurities come pouring out like a champagne bottle being opened, only there is no cause for celebration, and there will be no sweet nectar to enjoy when the fountain stops.

I relive that night as if I am there again, every intense detail coming forth, but it is the anguish of not being able to escape him or stop him from violating my most precious parts that has destroyed me. He took my power, he took my choices, my ability to determine when and where I shared that gift, and he mutilated my most secret place. He took the essence of what makes me a woman and staked his claim on something never offered to him. There was nothing left of the woman that man had met in the dark parking lot. I am still here in name only – my presence has been demolished.

Dr. Right stops Dax from trying to comfort me while the verbal bile is spewing forth, but when my words cease and the tears silently run down my face, he comes to me. Leaning into a corner on the bathroom floor he pulls me into his lap. He doesn't say a word, just allows his arms to provide a temporary shelter. She joins us on the floor, attempting to make eye contact with me. I try to avoid her, but my options are limited in the position I am in.

Her eyes are filled with unexpected warmth. She isn't looking at me like I am shattered. I notice for the first time that her eyes are a golden brown, a color I can't give a name to, but beautiful. I can see years of understanding and patience in them. I see my mother in them – God how I miss her, my father too, but when a child is wounded, it's their mother's comfort they seek. She sees the longing in my eyes. "What thought just crossed your mind, Cameron?"

My eyes filled with tears again, "Your eyes remind me of my mother's. I miss her. For a moment it was as if she was with me again. Like she had come to tell me I would be okay, to try to give me strength that I don't have anymore."

"Were you close to your mom?"

I smile at her memory. She was the most beautiful person I had ever known, not just physically, but her spirit was that of an angel even when she was living. She was vivacious, caring, smart, funny – people loved her because she was so genuine. "Very," is all I can muster.

"How long ago did she pass away?" I feel for the first time that I am talking to a friend and not my shrink.

I sigh, leaning back into Dax. "Eleven years ago. I miss her every day, my dad, too."

"Did they pass away at the same time?" she questions. I nod my response – another part of my life I don't share with people. My Fish know, of course, because they were there, but other than them, I can't think of anyone in my current life who is even aware the accident ever took place. "How?" Her question is short and to the point but is uttered with the most sincere regard for my memory.

Swallowing the lump in my throat, I give the Cliffs Note version of their death. We had gone downtown for New Year's Eve. It had become a tradition once I turned twenty-one. My parents and my long-term boyfriend, Chris, did the whole formal outing at the Hyatt, where we met many of my parents' friends and our friends to ring in the coming year. We left that night sometime around one; my dad was driving with my mom next to him, and Chris and I were in the back seat. As we left town, a drunk driver hit the driver's side of our car, going around sixty miles an hour. The impact caused our car to push into another lane, and the car beside us hit the passenger door. The car was completely crushed except for the bubble of the back passenger side seat where I was sitting, completely unharmed, not even a scratch." I can hear the sadness in my own voice. I haven't talked about that night in over a decade.

Dax almost whispers, not to anyone in particular, just in acknowledgement. "They all died on impact." He isn't asking a question, he is stating the obvious. A pain he knows well, a loss he has felt, a loss Dr. Right has felt. "I didn't know, Kitten." There is nothing to say, so I shrug my shoulders. There were times after the accident when I had wished I had died with them, the three people closest to me gone in an instant. Somewhere along the way, I took the anguish I felt at their loss, the anger toward the driver who took my loved ones, and set a fire in my belly that couldn't be extinguished. I vowed to live a life that would be worthy of their deaths. I had been the one given the chance to live.

At the time, giving my all to my career had seemed the best way to honor them, to become the best I could be, to shine publicly in a way that would have made them proud. But now, all that glitter is gone, and all that's left of me is an empty shell. I wonder if Dax and Dr. Right are reliving their horror in the same moment. I see how it had changed Dax – leaving Furman, leaving music, and taking on a completely different roll. I wonder silently if that's what my mom would want me to do: to redefine myself, to make myself new and whole again. I know beyond a shadow of a doubt she would, but I don't know what that will look like.

I am emotionally exhausted by the time Dr. Right leaves. I have moved to the couch from the bathroom floor when she makes her way out. We confirm an appointment for tomorrow afternoon, and she makes sure to remind me to journal before my appointment but encourages me to sleep first. Dax lets her out, but I can hear them at the door, "Thanks for coming, Shelly."

"She's going to get through this," her determination apparent in her voice. "She's as strong as you are. She just needs to find her way back on to the path. Give her time, Dax." He must have nodded because she continued, "I know you will, son. I see a light in her; she'll come out of the darkness." Whatever he says to her is so quiet I can't make out the words, and then the door closes and the lock turns.

CHAPTER THIRTEEN

I listen for his footsteps on the hardwood floors. There are a few, but then they stop at the base of the stairs. He must have taken his shoes off – the thuds on the floor are now muted. Curled in a ball on the couch, I watch him enter the room, sans shoes and t-shirt. He's nearly too much to take in. Clothed Dax has a looming presence, but seeing the beauty of his skin and his ink on his perfectly toned chest and arms, is enough to make me lose my breath. He is a walking art form. Kneeling beside me, he kisses me on the mouth. It is claiming yet somehow asexual. When he releases my mouth, he leaves his right hand on my cheek, his thumb stroking my cheekbone, his eyes searching mine. "You're exquisite." I have no response – he has seen me at the lowest points in my life, one of the ugliest I have ever experienced, just a short time ago. Yet here he is admiring me, and the way he says those two words tells me he isn't just talking about a pretty face. He is speaking to my soul. "Come with me," he says standing with his hand reaching out to me.

I follow without question, knowing wherever he leads me is exactly where I will need to be. Holding his hand, I follow a step behind him toward the front of the house. When we walk into the front room, he turns on the lights over the piano, dimming them enough to take the glare off the instrument. He lets my hand go as he takes a seat on the bench. I stand still not wanting to interrupt the moment. I have wanted him to play for me since I got here, but anytime I have brought it up, he has lightly brushed it off. Now here he sits, his feet bare situating themselves on the pedals, lifting the lid to expose the keys. He turns to me with an extended hand inviting me to the bench beside him. I join him silently, sliding in, not wanting to crowd him. "I haven't played since Jeremy died," is all he says before his fingers pose above the keys.

The most beautiful sounds I have ever heard come from his fingertips. The melody is sad, trapping me in darkness. It starts at a slow tempo, and I watch mesmerized as his fingers move across the keys. He seems to be telling a story, maybe his life story, through the keyboard with a melody that rises and falls with the highs, the lows, the melancholy, the desires, making up his life. The melody crescendos into a fiery rage, anger billowing from the opening in the beautiful wood, turning to destruction. His fingers suddenly pound out a fury that reverberates throughout the room overtaking my body. I can feel the emotion, the vibrations, in every cell of my body. Darkness slows as if night is falling on the author of Dax's story. I can't keep sight of his hands moving across the keys, one playing the depths of hell in a lower octave while the other races through the soprano notes. Haunted by his pain, I watch in awe, feeling the chords echo through me. Looking to him, I find his eyes are closed; he is playing from memory although I'd bet my life it isn't the memory of a piece of paper with notes composed on it. It is the memory of his life. He plays a despondent gloom, leaning over me, completely overtaking the bass clef. I watch his hands rise and fall, his emotions plummeting in a race against the keys; he pounds the ivory blocks so hard I am afraid they will break. Suddenly he stops, his eyes never open, his hands hover above the keys indicating he isn't done, and there is a period of silence in his life he pays homage to. He honors it as much as he does the rage, the hurt, the distress, the melancholy. His left hand begins to caress the keys, slowly as if the veil of anguish is being lifted from his life. When his right hand joins back in, it moves, gradually capturing light, bringing life back into the darkness, abandoning hell. It is relaxing, calming, then playful.

Without opening his eyes, never missing a beat, he slides me between his legs, arms surrounding me. The meaning is not lost on me; this is the part of the story where I am brought into the fold of his life. The banter between his hands continues until I feel his head fall back and chaos breaks loose on the keys. Uncontrollable heartache fills the room. Tears run down my cheeks as that night haunts me again, but this time he is there with me, surrounding me. He plays melodies I heard in my sleep, those he used to keep me with him even while I was unconscious, luring me back to him. His composition turns into a romantic descant, one with a slightly somber tone but filled with love, unquestionable, undeniable, a heartfelt connection – a commitment to my pilgrimage as part of his own. I lean back into him knowing it will limit his ability to continue playing for me, but I need him to understand that he has touched my soul, he has reached my inner spirit, the broken one I don't believe he could want, the most delicate part of my being. He slows until he halts altogether. He knows he's found me. He wraps my broken body and my damaged spirit into his arms, lifting me by the knees. My arms circle his neck.

Silently, he carries me to his room. He stands me up beside the bed; I watch his eyes, while he slowly reaches for the hem of my shirt. I close my eyes in acceptance reaching my hands above my head. When I feel the air move from my shirt falling, his hand comes to the back of my neck pulling me to him, his forehead touching mine. I wait for him. I can feel the heat from his breath on my face, devouring the security the embrace he has on my neck provides. His other arm sweeps around my waist, pulling my body to his. He flips at the closure on my bra, and I move back enough to allow it to fall down my arms to our feet. I'm tall at five feet and nine inches, but I still have to look up to meet his eyes. I'm lost in them. The green that comforts me, grounds me, is alive and warm tonight, in a way I've never seen them. A gentle smile shapes my lips, and he returns mine further snaking his arm around my waist making me feel tiny. He hesitates, giving me time to stop his approach, his eyes watching me for any sign of retreat. Instead, I move my hand to the back of his neck pulling him into me. There's a gentle sweep of his tongue across my lips, and I part them for his entrance. His perusal is slow as he makes love to my mouth. He worships my face like it's his salvation. There is no frantic rush or passionate overtaking. It is leisurely and sensual; he makes sure I know there is no pressure. I have all the time in the world.

He steps back from me, leaving me feeling cold, my nipples puckering at the loss, my arms dropping to my sides. I watch him watching me. I don't feel self-conscious or like I am on display. I feel adored, like he can see past all of the cracks, the chips, and the damaged outer shell to a beauty beneath he knows is there, even if no one else can see it. My heart aches for him, and I know beyond a shadow of a doubt I have never loved a man like I love Dax, and I never will again. As if my thoughts call to him, he steps back putting his fingers in the waist of my jeans. "May I?" he asks.

I unbutton my jeans for him, silently answering his question. He pushes them down, and I step out. He leaves me standing in my panties. I reach for him seeing the shock in his eyes; I haven't really initiated any contact between us unless it was sobbing in his arms. He stills, letting my hands roam his sides and his chest. When I reach his jeans slung low on his trim waist, I repeat his words, "May I?" He reaches down unbuttoning his jeans, duplicating my response. My smile spreads as his pants fall to the ground leaving him standing in his boxer briefs. There is virtually nothing left to the imagination. I knew his body was perfection. I'd felt him circled around me, every hard muscle acting as my fortress, but this is different. This is sexual in a way none of our other encounters have been. His erection is straining against the cotton, and it is as big and thick and tall as the rest of him. Holy hell.

I am gawking, my mouth hanging open in obvious awe. The smile has turned into a stupid high school grin. He laughs that barrel of a laugh I haven't heard in so long maybe since that day in my office I told him to leave packages with Julie. It shakes me out of my dick-induced stupor, jolting my eyes back from his penis to his face. "You're pretty fucking impressive yourself, beautiful," he says as his eyes graze my body. He grabs me playfully, scooping me into a ball before launching us both onto his king size bed.

We bounce, but he doesn't let go. He reaches down and pulls covers up to our shoulders before settling back in. Spooning has never felt so good, so safe. I can feel his heat all over me, and his shaft is tucked neatly against my backside. All of our nooks and crannies line up perfectly. Normally, we are in this position clothed while he traces circles on my tummy or up and down my side. Tonight, his hand is flat on my chest leaving his wrist between my breasts, my head on his bicep with one leg intertwined between his. There is no way I can retreat if I wanted to, which should cause anxiety, but instead I seem to melt into him further.

His voice is soft, warm like a quilt when he speaks. "I had no idea about your parents or Chris."

"I know. Most people don't."

"You're driven to reach some unobtainable destination because of them, aren't you?"

I don't know how he does it; he reads beyond anything I ever actually say to him, as if the words I speak are thoughts that come directly from his head. I manage to turn over to face him to have this conversation. "Yeah. It was the only way I could break free from the emptiness that settled in on me after their death. If I plunged myself into so much light, the darkness couldn't find me. I worked countless hours, ever the overachiever, to avoid the pitch-black realm I left behind."

"You feel like it found you again, don't you?" His eyes search my face in the darkness.

"Yeah. I don't know how to fight to get out of it this time, Dax. I don't want to be who I was."

"Baby, we will get you out of this. If it takes the rest of our lives, you'll be free from this." He hesitates before continuing, and I wait knowing he still has something he wants to say. "What do you mean you don't want to be who you were?"

I struggled to find words to piece together my random thoughts. "I, uh, don't think I want to go back to the bank, Dax. I don't want that kind of responsibility anymore. I don't want that kind of pressure. I need to find my light in a more peaceful life this time." I shrug a little trying to emphasize I don't really know what I am saying but his face says he gets it. "I want to resign."

"Okay." That one word shows me more support than I think anyone in my life ever has. Dax doesn't care if I am the CEO of a bank or a cashier at a grocery store. He wants everyone else to see the light in me that he sees. "Do you have a plan?" I shake my head because I don't. I didn't really know I wanted to resign, to walk away from that life, until the words came out of my mouth. The thoughts have been fluttering around in my head but like everything else in my life currently, they just seem like chaos trying to find a place to land.

"I have my parents inheritance, and I've saved most of everything I've earned since they died, so I guess I don't need to make a decision tonight."

"Have you thought about selling your house?" he asks as if he is questioning what I want for dinner.

I laugh. "I need a place to live, Dax."

"Cameron" he draws out my name as if I am missing something. "You are not leaving here. Ever." Other than Dax pulling me back to reality after a trigger, I haven't heard that tone from him since he ordered me to meet him for dinner.

"That's really sweet, but you need to get back to your life. I need to get to rebuilding mine. It's been almost four months. I should be moving forward toward stability. You can't coddle me forever."

"Is that what you think I'm doing?" There is an edge to his voice that is borderline irritated.

"Isn't it?"

"Fuck no, it's not, Cameron." I hate when he calls me by my full name. Truth be known, I've never liked my name. I've always thought it is overly masculine. "When I told you that you belong to me, I meant it. Where you go, I will be and vice versa. I'm not nursing an injured bird back to health to release it. I want every part of you. I've told you this more than once. I've shown you this, and I know you see it. You're scared of it. I don't blame you, Kitten, but you aren't going anywhere. If you want to keep your house for the time being, I'm good with that, but make no bones about it – you will never live in it again. You're furry little cats will drive me insane right here, in *our* home, although I do think we should try to come up with more appropriate names for them."

"I can't stay here, Dax. I can't depend upon you. I will have to be able to hold my own again." I'm becoming belligerent.

"Out of the question. You will never be on your own again. If you run, I will come after you. You're mine to protect, to comfort, to coddle, to love."

That last word has me stumped. I am choking on it. Other than the Fisheses, no one loves me, and no one has since the night my parents and Chris died. Panic strikes full force. I try desperately to unlace myself from him as the tears pour down my face, the never-ending trail of emotion that I don't seem to be able to overcome.

"You don't think I do?" I know what he is asking but just keep squirming. It isn't in fear of him hurting me. I am sure I will do that on my own. I know that if he says those three little words, makes me believe they're true, I won't ever recover from him. "Jesus Christ, Cam. I love you – every imperfection, every smartass comment, every wound, every triumph, every scratch, scar, every curve. Every. Thing. About. You. I cherish your dark as much as I crave your light. You are it for me, baby. Ask anyone who has seen us together – they will tell you they see it. You're the only one who won't open your eyes to it." I know it. I have known it. No one does this for someone just because they have admired him or her from afar. They don't put themselves in this position for an acquaintance. They put themselves in this position for someone they are invested in, someone they love.

Grabbing my face, he kisses me with total abandon. He pours every emotion he has for me into that kiss. I silently return his admissions knowing I am broken without this man. I will flourish with him, because of him, in spite of myself. "I love you, Kitten." I kiss his lips, snuggling back down into him, allowing sleep to take over.

CHAPTER FOURTEEN

The next morning, I resign from the bank. I have no idea what I am going to do with myself, but I don't have to figure it out right now. I woke up this morning determined to start to make small changes, progress in becoming a new me. After I formally resign, I shoot Rachel an email asking her not to share my inquiry with anyone, not the Fisheses or Dax. Rachel is a real estate agent, a damn good one, probably because she is so good with people. She has a knack for selling high-end homes, and while mine doesn't really fall into that category, I ask her to get back to me about whether she would take on the listing. I get an email back from her almost instantly telling me she has been waiting for me to approach her, promising secrecy. She says she'll have it on the market by the end of the week and will bring the documents for me to sign tonight at dinner. I want to be angry she has been anticipating my decision, but the truth is she knows me really well and obviously sees the strength in my connection to Dax.

After breakfast with Dax, I sit out on the porch alone to do my journaling before my appointment this afternoon. It is the first entry that hasn't been riddled with doubt and fear, the first holding a note of hope. I can't wait to share it with Dr. Wright. (Yes, I'm back to using her name in the appropriate manner.) I feel light; almost playful. Putting the finishing touches on the entry, I go back inside to find Dax standing in the kitchen with his back to me. He eats cookies standing over the sink to catch the crumbs, which I think is delightfully cute, although I doubt I'll ever tell him. I don't have any shoes on so it's easy to walk up behind him unnoticed. I snake my hands under his shirt and around his waist, settling them on his chest while leaning up to kiss his neck. "Hey, baby," I mutter as I bite him gently. I realize I've never used a term of endearment with him and suddenly become shy.

He leans over his shoulder to kiss my forehead, doing so with a mouthful of cookies. "Eww. You left crumbs on my head!" I'm swiping them off when he turns in my arms, swallowing the mouthful of sweetness. He puts his arms over my head and around my neck squeezing me like a boa constrictor. As he loosens his grip, his hands graze my sides, causing me to giggle. I see it the instant he realizes I am ticklish. I try to escape him, but he's too strong. By the time we fall to the floor, I am laughing hysterically, the muscles in my stomach aching, his smile the brightest I have ever seen it. When he has me laid out flat on my back, he is hovering over me. He stops tickling, realizing the position we are in, even though fully clothed, is completely erotic. I feel him harden between my legs as he moves to his forearms to take the weight off me. Using each hand separately, he brushes the hair out of my eyes that had gotten tangled there during the hysteria. Our eyes meet, and I can see the love he talks about in them gazing back at me. I could stay like this forever, lost in him. Hesitantly, he leans in to me, a gentle peck on the lips, then down my jaw to my ear, his kisses become more sensual as he goes, lips slightly parted allowing his tongue to grace my skin. When he reaches my ear, my entire body breaks out in goose bumps. It stops him dead in his tracks until I put my hand to his cheek telling him with my touch it's okay. When he continues, I move my hands under his shirt to his back, tracing the muscles which move with each shift of his body. I love how he feels under my fingertips, his weight on top of me. He continues to tease my neck while reality begins to slip away. My fingers trail lower down his spine while my bent knee allows him to settle in closer. My neck is my weakness;

it turns me on in a different way than any other part of my body being touched. A man has to take time to appreciate a woman's neck, meaning he's invested in something other than getting off. As he adjusts to my movements, his mouth finds mine; his tongue parts my lips at the same time my hands find his ass. With the first plunge from him, my hands drew him into me, grinding his dick onto my center. My pussy is wet, aching for him. I am aching for him. He rolls his hips into me as his tongue dances with mine. If we weren't clothed, one minor move and he would be inside of me.

He pulls back from me, panting. My chest is heaving. I want him to be inside me like I have never wanted anything before. He sits up on his knees giving me access to his shirt, which I fully intend to remove. I want to lick every inch of ink on his stomach, memorize every cut of muscle. When I reach for the hem of his t-shirt, he grabs my wrist. It isn't aggressive; it is a warning. I can tell by the look in his eyes he is hanging on by a thread. "Kitten, we need to talk before this gets out of hand." My shoulders sink back to the ground. I must have looked like he just slapped me across the face. I have never been rejected.

He extends his hand to me, pulling me off the floor as he stands. Mortified is an understatement. Embarrassed. Humiliated. Completely disconcerted. I turn to walk away, to escape what I am facing but he refuses to let my hand go. "Cam, I'm not turning you down." I think that stings worse than hearing him say we need to talk. "Baby, please come sit with me and listen."

"Just say what you have to say, Dax." I don't handle rejection well; I haven't had a lot of experience with it in any area of my life but certainly not with a man.

"No, I won't. You will come sit, and we will talk."

"Ugh, fine. Can we make this fast? We need to leave to go to my appointment."

"Cam, drop the sassy mouth, " I clamp my lips shut. "If you don't want to talk, then you can listen. I don't enter into relationships without discussions about my lifestyle and my expectations, but before we get to those, I want you to answer a question for me."

I wait for him to ask.

"When is your follow up with your OBGYN?"

When I don't answer, knowing my response will piss him off, he repeats the question. "I didn't schedule one, Dax."

"Why not?"

"Does it matter?" My snotty attitude has returned in full force. I know it's a defense mechanism, but it's a useless one with Dax.

He just gives me a look that asks if I am for real. He already knows the answer so why ask the question. "Well?" he asks.

"I don't want to go. No girl ever wants to go see their gynecologist."

"There's more to it, and I need you to tell me what it is…even though you know I already know the answers."

"Fine, Dax. I don't want some random man touching me there, and I'm not interested in being tested for every seedy disease known to man because some asshole violated me." He is probably expecting tears, but I feel stronger today so he's getting anger instead.

"Cam, I get tested every six months, not because I'm having sex and not because I have ever had unprotected sex, because I haven't. I do it because it's the smart thing to do. I do it so that I can protect my body and myself. I want you to do it so that you can protect yourself and your body. I want you to do it for us, not because of someone else. I want to be inside of you with no barrier between us, Kitten. So instead of making this about something in the past, make it about something in your future – in our future."

So much for anger – how the hell does he do that to me? How does he take me from one end of the emotional spectrum to the other in a few measly sentences, completely changing my perspective on the issue? I don't have to look at this as a reminder of the attack; I could look at it as a promise to my future.

"Secondly, I want you to make sure that you are physically repaired. You had a ton of stitches inside, Cam. I know they dissolve, but I don't want to cause you any pain, ever, but especially not because I didn't ensure you were healed."

I know he is right, but he has bypassed my major issue with the gynecologist. I don't want another man touching me there. I'm not sure what my reaction will be when and if Dax ever tries, but I sure as hell know I can't handle anyone else.

"Would you be more comfortable if I went in with you?" Either I need to do a better job of hiding my feelings, or he is telepathic.

"I don't want you seeing another man touch me either, Dax. I can't willingly open my legs for a stranger, even if he is a doctor."

"Is there a female in the practice?"

"Yeah. Would you go back with me if I went to see her instead?" I am acting like a scared child who needs her hand held, but he doesn't make me feel that way. He motions me toward his chair, pulling me into his lap, in my spot.

"Of course. Will you make an appointment before we leave?" I agree pulling my cell phone out of my pocket. He can hear the entire conversation; the receptionist is a little too chipper for my liking when she asks if I could come today at four since they had a cancellation. Dax nods, and I concede. When I hang up, he is happy. I just roll my eyes.

"We still have about an hour before we need to leave for Shelly's office. Do you want to talk about the rest now or after dinner tonight?"

"Aren't we supposed to go to dinner with the Fish tonight?" He nods. That could make for a really late night in and of itself. Add a meaningful conversation to it, and we might be up half the night, and it wouldn't be fun. "Now."

"Do you know anything about Dom/sub relationships other than the romanticized lifestyle portrayed in novels?" I shake my head, and he continues talking. "I've told you before I used to play actively in the club scene in New York. When I moved back to South Carolina, I left that behind. I don't have any desire to play publicly and will not share even the sight of you naked with another man. You've been all through the house; you know there are no secret rooms with sexual play equipment in them. I do like to bind a submissive. I do like to use toys we both enjoy. I do like to blindfold. And Cam, baby, I do like to punish. But mostly what I need from a sub is her total trust in me. You've given me that, and it is the greatest gift any man, Dom or not, can ever get from a woman. Sexually, I'm always in control. I will not surrender that. It is who I am wired to be. I want you to actively engage, but if we are in a scene, I control the pace, I set the parameters, and you trust me to take you where I think you can go. Do you have any questions?"

"If we enter into this, will we always be in these roles?" I say the last word skeptically. I honestly am not sure I can give up control.

"There is no if, Kitten, it's when. As far as our roles, we are who we are, baby. You are naturally submissive to me. You may never have been submissive to anyone else in the past, but you are with me."

"I was with Chris." It is a thought that somehow verbally leaked out of my head.

"I suspected you were. I also suspect that's why you haven't really dated or been in a relationship in a long time. You haven't been given what you needed for it to be successful, so you put your energy into other things. Cam, you have a natural inclination to please, but it's overwhelming with me. You give me a level of trust no other sub has ever given me. It's a true gift, one that I want to be careful with, one I want to honor, even if it means things go much slower than either of us want them to go."

"Have you had a lot of subs?" My question is shy, and the moment the words leave my mouth, I don't want to see his face. I'm not normally a jealous person, but the thought of another woman being with Dax shreds me.

"Not since I've been back in South Carolina. Only two. When we reached a point that it didn't work for us, I uncollared them, and we went our separate ways. I told you that I didn't date much."

"So that's it – this would be a relationship of convenience for you until it didn't work for us?"

"No, baby, part of what didn't work in those relationships was I wasn't in love with either woman. Yes, I loved them, held deep regard for them, but we were just very good friends who were attracted to each other and enjoyed playing together."

"Then why did you collar them?" I know enough to know what the collar means, what it symbolizes for the person giving it, what it means for the person wearing it, and what it signifies to those who see it.

"Just because I wasn't in love with them in a romantic sense, doesn't mean I wasn't committed to them. I very much was. I was monogamous, completely."

I nod as if in understanding, but really it is just to shut the conversation down. I feel inferior to these women whose names I don't even know. I don't know if I am jealous he has claimed them in such an open way or hurt that he hasn't done it with me. My insecurities started to creep in, and he will sense them the moment I acknowledge any of them mentally. "I need to go freshen up so we can leave." I recognize how somber my mood had gotten, and I can only hope that he will let it go for now. That will give me a reprieve until tomorrow, and maybe by then he will have forgotten.

"Kitten, what are you thinking?"

"Nothing, just that we need to get going." I can see in the way he draws his brows together he doesn't believe me.

"Complete honesty, Cam." It is a reminder. This is what our relationship has to be built on.

"Okay. I don't want to tell you what I'm thinking."

"Very well. Go get ready, and I'll wait for you in the kitchen."

CHAPTER FIFTEEN

I don't let him go into the appointment with Dr. Wright. He is shocked but just sits back down without saying anything. We go over my journal entry, and she is proud of the progress I have made and tells me after the breakthrough in the bathroom, which I consider a horribly muddled mess, that I will start to push through things. I tell her about my insecurities with Dax. She discusses our relationship with me as my doctor, then when she tells me our time is up, she says she wants to tell me something as Dax's friend.

"Cam, that man loves you more deeply than I've ever seen him love, and I've watched him with his siblings, my children, girlfriends, parents, grandparents, friends, you name it, I've seen it. There is no one, not ever, who has held his heart the way you do. While you think he needs to be careful with yours, and I agree, he needs to tread lightly, sweetheart, make no mistake, you need to be careful with his. He hasn't loved since Jeremy died. This is the first time I've seen him whole in a lot of years." She pats my cheek like a grandmother would do while I stand in stunned silence. She opens the door showing me to my escort, who extends his hand to me.

His smile reaches from ear to ear. I turn to look back at Shelly, because that is who she becomes in that moment, and give her a little wave and a gentle smile, telling her I understand.

"How was your appointment?"

"It was fine. Don't forget about my doctor's appointment. Do you know how to get to St. Francis East?" I ask changing the subject.

"That's the women's hospital, right?" I nod my head, "Then yes, I know how to get there." I direct him into the parking lot, but when he parks I tell him I want him to wait in the truck.

"What's going on, Cam? You haven't left my side in four months." He isn't upset, just wanting to make sure I am safe.

I'm not sure I am making the smartest decision. I knew when we were in Shelly's office he was within arms reach if I needed him. This would require me to go through a packed parking lot, into an elevator, sit in a waiting room for a group of doctors who notoriously run over an hour behind schedule, then undress, and allow someone I don't know to touch me. Hindsight is always 20/20. He let me go with my cell phone in hand and a promise to call if even the slightest panic arose.

Everything is going as well as can be expected. I haven't had to wait as long as I normally do because the office staff wants to leave at five o'clock. I peed in a cup for them, then donned my paper gown. They take blood to do the STD testing, and I sit on the table waiting. Dr. Nason and her trusty companion come in to the room – I had forgotten about the witnesses now required. Thank God, she is a female too. Dr. Nason has me lie back to do a breast exam then pushes on my stomach near my pelvic bones, confirming all is good. Then her assistant tells me to put my legs in the stirrups. Still covered by my paper gown and a sheet, I am making an effort *not* to pay attention in hopes that it will end quickly.

The assistant lifts the sheet to the tops of my knees and points the light at my vagina. The doctor knows she is looking at the trauma of a rape and what had been sent to my normal doctor via the hospital, but she didn't have the fine details that only Dax and Dr. Wright know. "There's going to be a little pressure," she says. As soon as I feel the metal, cold against my insides, I panic. The doctor continues doing what she was down there to do while her assistant tries to calm me down. I plead for them to stop, sobbing into the crook of my elbow. "Dax…" I whimper once as I pushed down on the call button on my phone. I hear his voice, but he isn't close enough. Calling to him again, "Dax, please…" The assistant pries the phone from my hand. The invasion has stopped, but I can't retreat far enough into myself. I hear her talking to him on the phone, telling him where to come to get to me. I hear him making a wake as he comes storming down the hall.

"Cameron. It's me. Open your eyes. Cameron. Open your eyes." My eyes follow his orders. "Look at me, baby. Find my eyes." His hands grip my face, forcing me to look into his eyes, to see the storm of green that is raging, not at me, but for me. Once he has me back with him mentally, he kisses my lips. "Baby, I need to put your clothes on you so I can take you home." I comply allowing him to dress me like a child. Anytime the nurse or the doctor tries to get near me, I flinch. He asks them to step back and let him take care of me. The assistant gives him some sass about leaving me alone with him after what had just happened. Dax responds, "Step. Back." I know not to cross him, but she must not have gotten that memo.

"Kitten, are you okay here for just a minute while I step outside to talk to the doctor?" I nod.

He steps out taking the assistant with him. They don't close the door, and I know that's so I can hear. He doesn't want me to think he is trying to hide anything from me. "Were you able to complete the exam?" he asks Dr. Nason.

"Yes, I didn't realize she had triggered, Mr. Cooper. The first exam is always difficult for rape victims. She was doing well through the breast and pelvic exam, when I inserted the speculum, she went into full blown panic attack."

"Was it metal or plastic?"

"Um, it's metal," Dr. Nason answers cautiously.

"Goddammit!" He curses. I can see him pulling his hair with his hands in frustration. He never loses his cool, but he just about splits himself in half over that one. If we had thought about it, which neither of us had, this could have been prevented. "Okay, what about the exam. Has she healed? Have her stitches dissolved? Her uterine wall was torn that night."

"Medically speaking, sir, she is in good shape. All of the wounds internally have healed. I don't see any long-term damage physically."

He doesn't reply to her, just turns to open the door. He takes my hand, leading me down the hall, behind Dr. Nason's assistant. She turns to point us to the cashier. "Do you think maybe you could just bill us this time?" he asks in a mocking tone, and she quickly assures him that they will.

Reaching the door of his truck, he presses the remote to unlock the doors. When I try to open the door, he puts his hand on it to keep it closed. I turn to look at him, leaning back against the door. "I'm okay, Dax." This episode wasn't anywhere near as bad as they have been in the past. The fact I'm walking instead of being carried should show him that.

"Kitten, when I heard you cry into the phone, it ripped me apart. I couldn't get to you fast enough. I'm sorry I wasn't there baby." I could see remorse written all of his face although it isn't warranted.

"I insisted you wait for me. This isn't your fault. I really thought I could do it. I really thought I would be okay. Please don't be upset. I know I failed, but I'll try again."

"You didn't fail, Cam. You have more courage than anyone I've ever met."

He is serious, but I laugh at him. "Are you kidding me? I'm afraid of my own shadow. I'm terrified to go out with my friends tonight. I was afraid to walk across a parking lot in broad daylight."

"We aren't going out tonight."

"I haven't seen my friends in days!" I wail, noticing a couple walking by us and realizing how my voice travels.

"It's been two days, Cam. Don't you think they will understand?"

"I'm sure they will, but I don't want them to. I saw the sun for the first time today, Dax, and I don't mean the actual ball of fire. I mean this morning when I got up my world wasn't dark. We laughed, you played with me, and it felt good. I need to keep feeling those moments."

"Then what changed? What happened at the house before we left?" I know he won't drop it. The man has a mind like a damn steel trap, and he isn't happy with how things were left although he agreed temporarily to drop it.

We are still standing in the parking lot. "Can we go home and talk about this?" I ask him.

"Fair enough."

Neither one of us says a word on the ride home. Dax quietly contemplates. I am rummaging through my mind wondering how the hell I am going to tell him what I was feeling this morning. He knows every thought wondering through my mind, so I'm sure he knows I'm waging war with myself sitting in the passenger seat. Hell, this is all an exercise in futility. My acknowledging emotion doesn't change anything; it just makes me emotional.

Pulling in, I stare at the fountain in the front yard. I love what it represents to him, and I love that he loved enough to need a memorial in his front yard. He loves deeply. I hop out of the truck when it comes to a stop. Dax doesn't need to say anything; I know where I'm supposed to go. I don't sit in his chair though. I don't want to be that close when I tell him how childish

I am. Once I settle on the couch, he positions himself at the other end so he can look at me. Then he waits.

"Do we have to do this?" I whine.

"Yes."

"I don't know how to say it."

"Then stop looking for the perfect words and just allow the ugly truth to come out."

"I was jealous." There, that is simple, to the point, and the truth.

"Of?" I'm starting to wonder if we could use any fewer words to have a conversation.

"Them."

"You're going to have to be more specific, Cam. There is no one in my life that you should be jealous of."

I hesitate. It's petty and juvenile. "Your subs."

"Why would you be jealous of them?" He is astonished. I have truly stumped him. For once, he hasn't anticipated what I had been thinking.

"Because they gave you something I can't. You had fun with them. You played with them. You cared enough about them to collar them." I refuse meet his gaze. I stare at the floor in hopes this would halt further questions.

For a moment I think maybe it has worked. But then I open my big mouth "Did you call them Kitten, too?" He is on me like white on rice.

"Look at me," I comply because I know I have no choice. Unfortunately, in doing so, he sees the tears threatening to leave my eyes. "I have never called anyone else Kitten. I told you that. Nothing about our relationship is even remotely like anything I've had with anyone else. I don't know how to make you see that. Do you want to know why I haven't attempted to collar you?" I shrug, not sure I really want to hear the answer. "First of all, you don't need that kind of drama in your life right now. Secondly, I don't plan to put a collar on your neck Cam, because I plan to put a ring on your finger, a permanent collar that binds you to me legally. If you want the collar we can certainly discuss it, but I'd like to know why it appeals to you. I know why it appealed to them."

"Everyone knew they belonged to you. That you chose them." It sounds petty even to my ears.

"Baby, trust me. Everyone knows I have chosen you. They're not so sure you have chosen me." He is chuckling, but I don't see the humor in it.

"I can't give you what they gave you, Dax."

"What do you think they gave me that you can't?"

"Sex. Fun. A partner, not a drain, or responsibility."

"The sex will come, love. I'm patient. I do have fun with you – we had fun this morning. But, I had fun with you long before today. I loved pissing you off in your office. I loved seeing you get worked up and then turn all shades of red when I didn't surrender to your demands. Cam, I love what I can be with you. Is it all fun and games right now? No, but it is real. You are definitely a partner, and you will be incredible the deeper we get into this, but you're wrong that they gave me something you can't. And believe it or not, any time you love someone, they become a responsibility, especially as a Dom. You give me something they couldn't."

"I don't understand."

"Cam, neither of those women ever had the faith or trust in me that you do. They never fully acquiesced, and that's why we only played. They couldn't be what *I* needed."

When I get nervous, which doesn't happen often, I tend to spout out whatever comes to mind. I felt it coming. "I resigned this morning." I slap my hand over my mouth as the last syllable comes out.

"Good. I'm proud of you. I wanted you to resign when you got out of the hospital, but I wanted it to be your decision, not one I forced on you."

"You wanted me to resign?" He has told me he didn't care what I did, but he hasn't pushed in either direction.

"Yes."

"Why do you do that?"

"Do what?"

"Answer with one word with no explanation."

"You didn't ask for an explanation."

I wait, but still he doesn't offer anything. I sigh, "Why did you want me to resign?"

He smiles at me, moving my bangs across my face, tucking them behind my ear. "I think you're destined for something bigger. I see more spark in you now than I ever did when you were cooped up in that building. I also want you available to me at all times of the day, and I want to be where you need me to be. Cam, I have zero desire to be away from you, ever. I told you before, if you want to work, great, do what makes you happy. If you don't, then don't."

"Can we please go out with my friends tonight?" Subject change. It's too easy to fall into Dax's lackadaisical life plans. I've never met anyone who does what they want to do just because it makes them happy. The spontaneity of it all confuses me.

He isn't giving in as quickly as I want him to, and a bit of the old Cameron comes over me. Before I think about it, I crawl across the couch, tossing my leg over his lap to straddle him, getting as close as possible before arching my back to look him in the eyes.

"You're playing dirty, Cam." Dropping my lips to his, I kiss him, coaxing out the response I want from him. "You think you will get your way with your sinfully sexy kisses?" He winks at me teasing me. With no verbal response, I lean in again, this time grinding my pelvis against his hardening dick beneath me, teasing his lips with my tongue. Softly inviting him to open to me, he accepts my invitation. With his hands on my hips, he pulls me into him again in an agonizing roll, while succumbing to my advances.

My hands find his hair, pulling him to me, allowing unrestricted access to his neck. Breaking the kiss, I continue to coax his arousal, nipping at his neck with open-mouth kisses, reaching his ear, "Please, baby," I moan into him.

His hands wander from my jean covered hips to under my shirt, skimming my sides. His thumbs stop under my breasts as he growls into me. He is fighting the urge to take this any further, but I'm waging war, not just to see my friends, but for him to claim some part of me physically. To stop my blundering, I want to feel needed, desired, and only Dax can give that to me. He seems so afraid he's going to cross a line I'm not ready to step over.

Leaning back, I pull on his shirt, raising it over his head. Next comes mine. Sitting in his lap, straddling what has become a massive hard on, I pull mine off before reaching behind my back to unfasten my bra, allowing it to fall from my shoulders before dropping it to the floor. His eyes haven't left mine – he is refusing to engage. If he doesn't look, he won't be tempted. "Dax…" I love how his name rolls off my tongue in invitation. I watch as his eyes begin to storm, witnessing the argument taking place inside him. His hands are nestled on my lower back. Taking them both in mine, I flatten them on my sides, moving them with my own toward my heavy breasts. His eyes bore holes into me, and his nostrils flare. He is fighting the temptation to give in with every ounce of willpower he has, but I won't be deterred. I stop his hands, using my own over his to squeeze the mounds, pinching my nipples. Tossing my head back, closing my eyes, enjoying the feel of his hands on my skin, even if it's forced. That is all it takes for him to lose his resolve. When his hands take over, I drop mine to his knees behind me, enunciating the curve in my spine, thrusting my aching breasts toward him.

He explores gently, lightly massaging, gently tweaking, waiting on a negative reaction, a trigger to tell him to cease-fire – his hesitation is agonizing. I can't break through to him with words, but his body is having a hard time resisting the physical encouragement. Rolling my hips again, I feel the hum on my skin right before his mouth encompasses my hard nipple. I can't stop the moan that escapes my lips when he nibbles at my peak. He moves to the other side, and it's just as euphoric. He gives each side ample attention, and I realize how close I am to the pinnacle from dry humping him on the couch. When I dig my fingers into his arm, it's as if I set off an alarm in his head. He stops suddenly, breaking all contact that he can. I see the panic in his eyes as he silently picks me up from his lap and sets me on the couch. Tagging his shirt from the floor, he tosses mine to me. "What time are we meeting your friends?" he asks as he stalks out of the room.

What the hell just happened? I clutch my shirt against my naked breasts. I had known when I started this little seduction he wouldn't allow it to go very far, but the reality of his stopping is like a slap to the face. I got what I wanted, at least partially; I managed to win an outing with my friends, but his rejection crushes any victory I might have obtained. Donning my shirt, I pad toward the stairs, making sure to evade him, to find refuge in my room.

My thoughts volley between what I want from Dax and what I feel like I need in life, to wanting to regain some independence and wanting to allow him to control everything. I overanalyze, think too much, and am hypercritical, at least the old Cam was. Part of me wants that back; part of me wants to find comfort in calling the shots. I've always dealt with difficult situations head on, but since Dax has become such an integral part of my life, I find myself just a bystander. I'm desperate to find some semblance of my life, and I determine tonight will be my first step. Mind made up, I set out for the shower.

When I open the shower door, Dax is sitting on the toilet lid. He watches me grab a towel and dry myself off before sheathing myself in the terry cloth. Ignoring him, I begin my ritual. He just sits reticently. He finally speaks when I turn off the hair dryer, giving my long locks one final brush.

"Kitten..." he starts to let out an explanation, but I'm not interested. I'm focused and for the first time in three months it's not on him.

"No need, Dax." I don't want or need his explanation. I heard it this morning and don't need to hear it again.

"You're taking this the wrong way."

"I'm not taking anything anyway. I'm getting ready to go out with my friends."

"We need to talk about this."

"No, Dax. We don't. You talked about it this morning. I got it loud and clear. You let me know when you are ready. Until then, I won't bother you."

"Why are you making me out to be a bad guy?"

"I'm not making you out to be anything. You think I need more time. I disagree. I'm certainly not going to beg you to touch me." My phone rings on the counter. I see Rachel's name on the caller ID and silently thank God for her interruption.

"Hey, Rach. What's up?" She proceeds to tell me the group wants to go to Marx downtown for dinner at seven. Knowing Dax can't hear the other side of the conversation, he has no idea what Rachel is saying, but he will hear me, and this is the easiest way to break it to him that he isn't going with me. "Great. I'll see you guys there. I can't wait for a girls' night." Her voice is stained with confusion when she asks if Dax is coming. "Nope, he's not coming tonight. It'll just be us." He stands grabbing something off the sink and launches it across the bathroom. When I get off the phone with Rachel, I turn to him.

"You are *not* going out alone. No. Fucking. Way. Cam," he thunders at me.

"You're right. I'm going out with four other women to a public restaurant on a Friday night where there will be tons of people." I know this is going to be a fight, but it is one I refuse to lose. He needs to see I am strong, not the broken version of me he cocoons.

"I'm going with you, or you aren't going." He stops moving, crossing his arms over his chest, daring me to tell him no. I love a good dare and even better a worthy opponent.

"Sorry, Dax. I'm flying solo tonight." My flippant response causes fire to brew in his eyes. I know he wants to protect me, but he was right when he said he couldn't be with me twenty-four hours a day. If I ever want to experience life again, I will have to step out of the nest. Tonight, I'm prepared to see if my wings have healed. "My friends all have your phone number. If something happens they will call you."

"Fuck no."

"Dax, here's the thing. I don't really need your permission. If you want to push the issue, I will just pack my things, take my cats, and go home."

"Now you're threatening me?" He's seething, and sadly I'm delighting in his torment.

"It's not a threat. If you think it is, continue to push me on this and see where it gets you. You forget three months ago I survived just fine on my own. I don't need a man to make me feel safe or worthy."

"Cameron, you are punishing me for stopping things earlier. Don't put yourself in harms way to get back at me." His voice strains to remain calm, but I know inside he is dying to scream at me.

"Don't flatter yourself, Dax Cooper, I don't give a shit if you want me or not. You are not the only man on earth, and if I have a physical need I want met, it won't be hard to get that itch scratched." It is a blatant lie, but I know by the slight flinch, he is debating whether it is a reality.

When he speaks again, I know I have driven my point home, and his words that follow sting. "I thought we had left the bitch in you at the bank. I can see I was wrong. You are not going alone, Cam. No matter how hard you fight, you're safety is more important to me than your happiness right now."

"Fuck you, Dax. This isn't about my safety; it's about your need to control me. Well guess what, I'm a grown woman. I need to find my balance again, and if that doesn't include you, then so be it." I don't know how this has spun so far out of control, but I laid down the gauntlet, and now I have to follow through. I hate the way he is looking at me right now, but if I can't prove to him that there is strength in me, nothing between us will ever progress. He will continue to handle me with kid gloves. I love him, with everything that's in me, but if I don't love myself I'm useless to him.

I stalk out of the bathroom leaving him behind. I throw on a pair of dark, boot cut jeans that fit like they were made for me, a purple billowy sheer blouse with a matching camisole underneath, and a pair of cowboy boots. With makeup applied, I glance in the mirror, and for the first time since the incident, I see ME staring back. I look good, but more importantly I look strong. I put on my confident air turning to walk out the bedroom door. He looms in the way, brooding, and steps toward me.

"Do you need me to fuck you to get you to listen to me? Is that what you want, Cameron? A cold, meaningless fuck? Will that make you feel desired? Will that fill the void?" His words hit me like a sucker punch to the gut. My hand stings when it hits his cheek. He stretches his jaw and rubs his hand over it but doesn't utter another sound.

"Apparently, I'm not good enough to be your whore, Dax. Point taken." I push him aside and run from the house. Jumping in my car, I steal a glance toward the house to see him standing in the doorway. He doesn't call out to me. He doesn't race after me. He just watches me pull out of his driveway.

CHAPTER SIXTEEN

My Fish know the moment they see my face something is wrong. They assume it is panic from being out alone for the first time, but ironically, that hasn't occurred to me. I hate fighting with Dax—I abhor it. I'm not much of a warrior; I don't need to be. I always find a way to get what I want, but with Dax, he won't give in, he won't let me manipulate him into giving me what I desire. That in and of itself frustrates the shit out of me, but to throw callous words at him just to get him to concede is not me. During the entire ride downtown all I wanted to do was turn around and run back to him, to apologize, but I resolve to see this through, so I can show him that I'm capable of moving on.

I tell them briefly about what had happened, twice in one day. They all kind of look at me stunned. "What?"

"Are you fucking kidding me with this shit, Cam?" Rachel is borderline pissed.

"What do you mean? Rachel, he rejected me – twice – and then proceeded to argue with me about going out with my friends and essentially told me I wasn't good enough to be his whore. Why are you taking his side?"

Piper chimes in, "I kind of see her point, Cam. He hasn't left your side, and he's worried about pursuing something physical in light of what you went through. I have to say, I think you're kind of being a bitch." She scrunches up one side of her face and shrugs her shoulders as if there is nothing else to say.

"What about you Charlie, do you agree with them?" I plead with her to side with me.

"I dunno, Cam. I think it's better to take it slow than to trigger some relapse."

"Well, fuck me seven ways from Sunday. I can't believe you guys are siding with him. I'm not asking him to sleep with me, although if I were, most men would just oblige. I just want him to show me some affection."

Sutton opens her mouth to speak then closes it. She hesitates before saying, "Cam, you know I always have your back, but you're wrong on this one. He's protecting you."

Luckily, the waiter comes to our table, interrupting the discussion I don't care to proceed with anyhow. The rest of the night goes like it always does – we laugh, talk about everything and nothing, have a few drinks, and close down the restaurant. When we get up to leave, I realize how late it is, how close we are to where the incident occurred, and can't help but feel strangled by the similarities in the evening. Sutton sees the anxiety mounting even if the others don't. She's always more in tune with what I don't say, reading my actions, and tonight is no different. She gives me a comforting smile before lacing her arm through mine. "Where'd you park, Cam? I'll walk you to your car." I want to tell her she doesn't have to do that but the truth is I don't know that I can make it there alone.

"We'll all walk with you and then drop Sutton off at her car, Piper at hers, and Charlie and I can go back to ours last because we rode together. That way no one's alone," Rachel is proud of her plan and to be honest, it makes my heart swell my Fish will never allow it to happen to another one of us.

Safely back in my car with the doors locked, I sit idling, wondering if I should just go home, or if I should go to Dax's house. He hasn't called or sent me a text. He let me leave. Maybe he wanted me to go, or maybe he was hoping I'd fail. A tap on my window sends my heart racing not to mention scaring the shit out of me. I look passed the hand rapping on my glass to the face of Fisher. Rolling down my window, "Fisher, you scared the shit out of me! What are you doing?"

"Everything okay, Cameron?" he asks in that tone officers use.

"Yeah," I hesitate, "no. I mean I'm okay, but everything's not okay. Damn, I talk too much."

He moves to eye level with me, "Did something happen?" I catch a slight glimmer in his eyes, something that hints at mischief, and then it hits me, holy shit.

"How did you know I was here, Fisher?" Son of a bitch. Dax hasn't called, come running, or sent texts because he has eyes watching me that I'm sure were sending regular updates.

"I saw your car."

"Bullshit! He called you, didn't he?"

"Who?" Now he's playing dumb. I have half a mind to jump out of my car and wail on him to get his attention.

"Cut the crap, Fisher."

"He was worried about you. He just wanted to make sure you had a set of eyes on you in case something went wrong. He said you were determined to go out by yourself tonight, which I have to agree, I thought was a horrible idea."

"So he sent you to be my body guard? Don't you have a job to do?"

"Not exactly, yes I'm on duty and haven't been with you all night, but I've checked on you regularly, and since I was downtown, Sutton had my number to reach me as well since I could get here faster than Dax could. I also bribed the lot attendant to let me know when you came out for your car."

"Sutton was in on this shit?" debating whose ass I should kick first, Dax or Sutton's, Fisher interrupts my thoughts.

"So, I'm going to ask you again, is everything okay? Why are you sitting here in the parking lot?"

I let out a loud humph, which seems to cause my shoulders to deflate. "I'm debating on going home."

"Sugar, Dax knows you've left the restaurant. If you sit here much long, he's going to get worried."

"No, Fisher, I mean *my* house."

"Ahh hell, Cameron. Don't make me call him and tell him that you went to your house. Do you know how bad that will go? He's been a mess all night. Every time I talk to him, it's as if he's struggling to breathe without you, afraid something will happen to you and he won't be there to protect you. I've never seen him like this. If you don't go home, he will kick my ass and then come find you."

"His house is not my home, Fisher, and I think you can hold your own. Where's Jackson? He's got your back, right?"

"You keep telling yourself that, sweetheart. Do I need to call Dax and tell him we are having this conversation and let him come get you, or are you going to be a good girl and go home to him? Think before you answer – I'd hate for Dax to punish you if you make the wrong decision." He says it with a wink, but it tells me he knows about Dax's lifestyle.

"I don't think I have to worry about him punishing me, Fisher. He won't touch me." I have said too much, but if my friends don't think it is weird maybe another guy will.

"Cam, you are all I have heard about out of that man's mouth for well over a year. I think I could have drawn a picture of you based on the details he described, having never seen you myself. I told him he was insane, that you obviously had no interest and weren't going to fall at his feet the way most women do. He refused to acknowledge your rejection. When I called him the night I found you, he went ballistic. I mean absolutely ape shit. I had to call in every favor under the sun to get him admittance into your hospital room, or he was going to get arrested. Don't you get it Cameron – he loves you. He's terrified he's going to push you too far too fast and lose you. Fight with him all you want, but as your Dom, he will make the choices he thinks are best for you, not the choices he wants to make to satisfy himself. The sooner you accept that, the better off things will be."

"He's not my Dom," I pout. It seems no one is on my side; I can't even get sympathy from a man regarding sex.

He laughs, "Yeah, sweetheart, he is. Now, are you going home, or do I need to call him and get my ass chewed?"

Ninety percent of me wants to tell Fisher he is on his own and pull out of the parking lot, but the ten percent that wants to see Dax wins out. "I'm going to have to apologize, aren't I?" I ask him.

"No, but he is going to make you talk about it." The smirk on his face tells me he is one, too. I wonder if Piper or Sutton would be interested in a Dom of their own.

"I'd rather just apologize," I roll my eyes. "I better get going. You might want to update him on my actual departure time so he's not freaking out."

"I've got it covered." He smiles at me as I start to roll my window back up. "Hey, Cam,

"Yeah?"

"If you let him, he will give you a life you couldn't have dreamed up. He will worship you, care for you, and protect you. But you will have to surrender to him." I give him a slight nod of understanding and roll up my window as he steps back from the car. I see him pull his cell phone to his ear, updating Dax on my whereabouts.

When I pull into the circular drive, Dax is sitting on the front steps, no shirt, jeans, no shoes, his elbows resting on his thighs, hands dangling in front of his knees. I sit in the car for a moment, taking in his form, his masculinity, his ink, the way his chest flexes when he moves his hands. Gathering my courage, I take a deep breath, exit the car, and walk toward him. All my bravado from earlier has faded. Unsure of myself, I search the ground like I will find answers there. When his feet are in my line of sight, I look up to a somber face.

Fidgeting, I break the silence, "Why are you out here?"

"I've been waiting for you."

"How long have you been sitting here?"

"Since you left."

"Dax, that was like seven hours ago."

"Yep," it is all he says before he jerks his hand out toward mine. Grasping it firmly, he pulls me to him, nestling me in his lap, burying my face in his neck.

"I needed to do this," he knows what I am talking about, "but I'm sorry I didn't address it with you in a more respectful way. My feelings were hurt, and I wanted to hurt yours in return."

"I know," he just strokes my back and holds my head to him. "Did you prove anything to yourself?"

"Other than I have a tendency to be childish with you, it felt really good to go out with my friends and feel somewhat normal. But Dax, I wanted to prove something to you. You treat me like I'm made of glass. I want you to see that I'm strong enough to get through this, that I will tell you if something is pushing me passed my comfort level. You keep telling me that my trust is the most precious gift I can give you, but when will you give it to me in return?"

"I do trust you," he whispers into my hair.

"No, you don't. You don't trust that I know what I need or know what I can handle. You want to treat me with kid gloves."

"Cam, the idea of pushing a boundary with you that we can't come back from is more than I can handle."

I sigh. I want him to understand how much I need to match the emotional connection I feel to him with a physical one. I want him to take the loss away and replace it with something beautiful. "I know, baby." It is all I can come up with. I don't want to argue with him. He needs to be as desperate for this as I am – if he's not, I'll wait.

He squeezes me. "I know what you're thinking, Kitten, and you're wrong." He spreads his legs, far enough to take my hand between them to touch his crotch, "Does this feel like I don't ache for you?" He is stiff beneath my palm, but his proclamation doesn't help ease my frustration. With a gentle squeeze, he seizes my wrist, bringing my hand to his lips, kissing my fingers. "I love you, Cam. I just want to protect you."

I don't return his sentiment; I just reach up to cup his face in my hands, kissing his sweet lips. "Let's go inside."

CHAPTER SEVENTEEN

The next few weeks are a lot of the same. I'm still seeing Dr. Wright two to three times a week and hanging out with Dax, his crew, and my friends. Dax always seems to have something going on – usually a project around the house that he includes me in. I had no idea how much I would enjoy physical labor, seeing the fruits of my efforts visually instead of in numbers and statistics. I adore working outside with him in the yard, planting flowers, pruning bushes – it's the first time in my life I've stopped to smell the roses. A complete calm has come over me.

I still don't venture far without Dax by my side. It's not that I can't, but I simply don't want to. The girls come to our house – that's a misnomer since it's Dax's house – a lot for dinner, and he has formed a bond with all of them, but he and Sutton are tight. I love all the Fishes equally, but Sutton and I just connect in a different way. He has that same connection with her – they banter back and forth, they annoy the shit out of each other, and act like brother and sister. He would protect her the same way he does me – he hasn't said it, but I can see it in how he looks at her and how he eyes Fisher when he gets too close to her.

Our group dynamic has changed drastically. I'm still in the fold, but I'm on the outskirts. Sutton is following my lead, but Rachel, Piper, and Charlie are still doing their own thing. I go out with them some, but the girls nights aren't as important to me as they once were – I want to be surrounded by people I'm close to, male or female. I want to be around Dax and his friends and family.

His brothers are hilarious and have become my human chrysalis. He has three; each so wildly different from Dax that you would never know they are related except for their looks. Moby is four years younger than Dax, and he has the same gorgeous features Dax has, but with blonde hair, brooding green eyes, perfect build from his job as a personal trainer, although not quite as tall. He is a joker through and through. At thirty-two, he is definitely the playboy of the group with a different girl on his arm every time we see him, and they are always drop dead gorgeous.

The next in the Cooper line up is Brooks, four years Moby's junior; he is the All American Boy. Holy hell, he has this golden blonde hair naturally highlighted, those same green eyes, and looks exactly like every fairytale boy you dreamed you'd take home to your parents in high school. He played football in college, graduated with honors, and is now some big wig at one of the BMW suppliers in town. Slightly reserved upon initial meeting, he's warm and a gentle giant when he gets to know a person. He protects me from the other three, Dax included, when they get rowdy, and I let him act as my shield.

Landis brings up the rear. At twenty-four, he is hella smart and basically a professional student. Dax says it's a ruse for him to slack off. Basically, he's getting a free ride with scholarships and grants, and his inheritance easily covers his living expenses. He goes to school and kicks back with his friends and brothers the rest of the time while he works on his Ph.D. in Horticulture at Clemson. What the hell does someone do with a Ph.D. in Horticulture? He's got the Cooper dark features, but he's the only one of the bunch with blue eyes instead of green, and they are luscious. If that boy ever settles down, he is going to make some woman quite happy.

The Cooper boys have all welcomed me with open arms and hearts. Each of them has formed a solid relationship with me in one-way or another. Julie was the only sister any of them had ever known, and she's surrogate. They're convinced I will be related legally and want to soak me in, forcing me to be one of them.

One or more of them is almost always at the house. I didn't come from a big family, and after my parents died, I craved the silence of living alone. Now that I've become a part of this brood, there's nothing I want more than to be a part of them.

There's another great thing about all the Cooper men – they each have a counterpart in the Wright family. Joey Wright and Moby are best friends with almost identical personalities. Jacob, better known as Jake, is Brooks' sidekick, and Landis and Julie have some weird platonic thing going that every one of Landis's girlfriends is jealous of. I'm not sure who gets showered with more protection, poor Julie or me. She's the baby; I'm the victim. Having seven large men always watching you, tempting people to look at you so they can intervene, it can be overwhelming. Luckily for me, my man is one of those seven, unluckily for Julie, all of those men are her brothers therefore leaving her with no men.

Tonight everyone is at our house, and I mean everyone – all the Cooper boys, all the Wrights, and all of my Fishes, plus Fisher. That makes for a loud and lively bunch especially since several brought their current girlfriends with them. I try to remember the girls' names as they have shown up at the house at random times but keep sticking my foot in my mouth calling them by the wrong name. I can't keep up with these guys and their escapades, so now I either don't address them by name or call them sweetie (nice and generic). This night is no different. Julie warns me not to try to keep up, so I quit while I am ahead. But, as the alcohol starts flowing, things start getting rowdy and lines start to cross. Lines clearly defined in the innerfold are not so clear to these wenches, looking at the men in attendance like they are meat at a butcher store and they can pick which ever piece they want to go home with, regardless of who brought them.

Typically, as the night wears on, the guys and the girls seem to naturally segregate – girls want to talk girl stuff and guys want to belch and do whatever guys do. Out on the porch, the girls are hovering, some on the steps, some leaning against the railing, some in rocking chairs, while the guys are playing corn hole, drinking beer, and relaying stupid stories that only a man would find amusing. I tune them in and out, usually tuning in when I hear Dax laugh or feel him look at me, and tuning out essentially at all other times. I'm more in tune with Dax when I hear these random girls, who each came here with a Cooper or a Wright brother, start comparing the brothers. I tune in when Dax's name is mentioned across the porch.

"Dax is fucking sexy as hell, and from what I understand, worth a mint. He owns all of this outright and doesn't have to work. One night with me, and he'd leave that little tramp who's moved herself in here."

She snorts as if she doesn't have a care in the world taking a long pull of her beer.

"I don't think so, Lizzy. She must have some sort of abracadabra pussy because he hasn't dated in years and never anything serious. Brook's says he's never seen him this way with a girl. I don't think you'd have a shot in hell."

Listening from the sideline, I want to tear these two bitches up, neither of them has a fucking clue what they are talking about, and I want to go run hug Brook. Instead, I just sit listening as if unaware that I'm the topic of their discussion, fuming but waiting to see where it goes.

"Wanna put your money where your mouth is?"

"You're not serious? His girlfriend is around here somewhere. You're just going to go hit on him?"

"Why not? I'm not married. He's not married. He's hot as hell, and I'd trade Jake in for the older version."

"Lizzy for Christ's sake, you don't really think Dax is going to have shit to do with you after you've been with Jake, do you?"

I can see the train wreck about to happen, but I can't stop myself from watching and do nothing to interfere. I know it is going to get ugly, but the girl is full on gorgeous, and I want to see what Dax will do. I know it's kind of trifling. Okay, it's a lot trifling, but I don't have an abracadabra pussy, at least not that Dax would know, since we haven't formalized anything between us. Yes, we still sleep together at night, but our relationship hasn't even gotten on track, much less pulled out of the depot physically. I'm not setting the test up; I'm just watching it unfold. Sutton plops down beside me, and I just motion for her to watch the two girls, Lizzy and whoever her friend is. She catches on quickly without explanation.

"Watch and see."

She stands, leaving the other girl sitting on the porch, and it also happens to be as Jake walks into the house. Sauntering her way off the porch, she heads towards Dax, who is talking to Fisher and Landis about who knows what. They are huddled in a man circle when she lays her hand on Dax's shoulder. As the circle unfolds, I'm out of eyesight, but I can see him. I don't know why I don't trust how he will handle this situation, but for some reason, I fear he will take her up on her offer because she's safe – it could just be sex, and she's not broken. I hate feeling this way. I have never defined my worth in terms of a man and certainly not in a sexual way. My identity has always been Cameron. I knew who I was – redefining that has been horrible and probably the reason for his continued refusal to move things further physically.

I watch her hand land right about his pec, in my nook on his shoulder, my safe haven on his body. It sends me reeling. I could not have imagined the anger rising in my body seeing someone else touch him. He looks over the shoulder she is touching to see who it is and in typical Dax fashion, he smiles at his brother's best friend's date. I can't hear what she says to him, but I see the look on his face fall, and then become angry as he drops his arms down by his side. She hasn't moved her hand, but she makes to move it to his face, and the hand not holding the beer grabs her wrist. Dax is no longer trying to conceal his thoughts on her approach.

"Lizzy? Is that your name?" She doesn't know it yet, but I have heard that voice, and it doesn't bode well for her. Fisher recognizes it too, as one Dax had used when screaming at him when he felt Fisher had let harm find me. Dax has never taken his eyes off the girl's face, so this isn't a show for me – he has no idea I can see what is going on.

He is still holding her wrist when she responds, "Yeah, you're Dax, right?"

"That's right. You also came here with Jake Wright, did you not?"

I watch as Brooks and Fisher back away from the scene, still within striking distance if they need to get to Dax but far enough away that they aren't involved.

"Yeah, but we aren't committed. We both see other people. I was hoping you might want to be one of those people." She is grinning at him from her platform heels trying her best to remove the stone face that has rooted in his features.

"You obviously know who I am. Do you know anything about me?" I can hear him losing composure as his voice begins to shake, it is barely noticeable, but it happens so infrequently even the slightest tremor tells me he is pissed the fuck off.

"I know enough to know I'm interested." The bitch bats her eyes at him. My mouth falls open. I look around to see if everyone is watching, but it appears that their only audience is the girl she had been talking to, me, Sutton, Brooks, and Fisher. At least four of us know this isn't going to end well.

"When you came in to my house with Jake, were you introduced to everyone?"

"I was." Her face sends the message she doesn't know where he is going with this.

"Then I assume you were introduced to my girlfriend, Cameron?" mental high-five and happy dance.

"I was, but where is she now? Don't you want some company?" I have never seen anything like this. I mean, I've heard some women are really this shitty to each other, but I have never seen it in person. I don't hang with a crew that would ever intentionally harm another woman – it's just a sisterhood creed. You don't do it.

"First of all, this is her home, and you're being disrespectful to not only her but to me. Secondly, Jake is like a brother to me, and even if I wasn't with Cam, I wouldn't tap shit his dick has been near."

"Damn, Brooks must be right."

"Excuse me?"

"Jess said Brooks said she must have abracadabra pussy because he's never seen you this way with a woman. You know she's just after your money. Why not play the field, have a little fun? Damn, Dax. Lighten up."

I see the fire in his eyes and am afraid of what he might do to the girl if someone doesn't intervene. I stand to make my way over, but Fisher catches my eye and just shakes his head no. About that time, Jake comes wondering back out of the house with a beer in hand, stopping to give me a side hug. I hold on just long enough for him to see the shit storm brewing in the yard.

Dax turns to Brooks. "What the fuck have you been telling people?" He drops Lizzy's arm to face him. She tries to put her hand back on his shoulder, but he brushes it off.

"Dax, man, don't blow a gasket. All I said to Jess is that I have never seen you like this with a girl."

"And the magic pussy comment? You had nothing to do with it?" His face is shades of red that verge on purple. I have never seen Dax this angry, and it seems to have happened in a split second.

"It's an assumption we've all made. You've never been serious with another girl – she must have some magic pussy. That's a compliment man." Their yelling has caught everyone's attention and my shame.

"Seriously, Brooks – do you ever think with anything other than your dick? Of all of us, you would be the last I would have thought could have made such an asshole remark." Dax lunges at Brooks, fists flying, and suddenly all of the Cooper and Wright brothers are pulling bodies apart. Dax gets in several good shots; I can see the blood on Brook's face from here. Had they not been pulled apart, someone would have gotten seriously injured.

"Fuck you, Dax. Having a good piece of ass isn't a crime. It was a compliment." Brooks is spitting the words out.

"Maybe for one of the whores you tag around with, but not for someone who's been through what she has been. Goddammit Brooks, I've never had sex with her – she was fucking raped a few months ago!"

The silence that ensues is deafening, but the crushing blow is when everyone looks my direction with pity in their eyes. As if time slows down, I watch each head turn in my direction, every Wright brother, every Cooper, their dates, and my Fish. Every single face etched with regret for me, pain, and sympathy.

When Dax finds my eyes, he knows what he has just done, but he can't take it back. This is what I had wanted to avoid at all costs, and it is evident in most eyes, they hadn't known what I thought they knew.

Jake tries to stop me, but I struggle from his grasp running through the house. I hear Dax screaming for someone to stop me, but I keep moving. I grab my keys and throw myself in my SUV pulling out of the driveway as Dax comes running around the side of the house. I can hear him screaming my name with the window down. I have no idea where I am going – all of my Fish are at "my" house. I reach for my cell phone to call Sutton, realizing not only do I not have my phone, I don't have my purse or any money and am sitting on empty. Fuck, fuck, fuck.

With no place to go for comfort, I go home. Seeing the 'for sale' sign in my yard makes me want to throw up. In less than thirty days, this will no longer be *my* house. I can always break the contract, but in reality it doesn't feel like home anymore. I'm sure Rachel can find me another house, perhaps in another county where not everyone will know that I was used. Fuck, Dax. Of all the shit he had to announce, I never thought he would violate that trust. I wander to the mailbox to retrieve the mounds of accumulated junk mail before unlocking the door to go inside.

CHAPTER EIGHTEEN

Most of my clothing is at Dax's house, but I still have enough here to make do for a few days – although no cell phone and no cash could really put a damper on how well I live. The fact is I'm not hungry tonight, and I can deal with the rest in the morning. Sitting on a stool in my kitchen, I sort through the mail, most of which is trash, but there are several pieces from my attorney. My stomach starts to churn before I open the first envelope. I haven't thought about any of this in quite some time – I have no clue how long it takes to take someone to trial, and my lawyer has little to do to prepare for the case. My attacker's lawyer, on the other hand, couldn't have picked a worse client. I haven't anticipated dealing with any of it on my own. Dax and I are rarely separated – he's always my wingman, but tonight I guess I'm flying solo.

I don't read the letters in order, not that it matters. One letter states the judge had set bail at $1 million dollars, and somehow the fucker had posted it. The second states I need to set up a time for DNA testing, which has already been done, but his attorney wants a third party to do the testing. The third is a bill – a large one for what little work I assume the guy had to do since it is all fairly cut and dry. I also now have a name for my attacker – Josh Fitz. I can't hold it in any longer. My face falls to my hands as I release the tears into my palms, screaming at how unfair the situation is to a god who has never listened to me to begin with.

Exhausted by my outburst, I slide off the stool when no more tears threaten to fall. There isn't much left in the house, but luckily, there are always several bottles of Riesling. Tonight, Mr. Riesling and maybe one of his friends are going to bed with me. I sit in the kitchen consuming the first tall guy, so I don't have to come back down to get a refill. By the end of that bottle, I am drinking straight from the next, and I am drunk. I ignore the sound of the doorbell over my loud music playing in the background. I don't care who it is; I'm not answering. The thought has not occurred to me that maybe I hadn't locked the door when Fisher appears in my kitchen.

My shoulders drop in defeat. "What? Did you pick the short straw?" my words slur together as I sling a cheap shot at him. He has never been anything other than kind to me.

"Cam, he's is freaking the fuck out. We've been looking for you for hours."

"Ironic, no one came to my house." I can't look him in the eye – I know I am being a bitch, but I can't stop it and don't feel like I should have to.

"That's because you don't live here."

"Actually, my name is still on the mortgage, at least for a couple more weeks, and my stuff still resides here, oh and look – I get mail here too!" I capture the letters from the lawyer in my hand waving them around his face. He takes them from me to glance quickly at what is in them.

"Holy fucking shit! Cam, I had no idea."

I let out a loud sigh and shrug, "Eh, I knew it was coming, right? I'd offer you some of my solace in a bottle, but I really don't want to share, and as an officer of the law you probably shouldn't drink and drive anyhow. I am going to bed. Would you mind showing yourself out?"

"Cam, why is it that every time you are separated from Dax, I end up being the one to have to break shit to him?"

"Lucky break, I guess." Fuck, like I know how Fisher gets saddled with this shit.

"Please call him."

"And say what? Thanks for telling twenty people you haven't fucked your girlfriend because she was raped? Or maybe I should thank him for being so chivalrous with little Ms. Tightbritches. Oh wait, I know. I can tell him how much I appreciate him getting into a fight with all of our friends and family around."

"That's not fair, Cam."

"Which part? Because they are certainly all true."

"You owe it to him to hear him out."

"I *owe* it to him? Is that my penance for him tolerating me for the last few months?"

I'm not being rational, and he is frustrated as hell. He keeps raking his hand through his already disheveled hair. I return to the fridge to pop a new top on my last bottle. I know I will regret the hell out of this in the morning, but right now is all that matters. I need to be numb to it all. Closing the door, I see him slide his phone in his pocket.

"Damn it, Fisher, for once could you have been on my side?"

"Sorry sweetheart, your safety will always come before our friendship." He sits down next to me when I lay my head on the cool granite countertop. Hesitantly, he reaches for my back, scooting closer so he can rub circles of comfort on it. "He loves you more than life itself, Cam." It's a whisper, but he knows I heard him.

We sit waiting for Dax's arrival, which I hear long before he walks through the door. His truck is loud and can be heard a mile down the street, but Fisher doesn't leave my side until he walks in the door. He looks like shit. With a black eye and busted lip, he looks as though he has been crying, but I can't say for sure. Fisher kisses my cheek and slaps Dax on the shoulder before walking out. Dax assumes his spot.

"Kitten?"

I look over at him but don't say anything. I am drunk, and the room is starting to spin. The moment he touches me it becomes too much as I launch myself in the direction of the sink to empty my stomach. He holds my hair while the endless stream of vomit makes it's way into the basin. When I'm done, I rinse my mouth, and he picks me up to carry me to my bedroom. Wordlessly, he undresses me and then himself, before pulling me into the comfort of my bed. We assume our usual position with his arm under my head and the other tucking me safely into him. I cry again, wondering if he will always see me as a wounded bird he has to heal, or if he will ever see the strong woman I was before.

"Can you tell me why you're crying love?" His words are soft and spoken with love; he wants answers but isn't pushing in his normal way. I shake my head slightly indicating no. He takes that as his cue to apologize. "I'm sorry about tonight. I lost my temper with Lizzy and Brooks, and it affected you."

He doesn't get it. It has nothing to do with his losing his temper – it has everything to do with him violating my trust, announcing loudly to the world I am trash he doesn't want to touch. I elbow him in the gut as hard as I can.

"What the hell was that for?"

"You think this is about you fighting with Lizzy and Brooks? Are you kidding me? Jesus, Dax. You told everyone there I am used and damaged – so much so that you hadn't even fucked your own girlfriend."

"That is *not* what I said."

"That's what I heard."

"Then you need to re-evaluate my words because that isn't what I said, nor what I implied. Cam, for fuck's sake. That girl acted like she wasn't in your home trying to hook up with your man – like there was nothing wrong with what she was doing, but Brooks – he fucking knows better. None of the guys knew any details about what happened to you, but they all knew it happened. For him to be so callous about a gift you would give me pissed me the fuck off! I would have beaten his ass to a bloody pulp over showing you so little respect. They all know, and I mean every fucking one of them, that you are mine. I would die to protect you, and if that means not having sex until it's right, then so fucking be it. I will not apologize for that, nor do I think it's shameful to say we live together but haven't fucked. I will care for you in the way you need, not the way other people deem necessary."

"What about me, Dax? What about what I deem necessary? When do I get a say in our relationship? When will you stop seeing me as a victim and start seeing me as a partner? I didn't break that night in the parking lot – I fought and I survived. I'm working like hell to get through it, but your treating me like I'm fragile makes me feel like it's all in vain – that no matter how far I come, you won't see passed what he did to me."

"I don't see what he did to you, baby. I still see the same woman I met months ago, the woman who could take on the world alone and kick its ass. What you don't get is that I don't want you to have to do it. I never want you to feel like you are alone again – that you don't have a backup system. I want to be such an integral part of your life and your make up that neither one of us makes sense without the other. The physical part will come."

"Seriously, it's been like six months, Dax. I want that connection. He took my power from me. He took my choices. I want to reclaim them."

"That's just it, Cam. You talk about wanting to take the power back, but you don't seem to get that physically I'm not geared that way. Emotionally, you don't want that control, so our daily lives work flawlessly because you let me lead, but I'm afraid for you to move past this. You need something I don't know if I can give."

"What are you talking about?"

"Cam, in order for you to regain control, you need someone to submit. I don't even think you have worked that out in your mind yet. You're so desperate for the intimacy you forget what you went through and will have to go through to get back. I've never been topped from the bottom, Cam. I don't know if I can do it."

"Baby, I have no idea what you're talking about in terms of power exchanges and bottoms or tops. I just know that I ache for you. Every day, every night – it's not about just having sex. I've gone years without sex. I want you to claim me. You tell me I'm yours, but I guess that doesn't include my pussy? I'm not trying to be crass, but damn, when did a woman ever have to beg a man for sex?"

He lets out a long sigh, gripping his hair with one hand like he could pull it all out in frustration. "I don't know what else to say, Cam. It isn't a lack of desire. I have to make certain you have what you need to move forward."

"How about an outside opinion?" The thought crosses my mind that Dr. Wright might actually have my back on this one. She's known for months how I feel about Dax and what I've wanted.

"What do you have in mind?" I can hear the skepticism in his voice.

"Dr. Wright."

"You want to ask your therapist about us having sex?"

"Yes, I do. I want to be completely open about both of our fears and what we want and ask her advice. If she says we should wait, then I'll shut up. If she gives us a green light, you have a decision to make."

"You realize you are asking me to tell my second mother about my lifestyle?"

"Yes."

"Fuck, Cam. You should know that by my agreeing to this shit how much I love you." He tucks me into his chest, tossing a leg over my thigh. His scent comforts me as I smile into his chest. "You want to answer a question for me?"

"Okay." I turn my head to look up at him.

"Why didn't you answer my calls tonight, return my texts, or call one of your friends to let them know you were safe?"

"I left my phone and purse at your house. I didn't have enough gas to go far, so I just came here."

"I'm putting a tracker on your fucking SUV. Next question. Why is there a contract pending sign on the for sale sign in your front yard? Were you going to tell me you put your house on the market?"

"That's more than one question." He responds with a growl that tells me not to push my limits. "You told me you didn't care what I did with the house, so I had Rachel list it. A few weeks later, I got a great offer on it. They close in about two weeks. I guess I didn't think it through, but I'm sure Rachel can find me another house pretty quickly."

Rolling me on to my back, he hovers over me, staring into my eyes with a look I can't read. "Why would Rachel need to find you another house?"

"I won't have a place to live." Surely, it is not lost on him that my house is going to belong to someone else.

"Kitten, you don't live here. You haven't in months. Why would you buy another house?" His tone walks a fine line between anger and control, self-control, like he is trying to not shred me with his words.

I shrug my shoulders unable to answer. The truth is I don't have an answer other than I keep waiting for Dax to decide he's had enough and leave. There's still so much shit to overcome, and I can't imagine him wading through it with me. At that moment, I realize I haven't told him about Josh Fitz.

"Josh Fitz got released on bond." Fuck me and my mouth. Every damn time I get nervous, shit just comes flying out.

"Who is Josh Fitz?"

I realize neither of us has had a name all of these months. I only obtained one hours ago through court documents. "The man who raped me." Wow – those were words I never thought would come out of my mouth, but they weren't weak, and I wasn't afraid to say them. I acknowledge what *he* did to me. He made that choice, not me.

"How the fuck did he get out on bond?" He doesn't wait for my reply but rolls off the bed obviously in search of his cell phone. I presume he is after Fisher, so I try to stop him.

"Dax, Fisher didn't know. He found out tonight when I showed him the letter I received from my lawyer. He's been out several weeks, but I didn't know because my mail comes here. I have a bad habit of not checking it since I pay all of my bills online."

"So that fucker is out on the streets and no one even called you?" I shrug; I mean what else can I say. "It's a good thing you sold this house, Cam. You're not staying here again after tonight. Knowing that fucker is lurking around, I want you with me at all times." I roll my eyes in the darkness; he couldn't have seen me, yet still says, "Don't roll your eyes at me, Cameron. I'm serious."

"How the hell do you know I rolled my eyes at you from across the room in the dark?" I giggle, which irritates him. I think he launched himself ten feet from the bed to land next to me.

He scopes me up as he hits the mattress rolling me onto his stomach. Pushing the hair out of my face, he takes my lips before answering, "I'm that in tune with you, Kitten. And you're a little predictable."

Nestling into his side, I reach up to him, hesitating to press my lips against his. I feel like I constantly beg for his affection. He senses me pull away and captures my neck with his hand. His eyes penetrate my soul before he takes my mouth with his. He says everything I feel in that kiss – it's mind blowing, and I feel it down to my toes, in every breath I take. When he pulls away from me, he stares for a minute, then kisses my forehead, "I love you, baby," he whispers into my ear. I want so desperately to return the words but find myself burying my body into his before I drift off to sleep to the sound of his rhythmic heart.

CHAPTER NINETEEN

The next morning things get real in a way I wish it hadn't. My bubble bursts with reality. Dax's phone rings at nine o'clock. My lawyer is looking for me, and when he can't reach me on my phone, he calls Dax. I listen as he tells me it is time to prepare for court and that he has the trial date. Josh Fitz's lawyer is trying to settle the case and wants a plea deal. I agree to come in and talk to him this afternoon about the possibility. Dax is livid I am even considering it.

"Cameron, if you let him plea, he gets out in a set amount of time. Why won't you fight against him?"

"He's not going to get life for rape, Dax. If I agree to a plea deal, I avoid going to trial. I avoid having to replay the events of that night in front of strangers. I avoid it being publicized. He still gets punished, and I get freedom."

"I just don't see how you can't want him to pay in the worst way a court can punish him! Fucking a, Cam – he violated you. He stole from you."

I know his ranting is out of love for me, but he is seeing this through a protective boyfriend's eyes, not through the lenses that lived it. He doesn't understand there are people out there who will believe I brought his behavior on myself by being drunk at two in the morning outside of a bar in a dark parking lot. Those people exist, and I will have to face their ridicule every day I step foot into a courtroom.

He throws himself onto the bed, lying on his back. I lie down next to him with my head on his shoulder reaching up to turn his head to me. I see his turmoil; it's visible in his beautiful green eyes. I hate it's there, but I need him to support me in whatever decision I make. "Baby, I need you to let me make this decision. I want you by my side. I want you with me every step of the way. But in the end, if I choose to offer a plea deal, I want you to agree it's the best thing for me psychologically so I can move on from this." My thumb strokes his cheekbone, trying to calm him the way he always does me. I think it's an effort in futility.

"If you could have seen what I saw that night, you would understand why I feel the way I do. If you had watched your lifeless body for eight days in the hospital, you might get it. He tried to take you from me, Cam. I want him to rot in hell."

With nothing to say, I just lie there, just being with him, feeling his pain like I know he feels every ounce of mine. It is almost suffocating to know he felt what happened to me that night, not in the same way, but in the same degree. I wish I had perfect words. I wish I could capture my feelings in music the way he does for me, that I could play him my life song. I wonder what he would add to the song he played for me that night.

"Will you ever play for me again?" It is random as hell, but he gets my quirks.

"Huh?" He props himself up to get a better view, not knowing what I am talking about because he isn't inside my head.

"The piano. The song you played for me. Will you finish it?"

"How do you know it wasn't finish?"

"Because your life isn't over." He looks at me with a smirk, grabbing me with his beautifully inked arm, tugging me to him with a full body press.

"Why do you assume that was a piece about me?"

"Wasn't it?" I raise my eyebrows to see him. Surely he isn't going to try to play it off.

"I didn't say it was or wasn't; I asked why you assume it was," Dax and his ever-simplified conversations.

"I don't know. It was as if you bared your soul to me that night. Every pain, every heartache, every triumph, every bit of happiness. You moved me between your legs when you met me in your song. I just thought it was. I was amazed you could play something so poignant that sounded meticulously practiced, but not have touched the keys in years. I was just hoping you would finish it for me."

"I can't finish something that isn't written. I would definitely say there are things that could be added."

"When did you write it, if you haven't played in years?"

"When I sat down at the piano with you."

"So, it was just kind of a free flowing piece that came to you?"

"I guess."

He must see the change in my face, one of slight sadness that I will never hear the music again. Not the way he had played it that night, even if he could remember bits of it, it would never be the same.

"Kitten, I can play every note again just like I did that night."

"How? If you didn't write it down, how can you play it again? You didn't write anything down that night."

"I play by ear. I have a photographic memory of sorts but not in the way you might be thinking. It's only with music. If I hear a song once, I can play it again, even something I didn't write. I can switch between instruments and play the same song in any key you want it played in." He makes it sound so mundane, but what a beautiful gift.

I smile at him, still waiting on the answer to my question. "Yes, baby, I will play for you again. Any time you want me to. But right now, you need to get up and get dressed. We have to go to Dr. Wright's office to hash some things out and then to the lawyer's office. Tonight, I want you in *our* bed. We also need to figure out what to do with all of your furniture since your house will not belong to you in a short fourteen days."

He has apparently forgotten I have virtually no clothing here, no cell phone, and no purse. "Kinda hard to do that unless you want me to put on what I wore yesterday. Or, I could wear my PJs to both appointments." I wink at him because I am stark naked.

"Hell no. Throw on your clothes from yesterday, and we'll run by the house."

After making it to his house, showering, and changing clothes, I return calls from all of my friends. I wish I had just called them on a conference call – it is the same song and dance with each one of them. They are all pissed I left without telling anyone where I was going and no way to reach me. How many times can you apologize for the same thing? Dax just grins like a jackass eating briars. He is gloating in their bitching. He loves that they felt the same way he did and is eating it up. I on the other hand want to smack the shit out of each of them and blame Dax for not calling them last night when he found me since he had a cell phone and I did not. None of them took that bait. Fuckers.

I click off with Sutton right as we pull into Dr. Wright's office, grateful that even at my expense Dax is in a better mood. My best guess is that one of us is going to leave here unhappy, and I pray to god it's not me.

Right before we sit down, Dr. Wright opens the door to escort us back to her office. Sitting, she asks, "So what brings you two by together?" Dax rolls his eyes and leans his head back on the couch, groaning in protest. "I take it Dax isn't happy about being here?" She looks to me for an answer.

"Dax doesn't want to have to talk to his surrogate mother about his sex life or his lifestyle," I grin wide. I have been in the hot seat so many times in the office talking about everything from my past to my present, the future, the rape, my girly bits, Dax, and anything in between that I am no longer ashamed of anything that comes out of my mouth. I didn't ask Dax to bring me to a shrink he knew personally; he made that choice. Now, he gets to live with the relationship I've developed. Asshat.

She laughs at my outburst while Dax just keeps shaking his head like he is a fifteen year old boy who is about to be chastised for making out on the family couch. "Dax is that true?"

"Just shoot me, Shelly."

"So if Dax doesn't want to talk about this, why are you here to talk about it?"

"He doesn't think I'm ready for sex and said some crap about me taking back the control Josh took from me."

She looks confused, "Who is Josh?"

"I found out last night that the guy who raped me is named Josh Fitz. I figure it is easier to call him by name than say 'the guy who raped me'."

"Dax, why don't you think Cam is ready for sex? She has come a very long ways since we started meeting. This is not a desire she has come to recently and not one she hasn't considered carefully. We have talked extensively about it." Cam one, Dax nada.

"No, I didn't say Cam isn't ready for sex. I said I don't think she is ready for sex with *me*. Big difference." He refuses to meet anyone's line of sight and continues to stare at the ceiling.

"Why would she not be ready for sex with you, per se?" Wait for it. Wait for it. This is going to be priceless. I can't wait to see the look on her face when he admits the kind of lifestyle he leads. Surrogate mother will beat his surrogate ass.

"Geezus, are we really going to do this?" He's exasperated and terribly embarrassed. My alpha Dom is a wuss. Damn, I love him.

"I think it's fair Cam understand what you mean. She has expressed concern you won't pursue anything physical with her because she thinks you believe she is damaged, or not good enough."

"Fuck, Cam, you told her that shit?" He sits straight up, piercing me with those gorgeous green eyes.

"I tell her everything. Why does that surprise you? I told her two weeks after I got out of the hospital. Wake up, Dax. You're the one who's late to the tea party."

"Dax, what Cameron has told me isn't the issue right now. The question is, why do you think she isn't ready for sex with *you*?"

"Because I'm a fucking Dom! I don't want her to feel like she's not in control. I'm afraid she doesn't understand what submission truly means, that ultimately she has all of the control." His outburst surprises even me, but Dr. Wright doesn't skip a beat – what a let down.

"Obviously, Cameron is aware of your lifestyle choice, and it doesn't seem to bother her. So why is it bothering you?"

"He took her choice from her. He took her ability to call the shots. I don't want to trigger that for her. I want to protect her. I need to protect her."

"Have you considered stepping out of that role while you two initiate a sexual relationship?"

"Yes."

"And where did that take you?"

"How much do you know about BDSM, Shelly?"

"More than you want me to admit," she answers with a sarcastic smirk that says she has first hand knowledge. Holy hell – score for Dr. Wright one, Cam one, Dax zilch!

"Jesus Christ, I can't believe I'm having this conversation with a woman who changed my fucking diapers and watched me go through puberty." He is quiet while he formulates what he wants to say. "I feel like Cam needs me to sub to her. I don't know if I can do that. I can't do vanilla. I can't do traditional. This is the only lifestyle I know. I have never let anyone top me."

"See he keeps saying this kind of thing – what does that even mean? I get that he's alpha-male, holy hell do I get it. I don't want him to be anything else. I don't want him to switch roles with me. I like to make him happy. I like to please him. I want to be on my knees in a submissive pose for him. I want him to want to want that with me." My voice cracks at the raw admission.

"Kitten, I *do* want that. I dream about you waiting for me, succumbing to my commands, trusting me with your body. You don't get what that type of role reversal could trigger for you. You haven't been in that type of relationship in over a decade and even then you didn't know what it was. You just thought it was kinky." He stands and starts pacing. Dragging his hand through his hair.

"Dax," Dr. Wright speaks to him to get him to return to the present discussion. "Are you opposed to trying to scene with her as your Dom?" He stops suddenly facing her, and I am gawking at her – what the hell are these two thinking. I am no Dom in the bedroom. "You could let her play, let her give what she needs in order to regain the control you feel she lost. Then venture out from there."

"You're serious about this shit Shelly? You really think I should submit to her? Christ, I can't believe I'm having this conversation. Do you know me at all?" He seems adamant he can't do what she is suggesting even though it sounds fairly similar to what he has suggested as well.

"Do you love her, Dax?"
"Of course I do."

"Then as her Dom, shouldn't you recognize her need for this and it be more important than your desire to not give it? Your job is to care for her and meet her needs first and foremost. She isn't going to out you to your friends or discuss it with other people. You aren't going to lose any of your street cred with the guys. Shouldn't you be willing to humble yourself in order for her to heal?" I see it register with him. It's a matter of pride for him. Point two goes to Dr. Wright.

"Look, Dax, Cameron. The two of you have to work through this together in a way that works for you both. I would suggest you discuss a scene that would work for you as a couple – one which fulfills the needs Dax believes you have and one addressing his fear of submission. You might be surprised what you come up with or how it plays out." He nods in concession, and I'm just confused. I don't want to assume his role. I want him to consume me.

We leave her office with a green light, but I don't feel the victory I had hoped for. In her own way, she agrees with Dax, she thinks I need to exert the control, to harness it before we flip the roles to one that Dax is naturally comfortable in.

After lunch, we go to my lawyer's office. This goes as well as can be expected. I don't know how plea deals normally work, but my lawyer is suggesting offering him fifteen years with no parole in exchange for a guilty plea for assault and battery of a high and aggravated nature. He says he could get up to twenty if we went to trial but could also be eligible for parole at some point. I look to Dax for his approval, but his face isn't readable. "Do you think he would take that?" I ask.

"My guess is they will counter with something else. Anything offered has to be approved by the court before it can be accepted, so the judge will still have to see it as just."

"Can you give us a minute?" Dax asks in his alpha voice that scares the shit out of me sometimes. The lawyer nods and vacates the office.

"Kitten, if you can get him behind bars for fifteen years with no parole, I want you to do it. I don't want you to face a trial."

"Okay." I am not going to argue with him. In my mind, I would have settled for ten, and might still have to, but starting with fifteen seemed to be where Dax I, so I will go with it.

"No argument?" I shake my head. He kisses my temple as he walks to the door to retrieve the suit. When he comes back in, Dax does the speaking, the lawyer says he will be in touch, and we leave.

We ride home in relative silence – neither of us wanting to address the elephant in the truck. I know to enjoy the ride because it won't last once we get home. Dax doesn't want to discuss this either, but he won't leave it sitting out there. When we get home, I try to sneak up the stairs when he heads for the family room.

"Kitten..."

Dammit, so close. "Yeah, baby?"

"Come sit with me." He calls out to me. I want to try to play dumb but it's useless; I won't win. With my hand on the stair rail, I let out a sigh, dropping my head in resignation. "I heard that, Cam. Come on."

In his chair, I attempt to sit on the couch, but he grabs my hand to pull me to him. Instead of going to his lap, I chance the floor. I need to be able to think straight, and it won't happen in his arms. I don't realize what I am doing; it is just instinct to kneel in front of him and lean into his leg. He strokes my head; it is soothing like a warm bath. His huge hand smooths my hair, his thumb tracing my eyebrow when he comes back to the top of my head.

"Are you trying to make this harder for me, sweetheart?" I hear the longing in his voice. He sees the confusion on my face.

"I don't understand?"

"Why did you chose to kneel instead of sitting with me?" There's a fire raging in his eyes. I recognize the lust burning there. It dawns on me I have assumed a submissive pose at his feet. I try to stand, but he keeps me where I am.

"Dax, I can't think straight when I'm folded up in you. That cocoon offers so much protection that I block out the outside world."

"But why kneel?"

"I don't know? It wasn't a conscious decision. It is just what seemed natural if I wasn't assuming a spot on your lap. Is it wrong?" The uncertainty in my voice causes his face to soften. He tilts my chin up so that my eyes meet his.

"No, baby. It's not wrong. It's exactly where I want you, but somehow we have to get through this before we can get there." I know what he means and regardless of how much I don't want to address this, if I ever want to move forward with him I will have to make my way through this.

"Okay, so let's just get this over with. What do I have to do?"

We talk for what seems like hours. I'm exhausted, but I think we have formulated a plan. I don't think either of us is comfortable with it, which makes me wonder why we are doing it, but instead of analyzing the hell out of it anymore, I just go with it. Tomorrow is the day.

~~~

I've tried to mentally prepare myself for this all day. Dax and I spent the day apart. He has been at the house, and I've been hanging out with Rachel and Sutton, who took the day off. We've done the girly thing indulging in manicures, pedicures, romantic comedies, and fattening foods. They know what's going down tonight, and in all honesty they have given me the confidence to go through with it. They agree with Dax that I need to resume control of my body. I was hesitant to tell them anything because I didn't want Dax to believe they thought any less of him, but he wanted me to have moral support and agreed to it. Oddly enough, neither thought of him as less than a man because he was willing to submit to me – they both thought it was swoon worthy. Figures, they aren't the ones who have to assume this role.

When I leave them, I step into a theatrical role of a character I don't know. Parts of me remember this strength; I've always had it in every aspect of my life. I was the Board Room Queen, a force to be reckoned with in the business world, strong, confident, vibrant. Over the last twenty-four hours it has dawned on me just how much that man stripped from me – how much of me he took with him that night. I'm still strong because I'm still fighting, but it's not a type of strength I recognize. It's much softer, much more subtle. Desperately trying to find the powerful confidence I once embodied, I force myself into the role I'm to play tonight.

CHAPTER TWENTY

I know he's there. He said he would be there by 5 P.M., and it's nearing six. The anticipation will only heighten his arousal. I left him instructions on where and how I expect to find him when I come in. It's odd to think I've been living with him and sleeping with him for months, but this will be our first truly intimate encounter. I know what he looks like, and he me, but I've never felt the heat of his bare skin pressed to mine, the touch of his fingers beyond the gentle caress he's offered in comfort, never heard the sound of his voice when he comes, or felt the tension leave his body after release. It's strange the connection you can build given the investment of time and patience. That's where we are. We have invested the time, and we have both certainly exercised the patience, but it's worn thin. I thought I'd be nervous, but the closer I get to our house the more intense the heat between my legs becomes. I'm calm. I know he will have followed my instructions to the letter. He wants this for me – he wants me to reclaim myself.

Rounding the corner, I hit the garage door button, alerting him I am home and hopefully skyrocketing his anxiety. It can be heard in the living room where he should be waiting. I pull the SUV into the garage, but instead of going into the house, I draw out the encounter stopping at the mailbox, trying to overcome my reservations and leave the doubt at the street. I hit the button on the garage door as I make my way to the front door.

With keys and the mail in one hand and my pocketbook in the other, I push open the heavy wood door, sound instantly filling my ears. The essence of Lichen Yu fills my ears, the dark notes of "Vengeance" reverberating through the sound dock. It instantly sets my mood taking me to a place I don't visit with other people – the confident-take-charge persona floods me. The music is raw, vividly wicked, and utterly sings to my soul. Entranced by the emotions in the notes, I walk by Dax, exactly where I told him to be. I don't notice his position, but I'm sure he can sense mine although he never moves. I set my things down in the laundry room, hang up my keys, and go through the mail while he waits. My mind wanders with the pungent ministrations of the piano while I enjoy a glass of wine. Turning the glass up, my focus goes back to the sub on the living room floor.

I feel the clicks of my heels on the floor. In his position he can feel them too, even over the vibrations of the music ringing. It's a cascade of sound – the piano resonates throughout the room and through me. I come back to him, approaching him at his head. His forehead is resting on the hardwood floor; his hands and arms shoulder width apart near his ears lying on the same hard flooring. His knees are spread wide lifting his ass in the air with maybe a foot of space between his cock and the hard surface beneath him. His back perfectly straight, feet pointed out like a dancer's, resting lengthwise from ankle to toe. From his head to the tips of his toes, his body creates the most elegant lines, graceful, poetic. All man rounded into a ball for my plying. I could stare at him for hours, engrossed in the words and lines inked into his skin, watching the rise and fall of his back as he breathes, noticing how his pulse increases as I stand in front of him. I can see the cadence of his heart through the vein in his neck. He's anxious, and the longer I examine him, the more pronounced that beat becomes. He knows I'm watching him, inspecting him, scrutinizing him. For him it's a painful process, awaiting my approval, but for me, it's empowering. Lingering around him, I move to circle his body; he hasn't so much as twitched, the only signs of his fear being the animated throb in his neck and the slight glistening of sweat covering his body. His thighs have to be aching from the length of time in the position I instructed him to wait in, but I can't help myself. Something changed in me the moment I walked in this room and saw him here. The need to punish him floods me – not him but man in general.

I pass his feet, taking a few steps back, enabling a full view when I turn back to him. I don't allow my eyes to focus on anything as I cast my vision in his direction until my eyes land on him. My heart skips a beat – he's glorious. His ass popped high in the air, spreading his cheeks so I can see his forbidden hole, one he knows I am going to take tonight. Allowing my gaze to take in all the details, I notice he's aroused. His balls are tight to his body, and where I expect to find his dick hanging between his legs none is visible, but I can see the outline of his chest sloping downward meeting his shoulders.

As I continue to circle him, "Rolling Thunder" kisses the air with fluid sound, and I casually trace my middle finger up his spine, as I round his body this time. In a painfully slow manner, my finger peruses his flesh, and I see goose bumps rise on his skin, but he never moves. At the last minute my nail grazes his side, triggering a shiver. I pull my hand away, stopping to stare at him. With two more steps I'm behind him, staring at his perfectly poised ass, and I squat so my hand is level with him. I can sense his anticipation and see him tense seconds before he feels the slap of my palm on his right ass cheek. He lets out the slightest sound, maybe a whimper, but it was too low to decipher, before he feels the second blow, followed by two more, alternating sides so they are both a beautiful pink that makes me smile. I smooth my hand over the marks, loving the feel of the heat radiating from my palm prints. Running my fingertips gently down the crack of his ass, I press a little harder when I reach his asshole, acknowledging I will be back for that area. I reach beneath him to cup his balls in my hand, and they're smooth as instructed. I can't help but continue reaching to find his cock pressed up against his stomach, rock hard and velvety smooth, and slightly wet at the tip. Bringing my wet finger to my mouth, I taste the saltiness and grin as I stand up.

Straightening my spine, hands behind my back, I utter the first words he's heard from my mouth since walking in the door. I almost don't recognize my own voice – it's filled with a coolness and authoritative tone foreign for me, at least sexually. "Up, Dax," it's a command he instantly succumbs to. Rising to his bare feet, even though I am in heels, he's still slightly taller than I am. With his back to me, my hand graces his hip in that spot I love, the mark where my thumb points downward to his dick. I stand facing him his eyes are cast downward. I tip his chin with my left hand, in an attempt to force him to make eye contact with me. The song changes as he raises his eyelids, unsure of whether he should meet my stare straight on.

"Confessions" fills my pores; the silence thus far in our encounter is perfectly balanced by the melody. My hand moves from his chin to his cheek to coax him to look at me. His eyes are stunning; it's not the color, although the green is deep. It's the emotion he's trying to hide. They're soulful; there is pain in them, coupled by lust and possibly fear. They shine bright, and he's eager to please; he wants to submit — for me. And that, is the most beautiful reaction I've ever seen. His eyes speak volumes as I search them. With a smile, I point toward the bedroom.

He walks in, stopping just shy of the bed, awaiting instruction. I leave him standing while I walk past him to our closet to ditch my heels before returning to the chair beside the bed.

"Dax, turn around." He does as he's told. "Kneel."

He's much more graceful than I imagined he would be as he lowers himself to the ground in front of me. I nudge my foot between his knees to spread his legs just slightly as he places his hands palm down on his thighs. Using my big toe, I work my way under his right hand with my foot while he watches me, never making eye contact. His hand instinctually wraps around my foot, thumb in the arch as he squeezes, and I let out a small moan. He takes a chance, without instruction, rubbing my foot with both of his hands. His calculated risk is a good one; the little sighs that escape my lips acknowledge that. I see the corners of his mouth turn up just slightly in a hidden smile, but I don't acknowledge it. I just allow him to rub the tension away from both feet before sending him to draw a bath for me. He is already clean; that was part of his instruction when he arrived, to do a thorough cleansing of his entire body, so I was free to explore. From the inspection earlier, he has done as I had told him.

Pouring bubble bath in the tub as it fills, he notices me in the mirror he's standing in front of. I see him catch a glimpse of me over his shoulder as I take my clothes off. With just the slightest rise of his brow, I know he's pleased at what he sees but remains mute. Tossing the rest of my clothes in the hamper, I meander toward him. He reaches out his right hand to assist me over the edge of the tub, and taking his hand, I step in, but I don't release his hand or his stare. "Do you like what you see, Dax?" His eyes snap up to mine. He hasn't been given permission to look much less ogle.

Hesitantly, he croaks out, "Yes."

"Yes, what?" I won't tolerate disrespect, and he is well aware of this; we agreed the role would be fulfilled as he would expect me to fill it when I am under his care. The slip is unacceptable.

"Yes, ma'am." I hear the sorrow in his voice; he knows he has made an error. It wasn't a huge infraction, but one that would definitely allow me to enjoy watching him squirm.

"Do you want to touch me?" My tone is coy, almost mocking. He can sense it. He knows he's going to be punished.

"Yes, ma'am."

"What do you want to touch first? My tits? My pussy? My ass?"

He's slow to respond, he knows I crave having my tits played with, but he is an ass man. While volleying with the decision to fulfill my pleasures or his own, I interrupt his thought process. "I asked what *you* want to touch first – not what I want you to touch first."

"Your ass, ma'am."

Turning around, I bend over, still holding his hand, "Go head, baby. You can kiss it, but I want you to kiss my ass like you would kiss my lips." He lets my hand go, lowering himself to his knees, hands on both sides of my hips, nuzzling my skin causing me to feel the stubble on his face. He kisses the cheeks of my ass with slightly open mouthed ministrations, and his tongue gently swipes my skin with each touch of his lips, while his hands kneed my flesh as he does. I stop his continued attentions by lowering my body into the hot water; he goes back on his calves in a kneeling posture. Motionless.

I close my eyes when I start to speak to him, allowing the piano notes of "Hope for Happiness" to take over. I feel the notes to the tips of my toes; they're elegant, feminine, yet all empowering. "Dax, you've had two infractions since I've been home." He opens his mouth to argue before snapping it shut. "Good choice," I warn. "Since you seem to want to debate this point, you flinched during inspection in the living room which earned you four swats, and you failed to address me as ma'am moments ago. Your discipline is critical to your happiness. I can't let them go without punishment. Normally, I would have you do something mundane, something you hate investing your time in, but I'm not interested in wasting my time or pleasure today. While I relax, you are to kneel where you are, spread your legs a little wider so your balls can breath, and slowly stroke yourself while I watch. Do not come, or our play ends here tonight. Do you understand?"

His Adam's apple bobs when he swallows hard. "Yes, ma'am, I understand."

I eye him keenly as his takes his still erect dick in his hand, slowly working his hand up and down the shaft. The color of his skin changes with each stroke to an aroused pink, the head swollen, further defining the ridge between it and the length. I want to take him in my mouth but resist the urge. "Tug on your balls with your other hand, Dax. Use your fingers to reach behind them gracing that sensitive skin right before your ass."

He begins to close his eyes, trying to fight the tug in his balls for release. "Open your eyes. I want to watch them as you fight the urge to come."

Getting up on my knees, I lean over the edge of the tub, and sudsy water drips from my breasts on to his knees as I continue leaning over, with my nose in reach of his ear. The water drips down his chest and onto his raging hard cock while he continues to stroke. I reach under his arm, around to his ass, digging my fingernails into his cheek, and I whisper, "Don't you dare come, Dax." There's a hitch in his breath as I lean back into the tub, stopping to run my tongue around the head of his cock, sucking the bulb into my mouth before releasing it with a loud pop.

I can tell he's struggling; his hand has slowed, trying to fight ejaculation. I can't help but smile. He's been stroking his cock for a solid ten minutes, riding the edge of release, the head continuously leaking a clear substance that calls to me. Interrupting him, I tell him to get my loofah and body wash from the shower. He's wobbly as he stands but does as he's told. I make quick work of my skin, washing away the remnants of the day. As I step out of the tub, he stands to hand me my towel.

"Dax, there's a box on the bench in the closet. Get it and go to the bed. Open the box, chose one, set it on top of the box, and lie face down on the mattress." He nods slightly as I start to pile my hair on top of my head in a lose knot. I grin a wide smile as "Epic Dance of Snow" comes through the speakers above the bed. It's an enchanting song when it starts, but the song following it, "Fires of a Revolution," progresses into a haunting diatribe. I know I have about seven minutes to get him where I want him before the darkness comes through. I want to penetrate him at the moment his mind is permeated by the sounds of the crescendo. It excites me thinking about the sensory overload I'm hoping he succumbs to.

 I find him, as told, face down on the bed. I look to the nightstand to see which dildo he chose. Smart boy, he didn't choose a small one but didn't go for the largest either. He went just this side of medium, to show he's willing to take the pain but realistic in what he can handle his first time. My heart swells with pride knowing how hard he is trying to help me. I'm counting my movements with each measure that sounds through the speakers. He can't see me as I put on the straps to hold the toy he's chosen in place; he can only hear my movement in the room. Once the straps are comfortably in place and I've secured the blue anal probe he selected at the apex of my sex, I nudge my knee between his on the mattress, climbing up his body as the music builds, the staccato of the keys, the bludgeoning nightmare in the melody just around the corner. I drag my body up his, allowing him to feel my breasts on his skin, my stomach pressed into the curve of his back, my rubber cock on his ass. I push myself up, stroking my hands from his shoulders down his sides, passing his clenched ass cheeks, smoothing my hands over his thighs and down his calves. Every inch of him is mine. "Who do you belong to, Dax?" I ask in a heated voice.

"You, ma'am."

"What parts of you belong to me?"

"All of me. My ass. My cock. From my head to my toes, it's all yours. You own me." His voice is breathy in anticipation. He knows it's coming soon – I'm not sure which of us is more frightened by the exchange about to take place. It's one neither of us can ever come back from. I can smell the fear on him, but I also know how much trust he has placed in me to give this to me, to commend this power exchange, and I won't violate that.

My hands slide back up his legs to his clenched ass stopping at his hips. My fingers dig into the front of his abs; it's not painful, but he knows exactly where I am and what I'm commanding. When I lift with my hands, his hips rise off the mattress, bringing his knees under him. He tucks his head into his folded arms still resting on the mattress in a posture of shame. The notes continue to escalate in the room, further reaching the base of the keyboard, the darkness within reach with highlights coming from several octaves up moments away.

I reach for the tube of lubricant and notice his hands tremble just slightly. I hesitate wondering if I'm taking him too far, but he has a safe word. I can't think long or my moment will pass. The musical selection was deliberate – every bit of it to escalate the experience to illustrate my dark night, order chosen in the play list to bring him to this moment. Timing all things perfectly was a big risk, if it takes longer than I anticipate, he will reach this moment on the after care side in my song choices. It just won't work. I had made the decision; he had come here making his decision. If he safe words, we stop; otherwise, I move forward.

Pressing a generous amount of lube in my hand and a dollop on his tight asshole, I proceeded. First to lather the object of penetration, second to try to relax him, even if just slightly, so it won't be so painful. With only a few bars left I line the tip up with his hole, seeing him tense, I reach around him where his penis is semi-hard further noting his anxiety. I cup his balls, working my fingers around them slowly, massaging them as I see his shoulders slump just slightly, running my hand up his shaft, covered in lube it makes for an easy glide, several times up and down, stroking his cock as it begins to grow and harden in my hand. The tension in his hips begins to recede.

I lean in closer to him, the music building, that image of fingers over the ivory keys runs through my mind; we are almost there. I lean down over his back to whisper in his ear, "Push back on me just a little." I feel the warmth of my breath on his skin as I speak. There is only a slight nod of confirmation when I sit back up, pushing passed the tightness, I hear him wince, but it is almost inaudible. I am slow but deliberate; breaking through at the exact moment Lichen Yu furiously runs the gamut on the keys. His dark ramblings in the notes reaching their pinnacle. Within less than sixty seconds the song ends and "End of an Era" begins. My movements match the music, the intro being slow, romantic, and beautifully robust. I rotate my hips, slowly dragging the dildo in and out of his ass as he claws at the sheets, never uttering a word. I watch his fists dig into the mattress. My hands roam his back, using the sides of his hips for leverage, enjoying the feel of his sweat-drenched skin under my fingertips, outlining his tattoos with my touch, and enjoying the burn in my thighs from the rhythmic motion of taking him. I love his vulnerability, the power I get from ramming my "dick" into his rim and taking his virginity there. I'm on the verge of climax myself from the pummeling the strap-on is doing to my clit.

"Dax, grab your dick. Stroke. Tell me when you can't stand it any longer but do not come." I'm panting. I'm close; I'm hoping I can hold out until he's there with me.

"Yes, ma'am." He mutters into the sheets. I see his arm move and know he is doing as told.

His body starts to shift as I pull him in one direction, taking his ass for my pleasure, and he pulls, taking his dick in the opposite direction. The music continues to work my frenzy and I notice he is stroking to the rhythm. He's found the connection I had hoped he would.

He staggers out, "ma'am…"

Knowing we both need the same thing, I demand he come. He stills as he finds his freedom, his body tenses with his hand still moving on his cock, he screams, "FUCK!" with two last strokes, his body relaxes as he comes in the palm of his hand. I ride through my wave enjoying the moans coming from him, but when he screams out it sends me crashing over the edge. I pull out of him aware of how sore he will be, and if not torn, definitely bruised. His hand is full of his own mess. I stick two of my finger in it, dragging them in it like it's peanut butter. Raising my fingers to his lips, he opens without hesitation and sucks the come from my pointer and middle fingers. Reaching for a tissue, I wipe the rest off of his hand.

"While I go clean up, relax. I'll be back in a minute." I smack his ass playfully as "Chariots of the Flying Kingdom" takes over. Hopefully he will capitulate to the composition and allow it to soothe him.

When I come back, he's on his back with his forearm covering his eyes. I'm not sure if it's exhaustion or shame. I sit on my calves naked, on the floor at the foot of the bed, waiting for him to break the silence. He finally removes the arm that blindfolds him, laying it next to his side; turning his head to me, he smiles. It reaches his eyes. It's breathtaking.

"Jesus, Cam – you're exquisite like that." I bow my head in the most submissive pose I've ever assumed.

I don't know what to expect from here on out. We only discussed the scene up to this point. The stress, the tension, is all leaving my body, as a flood of new emotions racks my body. There is sensory overload – shame, guilt, lust, desire, pain, seeping its way from my pores. My shoulders shake as the sobs escape. My head drops back as gut wrenching cries are discharged from deep within. He knew it was coming; he had known all along, but I couldn't see it, and maybe I didn't want to. I acknowledge the bastard left more than broken bones and stitches that night. He took an innocence, one I didn't grant him; he took my free will; he took who I was in that alley as if it was his to claim with no regard for the devastation he would leave behind. The ache is so great my chest throbs in pain as I gasp for breath.

Sitting up, staring at me from the edge of the bed, Dax slides to the floor. He shifts me to him and moves us to the bed. My cries have gone silent, but tears continue to roll down my cheeks. I find his eyes, and he is feeling every bit of pain that I am releasing, living every ounce of agony with me. I need him to replace the memories with something good, something whole, something created in love.

    His calloused fingers graze my cheek in a futile attempt to wipe away the tears that refuse to stop falling. Bringing me close to his side, I lay my head on his bicep, letting love pour through the tips of his fingers into my skin from my cheeks down my side, around the small of my back. Kissing my lips softly, my eyes close, his touch all that I can focus on. The music has ceased, and the room is silent, except for the sound of our breathing. The circles he draws on my spine become larger until I feel his hand cup my ass, fingers digging into my skin, pulling me to his hips. He is losing his resolve. He wants to connect with me in the way that I need him to.

    His hand drops to my thigh encouraging me to lift it over his, opening my sex like a flower blooming. I allow him to guide me with no resistance. His ministrations on my mouth move to my neck and collarbone. His breath is heavy on my skin, sending waves of sensation through me that I want to clutch, to hold on to in case I never get to feel this serenity again. With his mouth pressed against my ear, he whispers, "I love you, Cameron," right as he pushes himself into me.

I gasp as he fills me tossing my head back in unexpected ecstasy. He's slow, methodical, rhythmic, assuring the pace is one of passion and not torture. It is the gentlest serenade anyone has ever sung to my body. He continues to make love to me from the side ensuring I know I can escape I'm not captive, and I'm not here against my will. The gesture is not lost on me. I roll him to his back straddling him, my hair having come loose from my bun cascades around me in a veil. I never break our contact; the kiss is uninterrupted. His hands find my ass, cupping both cheeks, rolling me up and down with the sway of my movements, my plunging him in and out of me. As I feel my climax reaching the surface, I break from his mouth but continue the pilgrimage he started. He kisses my forehead and whispers, "Come for me, sweetheart." It is the gentlest command I've ever heard. They are the most erotic words I've ever heard spoken, and I let go, crashing around him, squeezing him from the inside out until he finds his release with me. My face buried in his neck, I ride out the pulses he provides within me as our pace slows. He kisses my temple as our bodies still. "I love you, Dax." The words slip out before I can process what I am saying. My entire body tenses in anticipation of his response. Terrified he will assume the words were a mistake, released in the heat of the moment, I try to quickly escape, to find refuge in the bathroom, but as I attempt to pull away he clutches my hand.

"Kitten, where are you going?" His voice is soft; sounding like the sun feels on a warm day.

My face flushes red, and I feel the heat of embarrassment in my cheeks. I don't respond to his question. He just told me minutes earlier he felt the same thing, but for some reason the words leaving my mouth feel like a violation, like somehow I had cheapened what he had just given me.

"Cam?"

I stand silently waiting. His bicep flexes as he pulls me toward him sitting up. I come to a resting spot between his legs, our naked vulnerability heightening my apprehension.

"What just happened?"

I suck my lip between my teeth as I refuse to speak; my insecurities overtake me. Palming my face he forces me to meet his stare. "I love you too, Cameron. More than I can express in words. I never thought I would feel alive again after Jeremy died, but you've given me that. You give me that daily through your sass, your wit, your banter, how you love, your passion, your strength. Don't be ashamed of whatever vulnerability you're feeling right now. I feel it too." He searches my eyes for what I assume is understanding. Finding it, he kisses my lips before waltzing to the bathroom. I watch his perfection over my shoulder until the door closes, confiscating my view.

CHAPTER TWENTY-ONE

I anticipate confusion in our relationship from both of us after he subbed for me, but it never comes. Not from him, and not from me. Several days pass, and my apprehension or expectation for strife to manifest itself seems to vanish. We had agreed before the scene we would not be intimate again before we met with Dr. Wright, which thankfully happens today. We both want to get professional advice on proceeding.

Hopping in the truck, I look to Dax. We haven't really talked about the scene, and I'm hoping we won't have to today, but I know that's not realistic. Dr. Wright will pick it apart bit by bit. I'm not sure which of us that will make more uncomfortable, Dax or me. He always seems to sense my apprehension. As he catches my gaze, his body pauses before he reaches to take my cheek in his hand. "Kitten, there's no need to worry. We're good."

I can't help but smile back at him. "We'll see how good we are when Dr. Wright starts asking you intimate details." I laugh half-heartedly at the thought, but he just winks at me before starting the truck.

I love that she's right on time. There's nothing more irritating than for a doctor to make you wait. They set appointment times for a reason, right? Oh wait, those are just for the patient to adhere to. We both make our way back, settling into the cushions on her worn couch. With my hands folded in my lap, he gently places his palm on my knee for reassurance.

Dr. Wright doesn't suffer pleasantries; she just jumps right in. "So the two of you were supposed to scene after our last meeting. Did you?"

"Jesus Shelly, way to get straight to the heart of the matter." The press of his fingers into my thigh alerts me to his irritation. Quizzically, I look at him; surely he anticipated this. I sure as hell did.

"Dax, there's no point in wondering around the edges of the issues. It was the assignment. You both agreed to it. You are both back here to discuss how it went, problems you came across, how to move forward, etc. We're all adults here." Her voice never wavers; it's smooth like a mother soothes a wounded child.

While it sets my nerves at ease, Dax simply looks to the ceiling. I would bet money that he is silently counting to ten to calm himself. I can't help it. A giggle parts my lips as I throw my hand to my mouth in an effort to catch it.

"Cameron, there's nothing funny about this." His voice is gruff. He's right; there is nothing funny about it, but I can't suppress the laughter, which is turning into a cackle. Something about the way he says my full name when he is angry just tickles my funny bone.

"Okay, you two. Let's get back to the topic at hand. Cam, did you scene?"

"Yes."

"Did the two of you talk about the scene before hand?"

"Yes."

"Cam, are you going to give me more than yes or no answers?"

I wish I could figure out how Dax avoids the hot seat. "What would you like to know? Those were yes or no questions."

"I'd like for either you or Dax to tell me about how you decided what sorts of things would come into play."

I take a breath so deep my shoulders rise at least two inches before solidly exhaling through my mouth. I don't make eye contact with Dax; it's easier this way.

"Yes, we talked extensively about what would or should take place. Do you want details?" She nods her head in affirmation, so I continue. "Dax thought it was important for me to see him as vulnerable, to take from him something he had not ever wanted to experience. I guess in a symbolic gesture of what Josh took from me. He offered me the one thing that made him most vulnerable that he had never shared with anyone else." My voice trails off. As I say the words aloud, I realized the significance of what he had done for me, what he had sacrificed. Tears flood my eyes and silently run down my cheeks as the impact hits me with such force that it physically steals my breath.

Dax shifts on the couch just enough to bring me to his lap and tuck my head into his neck. Dr. Wright silently watches.

His voice is the salve to my wound. "Kitten, don't cry. I gave you what I wanted you to have." The feel of his strong hand smoothing my hair warms me, softens my anguish.

"Dax, can you continue where Cam left off?" Dr. Wright waited patiently for an unobtrusive opening. "What did you offer her?"

"I'm not sure how much you know about Cam's life prior to the incident." He waits for her response.

"We haven't talked a lot about what her life was like prior, not in detail, generalities yes."

"She was this badass banker type. Prim, proper, suits, heels. You know – the type who looks like they would eat you alive to get to the top or they had just devoured their last meal while stepping on someone's face on the ladder. Don't get me wrong; Julie says she wasn't like that, she loved working for her, but that was the image she portrayed. She was strong, confident, and no-nonsense. Anyway, I wanted her to attempt to step back into that role."

"You know she will never be that same person again, don't you?"

"No, I don't need her to be that same person. I wanted her to find the confidence she had to be able to take me. I also wanted her to have the comfort of the scene being in our home where she knows she is safe. I offered her the only thing I had to give that would make me as vulnerable to her as she was to him – for her to regain her strength. I've never been taken anally. For a man, it's intrusive and took every ounce of trust I could summon to allow it to happen." I watch as his eyes hold her gaze. He does not see this as weakness and he won't look away from her. I reach up to his face drawing his attention away. He leans into my hand lightly kissing my palm before looking back to her.

"Cam did most of the actual planning herself. When we talked about what she wanted to get out of it, she didn't see the importance of being in the driver's seat but agreed to take the keys all the same. She owned the part, and I have to say, she took me to a place I've never been before. I wouldn't trade that experience for anything."

"Cam, do you think you can fill in some of the details about what you felt and the emotions you went through?

I slide out of Dax's lap back to the couch drawing my knees to my chest. Wrapping my arms around my legs, I rest my head between my knees. The words don't seem to want to come, but Dr. Wright just waits while Dax's paw finds a resting spot on the back of my neck, his thumb strumming a tune behind my ear.

"You know I thought the whole thing was silly. That is not who I am sexually. It is who I was professionally. I was nervous, scared. I spent the day with my friends, who mentally helped me prepare. Something happened the moment I walked in the front door. The role clicked when I saw him on the floor, waiting, kneeling for me, ultimate submission from an alpha male. He was beautiful, completely exposed, anticipating me." I blush remembering the curve of his back and the gap between his thighs.

"Music speaks to my spirit, so I spent hours picking songs to play during the scene. It helped me stay in character, helped me know how much time I had remaining, and I hoped it would connect Dax to me." There's a gentle squeeze on my neck, an acknowledgement I accomplished what I had set out to do with my playlist. He hasn't said so, but I'm pretty sure he was shocked by my choices.

"I spent time taking in his body, watching him breathe, enjoying the subtle nuances of how his muscles would quiver from strain. I took delight in knowing he had to be in pain from waiting on hardwood floors kneeling. His shoulders had to ache from being stretched. He never complained, never moved, he just waited, giving me all the time I needed."

I pause, allowing Dr. Wright to interject a question, "How long did you wait for her Dax?"

Shrugging, he responds, "I have no idea. She told me where to be. I was there as instructed and simply waited until she gave me further instructions."

"Was that hard for you?"

"Waiting for her is always tough. Not being able to touch her was agony, but she was in control. This is how she wanted to play, so we did it her way."

"Cam, I assume at some point you allowed Dax off the floor?" Her eyes are alight like fireflies. She will never admit it, but I think she's enjoying seeing this side of Dax, even if it's through a third party narrative.

"I did. I took him to the bathroom where I made him watch and touch himself but wouldn't allow him to come. I tried to think of things that would be hard for a man; things that would cause anguish, but not pain – you know, waiting on a woman, watching a naked woman but not touching her, touching himself but not allowing him release. I knew what he wanted me to get out of it, but I couldn't inflict pain on him intentionally so these things seemed to offer the same sense of control for me."

"I'm impressed with your line of thinking, Cam. It would have been very easy for you to lose your self-control, for something to trigger a flashback or negative response. Choosing things not demeaning or painful for him was a wise choice. I assume the climax of your time playing was the anal?"

Another hard breath in and back out, I look to Dax. His eyes meet mine with a softness I wasn't expecting. There's nothing but adoration behind them. "I don't want to give you all the details, but I took him from behind, and we both climaxed. I was worried he was going to be different. That somehow this was going to destroy us. I went to the bathroom to clean up unsure of what I would find when I returned."

"How was he when you returned?" She moves to the edge of her seat in anticipation of my response.

"He looked sated. Calm. He looked stunning." I look to him as I say the last words to see the expression on his face. I point at him, tilting my head, "That. That's exactly how he looked." I smile softly. I've never seen the look that Dax reserves for me. Every ounce of affection he has for me is spoken there.

"You saw love, didn't you?" The words interrupt my gaze. I turn to her.

"Yes."

"So where did the two of you take this after the scene? Was there aftercare of any sort? Did you discuss the scene or the emotions that came with it for both of you?"

I dip my head in shame as Dax drops his hand to my opposite hip pulling me to his side. He starts to speak, but Dr. Wright interrupts him. "What happened afterward?" There's concern in her voice. Our body language says it wasn't all roses.

"Sensory overload, I guess," I laugh, but there's nothing funny about the emotional outpouring I had that night. "Dax knew it was going to happen. I guess you probably did too. I naively believed all of this was unnecessary." I shift a little to pull myself away from his embrace. Even if it is only beneficial for me, being able to say this on my own is symbolic. "Every emotion I should have felt in the weeks after the rape engulfed me. I was overtaken with shame, grief, anger, pain. You name the feeling; I was immersed in it. They all ravaged my spirit at once, escaping through sobs and gawking cries. On my knees, I submitted to the emotions." I hold my head up; I won't admit defeat, not now, not ever – Josh Fitz didn't win that night in the alley, and he isn't going to win in my home or in my head.

"Dax, what was your reaction to seeing Cameron so exposed and defenseless?"

"She was the most beautiful thing I have ever seen. I've never had an experience so raw with anyone, much less a lover. I needed to show her I loved her, not just say the words. I probably shouldn't have done anything physical, but I thought that was what she needed, how I needed to communicate with her. I made love to her. Not as a Dom. Just as a man." His words echo in my head. The serenity in what he offers me, in always anticipating my needs, even when I don't know what they are myself, surpasses any peace I've ever known. This goes beyond loving someone; it's a binding spiritual transfusion. Our souls coalesce.

"Have the two of you talked about how to proceed from here?" Dr. Wright poses the question.

Neither of us answers.

"Dax, what are your thoughts? How do you feel about proceeding in a *vanilla* fashion?"

"I think it's necessary for the time being. She needs to have complete trust in me physically. I need to know if there are things that will trigger responses before proceeding in a Dom/sub partnership."

"Dax, I'm not a fragile flower. Yes, I have emotional breakdowns at times, but it's not because I don't trust you or care for you. I want to fill your needs the way you fill mine. Why don't you understand that?" My emotions are starting to get the best of me. I want to be able to move beyond this, to forget it ever happened, but every turn I take, someone is treating me like broken glass. My need to compartmentalize this far outweighs my desire to process it.

He stands at my outburst; I follow him with hands shaking with the infusion of adrenaline. I'm not backing down on this. I need to stand my ground. "Cam, this is so much bigger than just having sex. You think nothing will change between us, that you will handle me taking you to your limit. I don't want to see you break. I can't be the cause of that." He doesn't reach for me. He doesn't try to comfort me. His voice is stern, uncompromising. "If you want to enter into this type of relationship, start here. Quit questioning my decisions and accept they are what are best for you. If you want to make me happy, you want to be my sub, start with that simple task."

It is like a slap to the face. I realize he's right, which might hurt more than the idea of what he was presenting. I think of a Dom/sub relationship only in sexual terms. He lives this as a lifestyle, and I can't follow simple instructions. I know he's expecting me to fight. Hell, I'm expecting me to fight. Instead, I cast my eyes toward the floor with a whispered, "Yes, Sir," before resuming my seat on the couch. I feel the weight of his stare resting on my neck, but I don't look up.

Dr. Wright choses to intervene, breaking the tension in the room, "Our time is up for today, but the two of you need to discuss how your relationship will proceed going forward, not just physically but overall communication of needs and expectations. Don't be discouraged by this Cam; this lifestyle is a continuous learning process. The wonderful part about it is finding a Dom who wants to teach you and grow with you. Give him a chance to do that but trust you might not always see the reason for his actions. I can assure you any decision Dax makes in regards to you will always be *for* you, not for him, because ultimately, that's his responsibility…to meet your needs." She turns her attention to Dax, "And you need to try to clearly communicate your reasoning to her and allow for discussion until she freely gives over the control. It will come." Her smile is soft and motherly, as though she is trying to teach us to share, rather than coaching us in our sex life.

Dax extends his hand to me and taking it, I stand. "Come on, Kitten. Let's get out of here."

We walk in silence, hand in hand to the truck. He kisses my temple as he opens the door to help me in. "Don't be discouraged, love." With that he tucks me in and closes the door.

CHAPTER TWENTY-TWO

As I sit in silence, my phone scares the shit out of me when it rings five minutes into our drive. "Hello?" I answer after pulling it from my purse.

Piper is on the other end, but I'm having a hard time making out what she's trying to tell me. "Piper, slow down. What are you talking about?"

"Cam, have you seen the news?" she responds in a breathless voice.

"No, Dax and I have been in counseling. What's up?"

"I don't really know how to tell you this."

"Just say it. You've never been one for beating around the bush."

The sharp intake of breath is almost as loud as the exhale that follows. "The local news is airing your story."

"What story?" Having no inkling of what she might be talking about, I'm getting irritated with her inability to say what she called to say.

"Cameron, it was released that you were allegedly raped by Josh Fitz. They have also publicly announced your resignation from the bank, the sale of your home, and your presumed relationship with Dax, whom they are referring to as some sort of a delinquent." She speaks the words quickly and with little emotion, but I don't hear anything beyond that.

I drop the phone as panic takes over. My chest starts to painfully constrict, my heart rate sky rockets, and unable to breath normally, I gasp for air. Blackness swarms my vision as I hear tires squealing causing me to lurch forward, the seat belt catching me.

"Cameron?" I hear my name in the distance, but the voice seems so far away. I don't want to reach for it. I want to succumb to the quiet away from the physical strain my body is acquiescing to. "Cameron! Baby, come back to me." The voice is closer, but I just want to move from it. My head hits something hard, jolting me back to a semi-conscious state. "Cameron. Open your eyes and look at me." Dax. My beautiful Dax. I feel his hand on my cheek and one behind my neck, his forehead mirroring mine. "Look at me, Cam." His voice has a way of always returning me to the present, my homecoming. My eyes flutter open, but my vision remains blurry. His face is stricken with an emotion I can't place as my sight clears.

"Dax?" I sound pathetic even to myself, weak, vulnerable.

"Shhh. I'm here." Somehow he has stopped the truck and comes to my side, now cradling me against his chest. I allow myself to linger, to enjoy his woodsy scent, the feel of his arms around me, and the comfort his embrace brings. "What the hell was that call about?" he asks through borderline anger and robust concern.

"Oh, no. Piper. I must have hung up on her."

"Don't worry about Piper right now. What did she say to you that sent you into a tail spin?"

"My cocoon."

"What?"

"This protective little silky world you've had me encased in, my cocoon, is being ripped wide open and every intricately woven strand torn apart." I sit staring at the open sky past him, lost in the nightmare of what is about to become my reality.

"Cam, what are you talking about, sweetheart?"

"The news did a headline piece on me today. They named me, the rape, my resignation from the bank, and Dax...they mentioned our relationship." Slowly my eyes meet his. "I don't know how to begin to do damage control on this, Dax."

"We do it together. Let's get home and see if we can find the clip online so we know what was said and go from there."

My huffing tells him I'm not happy with this course of action, but I keep my mouth shut and let him lead.

"Kitten, when you get through this, you will spread your wings, and it will be exquisite. Let me help take you there, okay?" I love the feel of his hands on my face as his calloused thumbs brush my cheekbones. There's tranquility in it, as he takes me from reckless to Zen with a simple swipe of a finger. He kisses me on the forehead before pulling back to look in my eyes, "You good to head home or do you need a few minutes?"

"No, I'm good. I need to call Piper back." He closes the door while I find my phone. I return Piper's call, who is not surprised I reacted the way I did. She's gathering the Fishes for a meeting of the minds at our house tonight. I'm sure Dax will be thrilled to have all of their opinions on the table.

"So are they all coming over or just Piper?" He asks as soon as I hang up. His tone is lighthearted with a hint of sarcasm. He loves them as much as I do, well maybe not *as* much, but he knows what they mean to me.

"All of them." I reach out to take his hand. He in turn kisses my knuckles before settling our hands on his lap. The rest of the trip is spent in silence. Arriving home, he helps me out of the vehicle, leading me in the house by my hand. Assuming he is keeping me on a leash, I follow thinking we are going to the chair to talk, but to my surprise, he leads me upstairs toward our room.

"Dax?" I draw out his name in question, but he provides no answer. I want to dig in my heels in an effort to force one but realize this is one of those times I need to be compliant and allow him to lead.

"I wanna play with you. Nothing intense. Just something to get you out of your head and start to explore each other. There's not going to be any need for a safe word, but you always need to have one. If you need to stop, say 'butterfly'."

I'm dumbfounded. Thirty minutes ago he was arguing that I was not ready for this, and here he is entering into it.

"I know what you're thinking, Cam. Stop. Today will be about you following commands without hesitation in a respectful way. Nothing extreme. Do you understand?"

"Yes." My voice trembles slightly though not from fear; I'm drowning in anticipation. I immediately catch my first blunder following up my one word response with, "Sir." It earns a smirk from him as he cocks one brow.

"When we enter into play, it's always Sir. What is your safe word?"

"Butterfly."

"Take off your clothes. Wait for me on the bed. Kneeling. Head bowed." I don't respond verbally as he saunters off to the bathroom, but instead I move to the chair to neatly fold my clothes as I remove them. The sudden nerves I feel are a strange mix of emotions. The adrenaline is kicking in, the element of the unknown putting my senses on high alert, and my heart aches to avoid a mistake. I desperately want to please him – to show him I can respond without hesitation, to follow where he leads, to trust him in every action he takes. I can't just tell him those things. In his lifestyle, I must be able to demonstrate them.

Nude, I perch myself in the middle of the bed. This seems like a simple task until I realize I don't know where to kneel or what the position is. Do I spread my legs? Where do I put my hands? When I have kneeled for him before, it was never intentional. My heart rate accelerates as I fidget in an effort to get comfortable and presentable, trying in vain to remember how I was sitting after we scened before, but the details escape me. I still when I see him exit the bathroom casting my eyes downward. No longer able to see him move throughout the room, I rely on being able to feel him around me. His presence causes the hair on my arms to stand on end as if there is a slight chill in the room. I suppress the urge to shiver as he approaches.

It takes every ounce of self-control I have not to look up to find his eyes. I stare at the comforter on the bed as he leans in to me, passing my face; I feel the warmth of his breath in my ear. "Relax, Kitten." He coos as he pries my fingertips from the inside of my thighs where the nails had begun to leave marks. "You look stunning."

He steps back, leaving me in anticipation. The expectation of what might come has me almost panting for air, the desire for him to touch me overtaking my thoughts. The room seems to be closing in as if nothing else exists in the world; this finite space contains everything. The waiting proves to be harder than expected. I want to reach out to him, to pull him to me, to take the affection I crave, but that isn't my role.

"Lie flat on your back with your hands over your head and legs together." The sudden sound of his voice catches me off guard and jolts me to action. I do as I am told while trying to avoid eye contract, unsure of whether or not it's permissible.

"Good, girl," the words strike me as odd, juvenile, yet somehow it seems to be the highest form of praise I've ever received as my face heats and my heart swells.

His touch graces my hands as he begins to wind a silky fabric around my wrists but doesn't secure the material or knot it. "Hold on to the rung above you." I realize the material is currently symbolic of bondage while he judges my reactions to being captive. I try to steady my breathing as he finishes working the ribbon. He feels my apprehension. Soothing it with his voice, "Open your eyes. Don't lose sight of where you are physically. Not yet." His voice in my ears is an instant salve. I wasn't aware my eyes were closed. "You can watch, Cameron. Do whatever you need to do to stay present."

With a gentle nod of my head in confirmation, I watch him move to the end of the bed, where he repeats what appear to be the same movements, fastening my feet to the footboard in symbolic binds. "You're able to move your arms and legs, but I want you to keep them as still as if they were bound by knots you can't undo. Do not let go of the headboard." Unable to move from this place my anxiety quickly starts to ratchet, but as long as I can see him, I stay just this side of irrational. The moments I let my eyes close I begin to forget where I am. It's a fine balance.

My eyes follow him around the room, wondering, anticipating, waiting for his next move. He steps to the dresser, turning on the sound dock flooding the room with classical music. But instead of the dark, macabre selections from my scene, he has chosen a much lighter fare, whimsical almost. The corners of my lips draw up in a smile at his consideration for every detail. Facing me, he begins to close the distance between us, stopping at the edge of the bed. I notice something in his hand, and he catches me eyeing it suspiciously. "It's a flogger. It can be used for pain or pleasure. For now, we are only exploring pleasure, trust, and your ability to follow my instructions." His face is calm and inviting, my apprehension instantly leaves me.

Starting at my feet, he drags the tails of the flogger up the arch, tickling the sensitive flesh, my foot jerks in reflex. He instantly stops. My instructions were to remain still and not let go of the headboard. I focus in an effort to maintain control over my response to him. The trail of leather continues to the top of my foot, slowly up my calf, leaving a trail of goose flesh in its wake. I've become hypersensitive to any touch. His continued pursuit up my thigh, methodically, causes my flower to moisten and my back to arch. He doesn't stop, but I watch his face for signs of irritation at my movement but see none. Reaching my belly he makes the same trail back down my other leg to my foot. My eyes slowly fade to close as I allow the sensations to take over.

The chill in the air heightens the exploration when he moves from my legs to my core. Circling my belly button the flogger caresses one side, then the other, my collarbone, then my neck. I turn into the softness embracing my neck just as the tail escapes my cheek. As the leather leaves my skin, I inhale sharply, moaning at the loss, with a quick burst of air the tassels land on my right breast. Jolting my eyes open, where I expect to find pain, my nipple has pursed at the sudden onslaught of sensation, glorious sensation. Before it registers, he repeats the same stroke on my left nipple. Our eyes meet; he's looking for anguish, but finds adoration. My heaving chest and low moans encourage his exploration. The ribbons of hide drag the nerve endings to heights they've never reached. With the flick of his wrist, the knotted ends tingle my glory spot causing my shoulders to rise off the mattress, but my hands remain locked on the rungs of the headboard. The cry of ecstasy causes his face to twitch in a hidden smile. I lower my back; I desperately want to remain in control of my responses, but his expert use of this little toy is making it difficult. My clit is throbbing for attention, my breasts ache to be touched, and I long to kiss his supple lips. Watching him move, in his element, he's graceful, yet strong, and beautiful. His eyes focus intently on me, my body, and my reactions. He's yet to touch me with his hand or any other part of his body, but my mind is screaming for release.

"Dax," I moan in question, begging for him to bring me the release I need.

"Sir." With that statement he pops my clit again. As I open my mouth to question him, the flogger comes between my legs from a different angle, hitting the length of my pussy, the knots at the end of the tails perched at my entrance. Each stroke of the straps is a little bit harder but nothing painful. He has me riding the edge of euphoric bliss with a razor fine line between it and pain.

I cry out to him again, "Sir," but he ignores my requests. The lashes hitting all of the spots that make my flesh scream, my breasts, my clit, the soles of my feet. He is going to bring me to orgasm without ever touching me with any part of his body. "Please..." I draw the word out in hopes of him sensing my desperation.

"Do not let go of the bed and do not come, Kitten." It's still Dax, but his tone is different than I have heard before; the authority in it surpasses even that which has brought me out of triggered flashbacks, but somehow it is warm and inviting. I desperately need to please him, to show him I can do this, but I'm struggling not to let the sensations crash through me.

The ministrations continue, up and down my body, slight flicks of the wrist bringing torturous pleasure to my body. He knows I'm at the end of my rope, my ability to maintain control is all but lost. He's watching my face intently, but I can't focus on him. Every time my eyes close, the rolling through my pelvic region starts, the waves of orgasm struggling to reach the shore. Flick. Flick. Flick. My pussy is pulsing with desire, so wet I can feel it smearing on my legs. Flick.

Flick. My mind is blank except for the colors of pleasure. With eyes closed, I feel tears seeping down my face, yet they aren't tears of sadness – it's somehow a euphoric release. Unable to see beyond the feelings being perpetuated on my body, I hear him, "Come for me, baby."

My legs are pulled from their station, suddenly resting on his shoulders as his mouth orchestrates a melody on my clit that sends my body into a crescendo, clutching at the wood of the headboard, my hips buck as I have an almost out of body experience. As the eruption of the orgasm starts, my whole body warms, my mind blanketed in color, and I feel weightless. The feelings are surreal. I don't see him, I don't feel me, I just exist, floating somewhere in an existential realm. Time ceases to exist as I transcend to a place of warmth.

I wake as though I have been asleep, slowly coming out of what seems to be a deep slumber. I find myself wrapped up in a blanket surrounded by Dax's huge arms. I watch as the sleeve of tattoos move in a repetitive motion, his hand stroking my hair, his cheek pressed against my forehead. He must have felt me stir, "Hey, sweetheart. How are you feeling?" The sound of his voice is pure magic; there are days I think it alone could feed my soul.

"Hhhmm…" I don't seem to be able to formulate words. My mind is mush, my body lethargic.

Chuckling, "You've been out for a while." He hands me a bottle of water, which I attempt to refuse. "You need to stay hydrated. Drink." I oblige simply because I don't want to muster the strength to argue.

"Did I fall asleep?"

"No, just a touch of sub-space. It's unusual for someone to reach it so quickly. You're response was perfection, Cam."

"Is sub-space bad?"

"Not at all. It's a place some subs never achieve, but others want to get there every time they scene. It's exhausting on the body and the spirit. Do you feel that?"

"Yeah. I don't feel like I have the energy to lift my hand to scratch my nose, but it's an amazing weakness."

"You did really well. I was impressed with your ability to do as you were told. It's much more difficult to adhere to bonds that don't really exist than it is those which restrict movement. I didn't want to push your limits by trapping you but wasn't sure how well you would adhere to my demands. Even when you went into sub-space, you never let the headboard go. I had to pry your fingers off to hold you."

"How long have we been like this?"

"I don't know, thirty minutes maybe."

"Oh my gosh. I'm sorry, Dax." I start to scramble to a sitting position, but his arms clutch me to his chest.

"Sorry for what?"

"You have to be bored out of your mind sitting here petting my head while I basically slept." The laughter roaring from his is confusing me.

"Why are you laughing at me?"

"Kitten, I'm not laughing at you, but how could you think I would rather be anywhere else than wrapped up with you, soothing you, loving you. This has been a perfect afternoon for me. I love this."

I lean up to kiss his neck before settling back into my nook, just enjoying the feel of his arms around me, the heat his body provides, the protection I feel in his cocoon.

"Your girls are going to be here in about an hour. Do you want to take a shower before they come or just be lazy?"

"Lazy."

"Fair enough. What do you want to do about dinner? Do you want me to grill for everybody? I didn't figure you would want to go out to have this discussion." He kisses my temple at the end of his statement.

My heart falls as I remember the reason for my Fish coming in the first place. I shift in his lap to make eye contact, "Can we skip all of that and just ignore any of this is going on?"

"Cam, you knew it was going to come out at some point. You can choose to face it head on, or you can let it determine your path. The woman I know will use it to steer her course, not the other way around."

"You have more faith in me than I do myself these days."

"You'll get it back." With that he pops a kiss on my lips, encouraging me to get up with a pat on my hip. "Come on, we'll go downstairs and see what we can get together for tonight."

CHAPTER TWENTY-THREE

Two hours later, somehow my Fish have turned into an entire school, not only have my friends shown up, but Sutton told Fisher they were coming over and why, and somehow it resulted in all of the brood making an appearance. The Wrights, the Coopers, my girls, have all shown up in support. I am overwhelmed by the encouragement of people who know little about my circumstances but who all want to figure out how to help me deal with the public onslaught and put Josh Fitz behind bars.

When the topic of our gathering finally comes to mention, the opinions of each person are deafening. I feel myself retreating to escape the verbal assault. My Fish are used to talking over each other and everyone somehow still hearing what's being said, but add seven loud ass men, and a tiny Julie to the mix, and my brain can't function. Times like these make me realize how much of myself was lost that night; the ability to take charge and herd cats is a foreign concept. I find myself tucked under Dax's arm buried in his chest, taking comfort in the vibrations of his chatter while he talks to the group. Suddenly, there is utter silence, you can hear a pin drop. I look up from my hiding space to find everyone staring at me.

Sutton stares at me bewildered as Rachel's big mouth pipes open. "Jesus, Cammy, what's wrong with you? You aren't saying anything? How do you want to deal with this shit?"

I shrug my shoulders, knowing that's not an answer, before muttering, "I'm a little overwhelmed by all of this."

"You need to snap out of this shit, Cameron. You have a storm brewing around you, and we have to figure out how to deal with it. Your going all weak on us isn't going to help." Rachel doesn't mean to be harsh; she just says whatever the hell she's thinking, always has.

"Damn, Rachel. Have you forgotten what the fuck she's been through? Give her some damn space," Sutton barks, ever my guardian.

"I know what she's been through, and now is not the time for her to become a sacrificial lamb. She needs to dig deep and find the courage to fight her way back out of this." Her words cut through me like a razor blade. I'm not that person anymore – that fight no longer exists in me. Where there used to be strength, now lies terror; where there used to be control, now lies indecision.

"You two have no couth. Shut up. Cam, sweetie, why don't we all sit down and talk about this rationally? You can tell us what you want to do and what you want us to do to help you get through the trial." Piper has the sweetest heart, always the voice of reason, the mother hen. She will make an amazing mother someday.

Everyone follows Piper's lead as they take seats around the living room, some on couches, some on the floor, Sutton in Fisher's lap (I have no clue what the hell that's about), and myself at Dax's feet with his hand in my hair gently massaging my neck. He knows I'm overloaded and is silently trying to reel me back to a safe place. He leans down, whispering in my ear, "You look edible at my feet Kitten. I love you."

I look up to him, his smile warming me from the inside out as my cheeks flush. I can't help but return the look; he doesn't need me to repeat the words – he knows I love him, too.

"Okay, Cammy, where's the Boardroom Bitch? We need to summon her ass." Comments like this make me realize Rachel doesn't have a clue. My misplaced anger, every thought I've harbored, laying the blame on the Fish, it all manifests itself in this moment.

"Look, that girl doesn't exist anymore. I don't know how to fight this battle. You guys don't seem to get it – I've changed. I'm not the girl you've known for twenty years. My only thought is that Dax and I need to reach out to my lawyer in an effort to do public damage control. Surely he would speak on my behalf. I'm dumbfounded the news stations didn't attempt to contact him, or me, or Dax, for that matter, to get some sort of statement. I don't want to be the one that delivers a message to the media."

Moby decides this is the opportune time for him to throw out his suggestion. "Why don't you let me and Joey go downtown, Fisher can sneak us in, and we will take care of him for you. None of the other inmates would bat an eyelash at a man who raped a woman." I flinch at his use of the word rape as Dax's hand tenses on my neck; when I relax, so does his hand.

"Moby, you're an idiot. Fisher isn't going to let you into the cells to rough up an inmate. Besides, he was released on bond." Joey and Moby are like two little peas in a pod; they're both indescribably cute, but they're better suited to wooing the ladies than fighting crimes against humanity. At least Joey is smart enough to realize that as he refutes Moby's idea.

Suddenly, Landis and Julie are arguing with Moby and Joey, Rachel and Sutton are going at each other, Brooks and Jake are talking over everyone, and Piper and Charlie are formulating the taking of the new Troy on the couch.

"Stop it!" I scream.

"There she is," Rachel's beaming at my outburst. "I know that fire's still in you, girl."

"Shut. Up. Rachel. Damn it. This is totally out of control. You guys act like we can just take on the world, the media, and Josh Fitz on our own. There is a legal system to deal with; I have a lawyer. I have to find the least intrusive way to deal with this situation publicly and try to start to heal and move on. Please quit fucking fighting and spouting off ignorant plots." I huff, falling back into the tree trunks that are Dax's legs.

"Hey, Cammy?"

"Yeah, Charlie…"

"Instead of coming out publicly about your ordeal, why don't you join a foundation for rape victims, or start one of your own? You might assist with counseling needs or legal expenses, things many women, or men, wouldn't be able to afford on their own or have the resources to obtain. You have options most women don't have, and you have the education and connections to really build an empire with a trust or organization." Her voice is soft but so wise. She pauses waiting for my reaction, and I'm quietly waiting for her to continue. "Let your lawyer come out publicly. As you get more involved in a program, fight to get the recognition for the program rather than on your personal trauma. Listeners are always the ones to look out for – they plot while everyone else runs at the mouth.

With tears running down my cheeks I move to hug her. I speak as though we are the only two people in the room. "That's perfect, Charlie. Thank you."

Instantly, the group quiets down, and everyone acts as though we didn't have some intense conversation and just mingles like its just another night. I love this group. I never thought I would have family other than my Fish, but I'll be damned if Dax hasn't just roped in a gaggle of hot guys to warm my heart. Even if their ideas are barbaric, they protect me as if they've known me a lifetime, and they do it simply because Dax loves me.

CHAPTER TWENTY-FOUR

The next few days are a total whirlwind. Dax and I visit my lawyer, who agrees there needs to be a public statement made from our side. He also agrees that I do not need to be the one to make the statement. He puts us in touch with a lawyer in town, who specializes in non-profits so we can start to organize our new foundation. Dax and I have decided we want to do this together. Since he's not working, I'm not working, and we have the resources to get something established, why not make it our project.

Suzy Crane, the lawyer we were referred to, makes time to see us. When we arrive, I instantly take a liking to her. I have to wonder if we weren't referred to her because she has a passion for what we want to do. She is not a big name in the legal world, but we are small potatoes at this point, and right now, we need someone who will invest in this project, not just try to profit from it.

Walking into her office, she stands, coming around the corner of her desk.

"Hey guys! Douglas said he was sending a couple over. I'm Suzy. It's so nice to meet you both." Her smile is warm and welcoming as is her sweet Southern drawl. She is tidy, and it's impossible not to notice her schoolmarm look. She has to be close to us in age. I bet if she removed the glasses, wore clothes a size smaller, and put on just a hint of make-up, she could be beautiful.

"Hey, Suzy, I'm Dax. This is my girlfriend, Cameron." I notice instantly she doesn't melt when he talks to her, just maintains her comforting charm – another point for Suzy.

"Please, have a seat. Tell me what I can help you guys with today." She returns to her perch behind the desk, pen poised to note anything we say of importance.

Since this is my saga, I feel I should be the one to tell her why we are here. I silence Dax, who's ready to launch into explanation with a touch on his forearm and a glance in his direction. He closes his mouth and smiles.

"We are looking for assistance in setting up a foundation for rape victims. We aren't sure of the ins and outs of what we want to provide, but legal assistance and counseling would be at the top of the list. We need someone to help us to set it up but then continue with legal counsel as we proceed."

"The process of setting up a non-profit isn't a difficult one, the paperwork I mean. I'll give you a quick run down of the steps involved. I can certainly take you through each one and would be honored to continue working with you past the development." She looks to me before continuing. Suzy is racking up the points. She doesn't know my story, but maybe it's just women's intuition, but she knows this is personal for me. I can see the look in her eyes that tells me she 'gets it.'

"First, I would need to file a certificate of incorporation. Then you will need to select a board of directors. Cameron, I'm assuming based on your tenure at the bank you are accustomed to how those work." She recognizes me from the news. Without admitting she knows my story, she just relieved me of having to tell her by acknowledging she knows who I am. I want to be stung by that, but the fact is it just saved me the agony of having to tell her the details. "I would suggest a minimum of four people to start, but you will most likely need to grow that number as the foundation grows. Do you have a vision? A mission statement?" I shake my head no in response, feeling like we've got the cart before the horse. "Don't be discouraged,

Cameron. The desire to do this will bring all of this to light as you start to put pen to paper. Your board can help establish that goal along with helping write bylaws and board policies. I will need to file for a tax ID number and federal tax exemption. There are state and local non-profit regulations you and your board will need to study and follow to the letter of the law to maintain your status. You will need to open a bank account and establish check signing procedures; find office space; get equipment; hire a staff; and put your payroll system in place." She runs through her checklist quickly as I mentally make notes of everything she says, hoping Dax is keeping up.

"Cameron, your biggest task will not be the legal nuances or finding a space. Your biggest hurdle, and one you need to set your mind to quickly, is securing funds. You will need large donations to run an organization like this. I would imagine you have connections throughout the business community. You are going to need to call in every favor you have to get on-going contributions, and eventually you will need to have staff dedicated to fundraising. I would also encourage you to reach out to both the legal and medical fields locally to find lawyers, doctors, and therapists who are willing to donate their services. Pro bono work is something all professionals do, but you will have to put together an enormous list of providers to be able to continually serve victims. Recovery can be a long process, and if a therapist only donates four hours per month, one victim may get all of their services for months or even years." She pauses, allowing the information to seep in. "Do you have any questions?"

Dax chimes in, "What do we need to do in order to get started?"

"I will start to draft all of the paperwork, but I will need the name of the foundation before I can file. You will also need to establish a board quickly, but I don't have to have those names in order to start the process."

"I should be able to get you the name and the board members names before the end of the week. Does that work for you?" I ask.

"Absolutely. I'm really looking forward to working with you, Cameron. I think what you're doing is brave and desperately needed. Women need to know there is life after tragedy." She leans in to hug me, and right before I flinch, Dax grabs my hand, squeezing reassurance into me. She sees my discomfort and extends her hand with a smile instead.

The next few days are a whirlwind of activity. Dax has let me take the lead on setting things up, and in the process we have quickly established a board of directors. Currently, it consists of myself, Dax, Dr. Wright, Piper, and Fisher, each chosen for a different reason. Dr. Wright has agreed to head up the search for the medical community donations; Piper is a marketing and fundraising genius since that's what she does for a living; and Fisher, because of his years in law enforcement. It may seem like an odd group, but I know these are all people dedicated to the cause who will commit the necessary time.

We are already feeling the strain of needing additional people. We are using Rachel and Sutton to pound the pavement for monetary donations. Rachel has amazing connections to old money through real estate and new money through dating the men she helps find homes. She's already secured almost a hundred thousand dollars in recurring pledges annually. Sutton has tons of military connections, and while most of those people don't have the money to donate, her commanding officers have connections helping in large ways as well. Turns out, Dax has made connections in the music world with symphony goers and classical music lovers, not just in Greenville, but also with professors and people he worked with at Juilliard. Many of my banking contacts have come through with donations as well, but our saving grace is Johnston Inman, III. I worked with his father at the bank when I first started. After he retired a few years into my employment, his son took over his accounts and his law firm. Johnston Inman, II always had an affinity for me. His father was and still is a philanthropist, and he follows in his father's footsteps. Inman, Inman, and

Tucker commit to being our angel supporter. The Inmans donate a collective ten million dollars to be set up in a trust of sorts for the foundation along with their attorney services. Johnston Inman, II also appointed a member of his staff to scout for other lawyers to commit to pro bono work for the foundation.

Dr. Wright, however, has not been as successful as the rest of us. She has had a difficult time getting a variety of different doctors to commit to working with us. Since we are all volunteering our time at this juncture, I'm proposing to our board we invest in our own general practitioner and on-site psychiatrist. It would eliminate the problem of trying to piece together treatment for victims and ensure there is always someone around to meet our needs. We sanction Shelly to start this search process, and as candidates are identified we will interview them and proceed accordingly.

CHAPTER TWENTY-FIVE

"Kitten, what are you doing?" Dax hollers up the stairs.

"I just got out of the shower." The sound of a thousand bulls trampling up the stairs startles me until it dawns on me that the stampede is Dax, realizing I'm naked and wet. I turn toward the noise just as he comes barreling through the bathroom door.

I gaze up at his tall frame finding his eyes. They're fierce, and he's looking to play. Our time together has been limited with the start of Healing Wings. He doesn't say anything, just assesses my face. Slowly, I release the towel wrapped around my chest. As it falls to the floor, I follow, tucking first my right foot under me as I reach my knee, then my left. When my butt hits my feet, I cast my glance downward. Placing my palms on my thighs, I wait.

I watch his feet; they're bare peaking out from under this jeans. His toes are cute. I fight the urge to reach out to touch his leg, to run my cheek up his pants, to caress him. Instead, I wait. The time seems to drag on while he says nothing, the sound of his breathing captivating the room. I know he's turned on, but he has me on edge and will keep me here until he decides the time is right. Disappointment fills me when he turns and retreats from the bathroom. While I submitted myself to him, I gave him control, and he has not released me, so I continue to kneel on the hard tiles. The exercise in patience is far harder to maintain than the act of submission, although Dax would argue patience is submission.

I hear him tinkering around in the bedroom, and then I hear the sound the speaker makes when it receives power, and bluesy jazz instrumental sounds fill the room. I don't recognize the artist, but his music always sets the mood. The sound is slow, rhythmic, sensual. Whatever he has in mind will not be wild, intense, or out of control. Still staring at the floor, I see his shirt drop to the floor as his jean clad legs and bare feet appear in my line of sight again. Squatting so we're at eye level, he tilts my chin, forcing eye contact. He kisses me with abandon, the sudden onslaught of his lips on mine and his tongue dancing in my mouth. The pull and push of a well timed, intimate kiss. As he pulls away, leaving me breathless and wanton for more, he tugs on my bottom lips with his teeth. Releasing it with a nibble before popping one more kiss on my swollen lips. He rises to a standing position leaving me vulnerable at his feet. I look to him for direction, but he doesn't give any verbally.

He unzips his jeans, and as he does so, he extends his hand to me. Taking my hand, he uses it to pull his semi-hard cock out of his pants. He takes a half a step forward, and I'm sure he can feel my breath on his crotch. I feel it radiating back to my face with each exhale.

"Suck me off, Cameron," that deep voice returns and with it his insistence upon my obedience. I don't hesitate. My free hand reaches around to his ass, sneaking beneath the jeans that hang loosely around his waist, while the full hand slowly strokes him to erection. The feel of his skin on mine is like silk encasing steel without the cold edge metal would bring. Deliberate in making eye contact the moment we lock glances, I swirl my tongue around the head of his dick, holding his stare as I take the enormity of him fully into my mouth. His green eyes burn as I stare into them. He reaches his hand to the back of my head, grabbing a fistful of wet hair, encouraging my rhythmic motions, keeping the pace slow. He slinks in burying his head at the back of my throat, holding me still. "Swallow." I do as I'm told and am rewarded with a low moan I've never heard him make, as my throat tightens around him, my tongue lavishing the underside of him, pressing against his shaft as I comply with his demand. He pulls my head back mid-swallow, my mouth tugging on his dick. When his head falls back, his Adam's apple glides up and down his throat, and it's a seductive calling. I feel the vibrations of his moans. Digging my nails into his ass, he groans, and I pick up my pace, trying to bring him to the finish line. When I hear him growl, I know he's close. Cupping his balls in the palm of my hand, I reach behind them, unsure of whether this will get me punished, and stroke his forbidden hole with the pad of my middle finger. I ease into the opening, watching his face for signs of irritation. When none come, I press gently past the ring, curling the finger back toward me in a "come here" motion. Sucking his dick, my mouth continuing its pursuit of semen, I call his orgasm to me with the movement of my middle phalange. Three firm swipes against his prostate have both of his hands in my hair as he fills my mouth with his seed. "Holy fuuuuccckk!" He stills me with his hands, pulsating on my tongue, and I swallow, waiting for more.

He regains his composure freeing himself from the confines of my lips. I remain kneeling, my hands returning to my thighs. Grabbing the waist of his jeans, he pulls them over his ass, tucks himself back, and zips up before reaching for my hand to draw me out of my pose. I stumble from my time on the hard tile as my legs regain feeling, his free hand catching my waist, steadying me in front of him. "Careful, love." I find myself pressed tightly against his broad chest, one arm capturing my waist, the other cupping my cheek. "Where the hell did that come from?"

"What?" I question coyly.

"That..." he draws out the word. "Who taught you to do that with your finger?"

"I read about it in a book. I've never tried it before." I smile a shy smile at him hoping he liked it but too afraid to ask.

"I don't know what kind of books you read, but we need to invest in more of them." He assuages my fears with one sentence. Leaning down, he kisses me sweetly on the lips. It's funny – I haven't heard the music since he turned it on, but now it fills the space around us as he hums the tune, pressed to my mouth. "We need to get going if we're going to make it to your closing on time." He smacks my ass playfully, turning out of the bathroom.

"How much time do I have before we need to leave?"

He looks at the clock on the nightstand. "Roughly, five minutes." He gives me a shit eating grin knowing he took up all of my dressing time with his escapade. I can't help but smile back at him. I love seeing him happy and knowing I put the smile on his face, even if it means I will look like the wreck of the Hesperus when meeting the buyers of my house.

"Crap, Dax! I look like hell," I whine.

"No, baby, you don't. You do look like you've been thoroughly used though," he winks at me. "Come on. We need to get going."

I throw on jeans and a fitted shirt while sliding on leather flip-flops. Dragging a brush through my tousled hair securing it in a ponytail, I debate skipping makeup but then conclude there's no way I can pull it off. I grab my cosmetics bag and race down the stairs and am scooped up in beautifully inked arms. With my arms wrapped securely around his neck, I nuzzle into him. "I don't know how I got so lucky," I mutter into his chest. The truth is, I really don't know. I don't deserve him, and I sure as hell shouldn't have gotten a second chance with him after blowing him off repeatedly. For some reason, he hasn't figured any of that out, which suits me just fine. He makes my heart sing and my soul soar.

With a tight squeeze, "I love you too," is all he says. We walk out the door hand in hand.

The closing only takes about an hour, but I feel like my hand is about to fall off from signing the same shit over and over. One of my favorite things about Dax is his ability to sit patiently for hours at a time always waiting on me. He never gets frustrated, never complains, just waits as if there is no where on earth he would rather be than watching me sign form after form eliminating my home ownership.

As we're leaving, I comment on my observation. "How do you do that?"

"Do what?"

"You have the patience of Job. How do you do it? How do you sit and wait on me for hours or days and never get frustrated or irritated by it?"

"Cameron, I love you. I've known it for a lot longer than you have. I have been patiently waiting for you to catch up. Know this, I will wait for you every day for the rest of my life."

I stop walking, staring at him. "You don't mean that, Dax. The rest of your life is a long time. Let's not make statements that far in advance." I try to play the words off like they don't mean anything, but the truth is they do. They mean everything. They imply a forever I lost the day my parents and Chris died.

"I'm not having this conversation standing outside in a parking lot. If you wanna talk about this, get in the truck. If you don't wanna talk about it, get in the truck. Either way, I'm not having a discussion about our relationship in public." The edge in his voice tells me he's pissed off, but for the life of me, I don't know what I said to make him angry.

Closing the door to the truck, "Dax, why are you so angry?"

"Why am I angry? Why do you think I'm angry, Cameron?" His hands gripping the steering wheel so tightly that his knuckles are white.

"I don't know? Really, I don't."

"What do I have to say to you to get through your head what my intentions are?"

"Dax, you hardly know me. How can you make a proclamation like that? You say these beautiful things, and I don't mean to belittle them, but I don't want to cling to false hope. It's not realistic." I plead with him to understand.

"I know you better than any of your friends do, and they are your family."

"How can you say that?"

"Cam, knowing you isn't about the number of years I have counted you in my life, it's about the intimacy in which we've shared in the times we've had. I was with you as you clung to life. I've held you when you've been scared. I've loved you when you were broken. I see the sunshine in your spirit, and I love your soul. It won't matter if I make that proclamation today or in ten years. There is no one on this earth closer to you, and that scares the hell out of *you,* but it makes me feel whole."

I'm speechless. No man has ever professed any sort of love for me, and if one had attempted to, I would have cut him off and promptly quit seeing him. I haven't had room in my life for relationships that required nurturing. If I'm being honest with myself, I have refused to let anyone get that close to me for fear of losing him.

"I know what loss like you've endured does to you, baby. I know what kind of walls you erect to keep that level of pain out. But the truth is, I scaled your walls while you were unconscious, and since then you've built them higher with me on the inside. As much as you don't want to admit it, you like the protection you feel I offer you, you like feeling like there's someone as strong as you are standing by your side, someone who allows you to step back and carries the burden for you."

Tears pool in my eyes, quietly spilling over onto my cheeks. I choke on the words trying to get them out, "No." He tries to interrupt me, but I hold up my hand to silence his protest. "No one has shouldered my burden." My words are broken as I try to get out what I need to say. "I haven't depended upon anyone because I haven't needed to. It scares the hell out of me that you could be *that* person because I thought those people left me years ago. I never thought anyone would come close to the love my parents and Chris gave me. I know beyond a shadow of a doubt you love me as fiercely as they ever did, and if I want to be honest, I know you always will. What I don't know is why."

"Why does anyone fall in love? Have you ever sat back and thought about the process of loving someone? It's not a controllable emotion. My heart was destined for yours. Stop trying to control it and allow it to control you. Let the love that's between us guide who you are, how you grow, and what we become."

I don't have any other words. I push myself across the cab of the truck, leaning into him to capture his lips. His hand hits the back of my neck, his grip telling me he's in control, the kiss telling me he's in love. "I'm sorry, Dax. I'm not good at this. Please know I love you."

"I know you do, sweetheart. I love you too but, baby?"

"Yeah?"

"You're going to be punished for that shit tonight. Just prepare yourself."

"Punished? For what?"

"Questioning what I tell you." There's playfulness in his eyes. Maybe punishment will be fun.

I smirk at him. "Don't think being a brat is cute, Cam. I didn't say funishment. You won't enjoy what I have in mind."

My face scrunches in disapproval. He laughs at me before starting the truck. "You ready to go meet Rachel and look at office space?"

CHAPTER TWENTY-SIX

Looking at office space loses its appeal after the second building we go into. This is about as much fun as a poke in the eye with a sharp stick. My patience is wearing thin as I near my breaking point. "Rachel, none of this is what I had in mind. I don't want to be in a building where other people run businesses. I want to be secluded where our organization is the only tenant. The people who come to see us don't need to feel as though they're on display walking through the halls, feeling everyone knows what they are in the building for because they are going to the floor we occupy. They need anonymity. Downtown Greenville doesn't offer that in a high rise."

"Look, Cammy, these are spaces offering us discounted lease rates for being a non-profit. I think as a courtesy you owe it to them to look at the space they offered. Quit being a whiney bitch and suck it up. Welcome to the reality of starting a business and the bullshit details involved in that process."

"She's right, Cam. You may see something that really wows you for the price." It doesn't happen often, but every once in a while I want to pop Dax in the mouth – right now would be one of those times! I am not interested in his rational thinking. I glare at him indicating my disapproval of his agreement with Rachel. "Keep it up, Cam. We have all night to work out your attitude." Holy shit. He just threatened me with punishment in front of my Fish.

Rachel dies laughing. She gets the death stare, too. "Bitch, I'll remember this," I growl at her.

"You're just mad because there's someone around now who can contain you, and I'm eating that shit up like it's a damn buffet. Dax just became my new best friend."

"Hussy, you don't have any friends. Your mama pays us all to hang out with you and has since high school."

I continue pouting while the two of them hack it up laughing at my expense. I love them both, but I'm over all of this crap. I deplore shopping, and this is an enormous shopping trip I want to end. Visiting two more high-rise complexes downtown with resounding no's, Rachel assures me the last stop on our list is what will fit the bill. Driving through the streets of downtown, we head into the legal district where the law offices reside in historic homes. She pulls into the driveway of a craftsman style cottage. I know before we even walk in the doors we just pulled up to the new home of Healing Wings.

It's a large chocolate brown house off Earle Street with white trim and white columns. The front door is solid leaded glass with an intricate floral design, and the hardwoods are warm and inviting, reflecting the sun from every angle. There are tons of windows allowing light to flood the space. The ceilings are high and the paint colors neutral. Inside, the rooms have all been sectioned off to become offices, but the front room is open leaving a space for a reception area. There's a small kitchen in the back and multiple offices upstairs. There's also an additional building in the backyard, smaller than the house although similar in style. It's a single room that mimics the larger house with the same hardwood floors and tan walls. My mind is racing with the possibilities the entire house and bonus house offer. It's perfect for what we need right now. In time, it might not be large enough, but for now and the foreseeable future, it is more than enough space.

I haven't said a word since we got out of the car; Dax and Rachel haven't shut up. Rachel looks to me as we are getting ready to leave and asks, "So what's the word, Cammy? Do you like it?"

"It's perfect. This is exactly what I had in mind." I don't think either of them expected me to be satisfied with anything today. Dax simply smiles.

"Fantastic. I'll call the owner and get the paperwork drawn up. I'll let you know when it's ready for you to sign. I guess you'll need to get it approved by the board, but I doubt you will have any issues with that. With that my friend, we are done for the evening. Go home and enjoy your man."

CHAPTER TWENTY-SEVEN

As expected, the Board approves the paperwork for the rental space downtown, which sends me into a flurry of activity, everything moving at the speed of light. While I am busy setting up a help hotline and securing volunteers to man it twenty-four hours a day, my team is still out searching for donations and benefactors, and Dr. Wright is in the throes of interviews. I am amazed at the number of candidates she has to choose from when this becomes a paid position instead of volunteer.

My phone rings, and Dax grabs it off the counter. "Hello?" he answers.

"Hey Dax, it's Shelly. I just wanted to call you guys and let you know that I have narrowed the applicant pool down to three general practitioners and two psychiatrists. Can you get with Cam and find out when the Board wants to interview?"

"Yeah, I'll talk to her and have her send out an email to find out what date works best for everyone. Do you want to do group interviews?"

"I think that would be best and would require the fewest interviews for the candidates. They are all currently working in practices in Greenville, so it probably would make sense to try to hold them after hours or on a weekend. Talk to her and see what she thinks, and I will set them up."

"Sounds good. I'll have her get back to you," and with that he disconnects.

"Cam?" In the living room, I overheard his conversation.

"Yeah, baby?" I call out.

"That was Shelly. She wants us to set up a time to meet with the candidates for the center."

I walk into the kitchen, stopping in my tracks when I catch sight of him. There's something about him that always stops me in my tracks. He's beautiful, but it's more than that. Every time I look at him, I see strength and a love that is so powerful I wonder how he contains it.

"Hey, sweetheart, what are you looking at?" He doesn't get it. I doubt he ever will.

When we met, I was positive he knew the power he held over women, but after getting to know him, spending so much time with him, I now know he's completely oblivious to what he does to me. He doesn't seem to notice or even care about other women, and there are tons of them out there who ogle him everywhere we go. His eyes are always set on me, as if no one else in the world exists.

Walking to him, I meet his body leaned against the counter, pressing my front to him. I lift up on my toes to kiss his jaw. Even as tall as I am, it's still a stretch. His arm comes around my lower back, eyes watching me in wonder. "You," I state plainly.

He dips down to kiss my neck, pulling me in closer. "Damn, you smell good."

I smile, resting my forehead on his shoulder. This isn't the reason he called me in here, but I can't think straight with his bare chest on display, his jeans hung low on his hips, his feet bare. That notorious V calls to me like a siren. I push back from him slightly, taking him in, moving my hands to cup his hips, thumbing the indentions that lead to his masculine treasures. His eyes sparkle with acknowledgement of what I want. It's as if I'm starving, and his body is the only thing that will satisfy my hunger.

"Cam?" he questions.

I don't respond. My fingers move to the button of his jeans, undoing them, watching his eyes. The zipper slides down. The house is so quiet I can hear the pull of the tag on the metal teeth. He watches me as though I have become his prey instead of him being the hunted. Pushing the material over his ass, he allows his pants to fall to his ankles before stepping out of them. I step back to admire his form, the ripple of his stomach, the tensing of his biceps, the clenching of his jaw, his cock moving to stand at attention. In the blink of an eye, his posture changes, his tone suddenly stern, "Take off your clothes."

I react instantly pulling my t-shirt over my head, feeling the weight of my breasts as I lower my arms, tossing the shirt to the ground. Standing in panties, I hook my fingers in the sides, maneuvering them down my thighs, maintaining eye contact. I step out of them as he holds his hand out, taking them from me as he turns me around, my back to him. "Put your hands behind your back." I do as I'm told, and the moment my hands reach their destination, he ties my panties around my wrists, securing them.

Immediately, he recognizes my apprehension; he's never bound me in a manner I wasn't free to escape, and my anxiety begins to escalate. I feel his breath on my shoulder and his hands secure on my waist. "You're safe, Kitten." The heat of his words in my ear begin to lessen my fears, but he knows I need to be able to see him to maintain my composure. Testing my limits, he bends me over the counter, my breasts press flat against the cold granite. "Do you remember your safe word?"

"Yes," I pant, attempting to maintain my composure, knowing he is pushing my limits. I want to be able to do this for him.

"Tell me what it is, love," his Dom voice ringing through the kitchen, reverberating off the walls. There is a hint of comfort and a level of fear I can't seem to differentiate between.

"Butterfly."

No other words are exchanged between us. Using his foot, he moves my legs apart, opening me to him. I expect him there, but the shock of his hands hitting my spine between my shoulder blades surprises me, causing me to lift up from the counter. Firmly, he pushes me back into position. His hands glide freely down my spine, then up my sides, teasing my nerves into hyperactivity. Every stroke of his fingers escalates my desire for him, as he moves down my hips to my thighs, passing my knees, and reaching my ankles. My center heats, the wetness almost uncomfortable. His fingers find the pool of longing nestled in my folds as he spreads my lips open, easing two fingers into me, using my natural lubricant to help him inside. Slowly driving them in and out, hitting a spot of ecstasy with each plunge, dragging past it with each withdrawal.

I can see parts of him in my peripheral vision, but as he lowers to a squatting position, I lose sight of him. When his tongue joins his fingers, I know exactly where he is, as he lavishes attention on my clit, continuing to explore with his fingers and bringing me to the edge quickly. As I writhe on the counter on the verge of coming undone, he commands me, "Be still. Do *not* come."

This is an exercise in futility. With his continued ministrations, I will not be able to hold on to control. I shift slightly trying to alleviate the sensual torture to my pussy. I feel the smack before I hear it, and my ass burns with heat from his hand. As I jerk up, there is a second slap, equally as hard in the same spot. As the warmth almost sends me over the edge, his pilgrimage never slows. I feel the muscles deep within starting to roll, tensing in anticipation of the orgasm I won't be able to stop. I whimper. Smack. Then, he's gone, removed from every surface of my body leaving only the sting on my ass cheek.

I hear him walking out of the kitchen, his feet softly marking time on the hardwood floors. I know better than to move. He left me here for a reason although I'm left not knowing what it might be. Panting, frustration mounting at my need for release, I hear him making his way up the stairs and imagine him rustling around in our room but can no longer make out where he is in the house.

With my face still pressed against the cool stone, my breathing becomes erratic. I realize it's not rational; I can move if I need to, but the anticipation of his return is morphing into panic. I try to find something to calm my fears, searching the room with my eyes before landing on the clouds dotting the sky outside. The sunshine and blue canvas begin to sooth my ravaging fears. Lost in the setting, I don't hear him approach.

"Cam, are you okay? Baby, you're sweating." His words don't register, but his voice does. His eyes are filled with concern. I smile at him, making eye contact, drawing me away from the serenity of the sky. He wipes my face with a towel kissing my temple. I catch a glimpse of him, realizing he's been wondering around the house naked.

Behind me again, trailing kisses down my spine, it takes every ounce of self-control I have not to arch my back in greedy need. His hands are everywhere and nowhere at the same time. Lost in sensation overload, I struggle to stay present. The desire to close my eyes and succumb to the pleasure is almost too much to resist. The cool feeling of wetness brings me closer to awareness. Startled by unexpected cold, I turn to look over my shoulder.

He's staring at my ass, slowly warming the lube he has dropped there, rubbing it around my opening. I watch without his knowledge as he strokes his cock. I lower my head, allowing him the freedom to use my body in whatever way he sees fit. His head finds my slit, and he rubs his length in between my lips, coating himself in my sex. He slips in momentarily, my pussy welcoming his thrusts. Slowly, methodically, he moves in, out, in, out, his thumb still circling my ring, the movement slowing as the pressure from his finger builds before it slips passed the barrier. The jolt of pleasure lifts my upper half off the counter.

"Down," his voice is cool and controlled, immediately telling me he's serious.

With my hands still bound by my panties behind my back, I am left with little room for maneuvering. I'm at his mercy when he slips out of my pussy, poising his cock at the other entrance. One hand is at my hip, while the other holds his shaft, pressing gently. I relax, pushing back against him, encouraging his entrance. The initial burn is intense, but I bite my lip to keep from crying out. Balls-deep, he draws his body to mine, lying flat across my back, whispering in my ear, "I want to hear you moan." Then the heat of his pecs is gone, and his hips begin to move, one hand wrapped around me exciting my nub while the other digs into my hip almost painfully.

I cry out the first time he slams into me; he has been gentle until this point, but now he's taking what he wants from me. The harder he pushes the greater my need for him to probe is. My moans turn into cries. Unable to move, my head lifts, stretching my throat, the pleasure hanging just this side of pain. Unintelligible words. Animalistic cries. The louder my wails become the harder he pushes. When his fingers penetrate my lips, deep within my womb, pressing, stroking my favorite spot, the euphoria takes over, and as I sink into subspace, the orgasm consumes my body. Dax's release may have come minutes or an hour after; time ceases to exist, and I am lost in a sensual space continuum. As my body shakes off the adrenaline, I hear Dax in the distance erupt when his orgasm fulfills him.

Releasing my bound hands, Dax pulls out as his dick softens, lessening the pain of the retreat. My hands fall to my side, and I realize my shoulders ache from the unnatural position they have been in, but I'm powerless to do anything about it as I lie motionless on the counter. He rubs my shoulders, aware of my needs, rounding the joint as he moves each of my arms relieving the tension that has settled in them.

With no words uttered between us, he scoops me up into his arms, carrying me like a sleeping child, to his chair. Sitting down, he wraps us both in a blanket, cuddling me to his chest, tucking my head into the nook. The security this offers me is unsurpassed by any other. There is no place I would rather be than in this place of vulnerability, naked, encased in his strong arms, his chin resting atop my head, knowing beyond a shadow of a doubt, he will protect me at all costs, love me with a fierceness I don't deserve, and cherish me forever. The emotions become too much as my eyes release what I can't verbalize. When the tears hit his chest, he pulls back to find me smiling at him, looking into those sage green eyes, I can't contain how much I love him. My heart swells almost painfully wondering if I will ever be able to show him what I feel for him. I never want him to question my devotion to him. I want to serve him, submit to him, be everything he needs from me. "I love you, Dax." I choke out.

"I know, baby. I love you too."

CHAPTER TWENTY-EIGHT

After receiving responses regarding interviews, we agree collectively we would rather dedicate an entire Saturday to interviewing than stretch it out over several days. Shelly schedules all five of the candidates for both positions two hours apart with a break for lunch. This is going to make for a really long day, but hopefully, at the end of it we will have chosen our first two employees and have a date set to open the facility.

Settling in to what we have established as the boardroom in an office upstairs, Shelly introduces us to each candidate, and the conversation flows easily between the group and each prospect. None of our interactions seem like interviews to me – more like we are having great conversations with new friends. The most important questions I pose to each candidate relate to their interest in working with Healing Wings, their motivation, and their commitment to this facility. Everyone in the room has asked questions all day, yet no matter how I phrase the question, each time they watch my reaction to the candidates' responses with baited breath.

Shelly has chosen candidates we can't go wrong with, no matter whom we choose, and there has been little time for us to discuss the previous candidate before the next comes in. I don't know who each person's pick is for the general practitioner position, but the deal is sealed with the psychiatrist when I pose my question for the last time of the day to Dr. Hope Maxwell.

I'm quiet throughout the majority of the interviews, listening, taking in what the candidates have to say, watching how they interact with the group, making certain to note how I react to them. Do they intimidate me? Am I afraid of them? Would I let them touch me, because if I won't, people who seek our help won't either. When the opportunity presents itself, I ask Hope, "What's your motivation to work here? What would be your goals as a contributor to Healing Wings?"

The look on her face softens when her eyes meet mine. I see it instantly. She's a survivor. "I've known this pain, Cameron. It's the reason I got into psychiatry to begin with. I was molested repeatedly as a child. When I finally found the courage to tell someone, my parents got me help. My counselor was my saving grace. I teetered on the edge of suicide as a teenager hiding the shame. She invested in me. As I began to heal, it became the only thing I ever wanted to do with my life. I never want anyone to experience what I went through, but if it happens, regardless of whom the person is or what his or her station is in life, I want that person to find refuge with people who survived and came out on the other side stronger than they were going in. I specialize in sexual trauma for this reason. It's not a job for me; this is my life's passion. I experienced so others could find healing."

My friends all have tears in their eyes, knowing there is someone in my presence that is a kindred spirit, someone who made it and is now making a difference. My decision is made. I only hope the others feel the same. I hug her as she leaves, realizing this is the first person I have touched other than Dax since the rape. He knows it, and I assume my friends do, too, because I haven't hugged them since they left the bar that night.

I return upstairs after letting Dr. Maxwell out and locking the door. Walking into the room, all voices stop. Piper speaks first. "Cam, we think Dr. Maxwell is the obvious choice for Healing Wings."

Taking my seat next to Dax, I look around the room. I wasn't gone that long and wonder what was said in my absence. "That decision was reached quickly."

"She was the only person we spoke with today whom you openly embraced not just physically, but it was obvious the two of you connected. Don't you think it would be beneficial to have people on staff who have experienced things they will be working with?"

"I'm totally on board with the decision, just surprised it was made so quickly. The other guy was equally as impressive, don't you think?"

Shelly interrupts our back and forth, "Cam, you know it's imperative for victims to be able to identify and interact with their doctors. I think our first hire should be someone with experience in the field."

"I'm not arguing at all, just want everyone to know I'm open to discussion. This doesn't have to be *the* person because I connected with her."

Dax lets out a loud laugh, "Of course it does sweetheart. This is your dream. You will be here daily working with these people. The board just needs to support your decisions and make sure you are making wise choices. Shelly brought the candidates she felt were best qualified, so picking who you *like* is exactly what you should do."

"Okay. Dr. Maxwell it is. What about the GPs?"

The group settles on making an offer to Dr. Matthew Moore after a discussion of his extensive background in obstetrics, which might prove to be helpful, and his glowing references, specifically mentioning his bedside manner and his ability to interact with patients.

Shelly agrees to make the offers Monday. She also tells me that once Hope accepts, she will have her take over the setup and scheduling of the hotline and securing additional part-time resources for pro-bono work. Dr. Moore will also be responsible for assisting in recruiting medical assistance outside of our practice. It totally escaped my attention we also need insurance of more than one variety. Luckily, Shelly was all over that as well confirming that we need to sign and fund the general liabilities, workers compensation, and malpractice coverage. I'm floored by the cost of this stuff.

First thing Monday morning, I get a call from Shelly confirming both Matt and Hope have accepted our offers, and she has paid the insurance premiums. The doctors will start in a week, and we will officially open three weeks later. When they start, their focus will be recruiting additional physicians to help us with overflow, and Hope will be working on maintaining the hotline.

Suddenly, or not really, but it seems as though this has all happened in a matter of hours instead of the months I've invested in it, I'm working daily at the center trying to get things ready. Piper has been working in the office with me. Since she does contract work, she's able to work from anywhere, so she's been coming in and making contacts with hospitals, doctors, psychiatrists, psychologists, and any counselor she can find to let them know of our services. Several have already said they have referrals as soon as we are able to accommodate them.

Dax is working in the facility as well, painting, assembling furniture, buying supplies, and anything else we need. He's spending a lot of time with Shelly, who has also taken up a part-time residence at the center. She's nearing retirement and doesn't really ever want to stop working. Everything about her amazes me, but when she admits to me this is the type of thing she has always wanted to be involved in, my heart soars with the prospect of her being available to people who come to us. She's been amazing with me and still is. Dax won't tell me what they are working on, but the mystery project is housed in the building behind the main house, now sequestered by the duo. I was intrigued initially, but Dax kissed me on the forehead and told me it was a surprise, so I let it go. They are excited, so I'm happy, and I'm sure whatever it is will be brilliant.

Lost in thoughts of Dax and Shelly, I don't hear the front door open. Moby scares the shit out of me. "Hey, Cammy." His bright smiles shines down at me sitting at my desk.

"Jesus, Moby. You scared the crap of me," I say throwing my hand to my chest.

"You guys need to get a bell for the front door or something to let you know when people come in." I nod in silent acknowledgment. "Where's Piper?"

As if she is summoned by the sound of his voice, "Hey, Moby. What are you doing here?" I'm perplexed by this exchange. Moby has been here a couple of times but always with Dax and usually in some sort of powerhouse move like delivering furniture. To my knowledge, he and Piper have never had a one on one conversation, so I'm a little befuddled, but instead of questioning it, I sit silently and watch it unfold.

"I was helping Dax out back and wanted to see if you wanted to grab some lunch?" His eyes have yet to leave her face, and his smile hasn't faded. Moby is a joker, always the life of the party, and honestly, I can't say I've ever seen him with the same girl twice. He's beautiful, and he is well aware of the fact women swarm to him, but not in an arrogant way. He's as sweet as can be, but it makes me wonder what his interest in Piper is. She's shy, sweet, and motherly – not at all his type – beautiful, but not the sorority girl we usually see him with.

"Sure, let me grab my purse," I'm still watching the scene unfold. Realizing my mouth is slightly ajar, I snap it shut as Piper returns.

"Hey, Cam, you want me to bring you anything back?"

Before I can answer, Moby breaks in, "I was hoping I could have you for the afternoon?"

The look on her face is priceless, and I wish I had a camera to capture it. She's confused by his presence, too, but apparently lunch didn't set off the alarms. The thought of the entire afternoon, however, has her eyes wide. She looks to me for an answer, and unfortunately, I'm not sure which one she wants me to give. Since she isn't an employee of the center, I wave her off. "Have fun you guys!" I call as Moby takes her by the hand dragging her out the door. She looks over her shoulder giving me the, *I have no clue what is happening but will be calling you later* look. I giggle as she closes the door behind her.

My stomach growls as I hear the back door open and huge tattooed arms enfold me from behind. Kisses on my cheek and his woodsy smell automatically make my eyes close to savor the moment as I lean back into him. "I'm starving, Kitten. Did you bring anything for lunch, or do you want me to go get us something to eat?"

"Moby was just here," I blurt out.

Nuzzling into my neck, biting my skin playfully, "I know, baby, he was helping me out back."

I crane my neck allowing him better access to the places which heat up my core. "He took Piper to lunch."

"Cam, I'm really hungry, so either tell me what you want for lunch, or you're going to become my lunch," he groans into my neck, the vibrations from his words sending heat to my girly parts.

"Mmmmm. That's tempting, but since I'll have you tonight, I want one of those new pretzel burgers from Wendy's, the one with bacon."

"That's disgusting. Do you have any idea how much fat and grease are in that?" Dax eats a diet I'm afraid rabbits couldn't live on – lean meats, fresh veggies, and fruits – nothing processed. He also works out to maintain his physique. I, on the other hand, am blessed by my mama's genes and eat whatever I want and stay thin. I don't indulge in the finer things in life often, especially not since meeting Dax, but when I want a greasy burger, I want a greasy burger.

"You're right, make it a combo with large fries." He pulls away from me turning my chair to face him. I know he's hoping I'll change my mind simply because he doesn't like the smell of fast food, but when he doesn't get the response he wants he acquiesce. "Oh, and a Frosty!" I giggle as he realizes I'm pushing his buttons.

Kissing me on the forehead, "I wouldn't do this for anyone else," and he walks out the front door. I can't help but follow his figure as long as I can see him. Everything about him makes me feel loved, the way he talks to me, the way he touches me, his investment in me, to his going to get me fast food when he hates it.

Basking once again in my Dax coma, my cell phone startles me back to reality. Thinking it's Dax trying to talk me out of my lunch selection, I smile reaching for the phone. When I see my lawyer's name, my smile fades a bit; nothing on the other side of this call can be good.

"Hey, Douglas," I answer trying not to let him hear the anguish in my voice. He's a nice enough guy, but all of my dealings with him center on Josh Fitz, which just makes him like the gynecologist. He's a necessary evil but you're glad you only see his ass once a year.

"Hello, Cameron. I hope the day is treating you well." Who the hell talks like that? Just because I'm paying him to talk to me doesn't mean it needs to be so formal.

"I'm good, how about you?"

"I'm well. Thank you for asking." Seriously, I appreciate professionalism, but this guy knows the most intimate of my secrets and the darkness that plagues my soul. "I'm sorry to call you in the middle of the day, but I was wondering if we could schedule some time for you to come by my office?"

"Yeah, I guess, is something wrong?" My heart rate immediately starts to accelerate, panic setting in, my fear rising to the surface.

"Well, there's been some feedback from Mr. Fitz's attorney I need to discuss with you and would prefer not to do it by phone." It's not in the words he uses, but there's an edge to his voice telling me what he has to say isn't good. I may detect a note of pity or sympathy.

"What's happened?"

He sighs realizing I'm not coming to his office and waiting for this information. There are some things about me that will never change; first and foremost, I get what I want when it comes to business, and my relationship with Douglas Drake is just that – business.

"It seems that Mr. Fitz has decided to take his chances in court with a jury. He has refused the plea we have offered him. I'm sorry, Cameron. His attorney tried to reason with him, but he refuses."

I'm utterly lost in his words. What moron would think any group of his peers would side with him on a cut and dried rape case where there is so much evidence against him, including an eyewitness! "W-w-what?" I stammer. "I don't understand. How can he *not* take the deal or counter or something? Why would he *want* to go to trial for *rape*?" I emphasize the last word more for my own satisfaction than his. It dawns on me, "He's going to try to plead temporary insanity, isn't he?" I'm practically screaming into my phone.

There's silence on the other end. I'm sure Douglas is waiting to see if my tirade is over before responding to the endless stream of questions I've thrown at him, none of which really have any answers.

"I wish I had answers for you. I want to be very honest with you, Cameron; he has one of the best lawyers in town. I've seen him win cases like this that for all practical purposes should have been over before they started. I just want to let you know where we stand and that I'm working on building the case against him. If I need you, I'll call. We will need to set up depositions with you, Dax, Officer Patrick, the attending physicians at the hospital, and anyone else in the police report that was there that night. I'll keep you abreast of my progress. You have a strong case, Cameron; you were able to identify him in a lineup. Don't get discouraged but get brave."

"What do you mean?"

"Get ready to testify." His voice is solid; there's no option, and this isn't open for discussion. "I'll be in touch soon. Please call me if you need me." We disconnect, and I sit in stunned silence.

This is exactly what I didn't want to happen. From the day I woke up in the hospital, this is what I tried to avoid. The public humiliation, the degradation, the stress, the continued trips down a broken memory lane, all of this is a darkness in my life I want to go away. I expect tears to come. I expect panic to set in. Instead, I find myself with my forehead on my crossed arms atop my desk. Closing my eyes, I wonder where I went wrong, what decision had I made to bring me to this point?

I drift back to the recesses of my mind and find myself as a teenager in my parent's kitchen, baking Christmas cookies with my mom. My heart aches for her – I miss her desperately, more so now than I have in years. After the accident, the first year was tough, but I resolved to use the tragedy to better myself; this is like losing them all over again. Sometimes you just need your mama, need to feel her arms around you, cradling your head as you cry on her shoulder. Silent tears leak from the corners of my eyes as I mourn her again. I miss my Dad and Chris, too, but this would never have been something I would have gone to them seeking comfort; I would have been all over my mama.

I don't hear the front door open. "Hey, baby!" Dax calls out as he walks toward my door. "Do you wanna eat in there, or the kitchen?" I raise my head meeting his glance just as he reaches the door to my office.

"What the hell happened?" Cameron. "I was only gone ten minutes. Why are you crying?" The questions rush out as I stare at him. "Answer me, sweetheart." His hand cups my cheek as the tears slide down in a steady stream.

"I miss my mama," I sob.

"Oh, baby. I'm sorry." Pulling me to his chest, he tries to comfort me the only way he knows how, by simply being there, holding me, proving to me I'm not alone. With my head pressed firmly to him, "Did something happen that brought this on?"

"Douglas Drake called," I feel his arms stiffen around me, his body tenses waiting for more information. "Josh Fitz rejected the plea. We're going to court." I look up to meet his eyes and see rage, a fury I've only seen in him when my safety is threatened and it's a look that should bring me comfort but scares the shit out of me. "Dax, he says I have to testify. I just don't know if I can do this. I want my mama. I want her to hug me and tell me she loves me. I want her to protect me like she did when I was a kid."

Switching places with me, Dax sits in my seat, putting me in his lap. "I can't imagine how much you miss her. I know I'm not much of a replacement, but I love you more than anything in the world, Cameron. I'll hold you, hug you, protect you, and stand by your side. We will get through this together. I promise there won't be one moment you have to endure any of this by yourself."

"I never wanted to endure any of it, Dax. This is exactly what I didn't want to deal with when you wanted me to go to the police station to identify him. Don't you see that? Everyone will know what happened, that he violated me. There will be people who believe I deserved it because I was downtown late at night outside of a bar. This is going to get ugly before it's over, and what will it do to the center?"

"You started this so that other people would have a place of refuge, to seek counsel, to get help. While I realize you don't want your personal life on display for everyone to make judgment calls, the fact is this is why you are doing what you are doing here. This is the reason for Healing Wings. How you handle this trial, the media, your own preservation, all of that dictates where you go with the foundation. You aren't trying to use this for personal gain; you are fighting back, giving other people hope when they face the same darkness, many of whom will never have their day in court." He lets his words sink in while I sit in his lap cowering in his embrace.

"Cameron, you are the strongest woman I have ever met. I thought Shelly was until I met you. Losing Jeremy just about destroyed their family, but she held them all together. But you, there is a strength inside of you burning to get out. When this is over, and you spread your wings, you will absolutely soar. And, baby…I can't wait to watch you fly."

We eat lunch in relative silence. I love that about him; there is never a need to fill the void. I'm chowing down on my French fries and cheeseburger when I catch him staring at me. "What?" I ask with a mouth full of meat and bun.

"You are the most beautiful creature I have ever seen, but that line of grease seeping down your chin is gross, Cam." He giggles as I roll my eyes.

I set my burger down, swallow my food, leaving the grease coating my lips and dragging a line down my face. Leaning over the desk, I capture his face with both hands and plant a sloppy, grease-laced, kiss right on his lips.

He pulls back laughing, wiping his mouth with a napkin as I do the same. "That is so foul. I can't believe you just got that crap all over me." His phone pings with a text. He glances down at it before looking at me with a smirk on his face.

I raise my eyebrows in question. "Moby wants you to bring Piper's stuff home tonight. He says they'll drop by to pick it up."

"What the hell, Dax? What's going on with Moby and Piper? And don't tell me you don't know anything because I'm calling total bullshit on that just by the look on your face."

"Eh, he likes her."

"That's it? That's all you're gonna say?"

"It's not my story to tell. Maybe you should ask Piper about how well they actually know each other."

"Oh my god, you have gossip, and you're not sharing!"

"Men don't gossip."

"Apparently, they don't get lucky either," I give him an eat shit grin and wink at him as I stand up and toss my trash in the garbage can.

"Oh, is that so? You're going to cut me off?" I hear the playful tone in his voice; he knows I'm joking. I can't believe he's withholding information from me about one of my Fish!

"Dax," I draw his name out in a long whine he I know he hates, "tell me what you know," I slide into his lap, straddling his frame facing him. Throwing my arms around his neck I start to kiss him, using my powers of physical persuasion, slowly grinding into him. Tangling my fingers in his hair, I tug back ever so slightly. There's a line of aggression that turns him on, but I'm careful not to cross it. As I nip at his neck while circling my hips, his hands find my hips, and his fingertips dig into my flesh. I'm getting to him, and he knows there's nothing he can do here, so either he gives me the information I want, or his blue balls will get worse.

"Fuck, Cameron. Quit. I can't take this shit here." He growls out the words.

"Tell me what I wanna know," I tease.

"Fine. They talk on the phone a lot, text, and they've gone out a few times. That's all I know, seriously."

"You've got to be shitting me! Piper Pritchard has been dating one of your brothers, and you didn't tell me? Hell, she didn't tell me?" I'm acting all put off, but the fact of the matter is I'm thrilled. I adore Moby and obviously, I love Piper. "How did I not know? How did it even start?"

"All I know is that night we had the cookout, the two of them were chatting about fitness. He told her he did personal training and offered his services. She called him the next week, and they've been working out together several times a week since then. I don't know when it turned into dating, and that's truly all I know. Guys aren't like girls; we don't do details."

"That little hussy. I wonder if any of the Fish know?" He shrugs completely ignoring my tirade.

"You can grill her tonight when they come by. I told Moby to plan on staying for dinner."

"Eeeppp. I knew there was a reason I love you."

"I hope it's more than my presenting you opportunities to harass your friends about their sex lives."

"Nope. That about sums it up," I wink at him hugging him tight around the waist.

CHAPTER TWENTY-NINE

My opportunity doesn't present itself. I think Piper knows I planned to interrogate her. She came down with a migraine and sent Moby by himself. As much as I love him, I can't do it. I can't bring myself to grill him for answers, and no matter how many times I give Dax the *look* to get him to ask, he just smirks at me and shakes his head. I'm like a kid waiting on Christmas morning for the go ahead to open my presents; I can't sit still and am having to restrain myself from talking to Moby. I figure the best thing I can do is remove the temptation, but since I can't ask Moby to leave, I kiss Dax on the cheek, hug Moby goodnight, and set off to take a bath.

Piper hasn't made an appearance today at the center, and when I text her to check on her, she says she legitimately has a migraine and has been in bed since late yesterday afternoon. I tell her I'm not going to push the issue now, but when she's feeling better I need the low down on Moby. She assures me she will give me intel but swears me to secrecy; it appears the other Fish don't know.

We have a board meeting this afternoon, and I'm really hoping Piper makes it in. Since our board is currently small, every opinion matters, and we have a big decision to make today. We have also asked the two doctors on staff to join us. As the other members come strolling in, I find myself chitchatting with them in the front room. Dax opens the back door, coming to me, securing an arm around my waist as he says hello to Fisher, Hope, Matthew, and Shelly.

"Sorry I'm late. I was finishing up out back. Where's Piper?" Dax coos in my ear.

Just as I'm about to tell him I don't think she's going to make it, she saunters through the front door with Moby behind her. "Damn, Pipes, you look rough." She gives me a smartass-glare.

"I told you I feel like crap; did you think I was lying?" she retorts.

"Well yes, actually, I did." I can't help but play with her. She's always the responsible one. I know if she wasn't here today it was truly because she couldn't be here. "Hey, Moby..." I draw out his name giving him a look that says, *what have you been up to today?*

"Hey, Cam. Sorry to interrupt your tea party, but Piper didn't think she should drive, so I offered. I'll wait down here while you guys do your thing."

Dax beats me to asking him to join us, which he readily agrees to. There's just something about Moby that I've always liked. Yes, he's easy on the eyes, but it's more than that. He's funny, always making everyone feel comfortable, and loves fiercely like all of the Cooper boys do. When someone is brought into the fold, it's as if that person has always been there. I know that if he ever settles down, whoever is lucky enough to snag him will be treated like a queen.

I watch him walk with Piper upstairs, keeping his hand on her lower back, carrying her backpack with her laptop in it. I glance over at Dax, who shakes his head knowing what I'm thinking. He grabs my hand to follow behind them.

Once everyone is seated, each of us updates the group on our progress with our projects. I'm amazed at how well things are going. Hope and Matthew both tell us about the other physicians they have secured to work with the center and have worked out schedules with them for volunteer time. Hope has the hotline fully staffed twenty-four hours a day as well and has dubbed it the Wings Network. I love her exuberance. Matthew has the same drive. Listening to him talk, I realize that we made the perfect selection with these two. They're amazing and devoted to this. Shelly has turned over her reins to Hope and Matthew in favor of the legalistic paperwork and insurance nightmares. She has also taken on the accounting for the group but mentions it will quickly go beyond anything she can handle. "I've been talking to Suzy, the attorney, and she agrees we either need to hire an accountant to put on staff or we need to hire an accounting firm, but realistically, we will need both in a short amount of time." We all agree to hire an accountant now and let that person be responsible for helping find a firm to work with us.

I fill everyone in on the fundraising that's been going on. The group is dumbfounded by the support the community has offered, and the one thing we thought would be an issue isn't proving to be. We have more than enough money to sustain us for a couple of years assuming we get no additional funding. My opinion is it's time to hire a full-time fundraiser/marketing guru who works solely for Healing Wings.

"I have talked to several marketing firms about outsourcing our needs, but the fact is that even if we do that, no one is going to seek funding for us." I look to Shelly and ask, "I know you are really busy, and if you don't have the time to add this to your plate, let me know and I will take it on, but would you be willing to do the initial interviewing? I've gotten several names from the firms I've contacted."

Shelly opens her mouth to reply to my question when Moby chimes in, "What about Piper? Why would you go outside for marketing when that's what she does?"

"I have thought about Piper, but she really is primarily marketing, and we need someone to do fundraising as well." I reply.

"Rachel could do the fundraising," Piper adds.

"Do you know if Rachel would even be interested? I hate asking her. I don't want either of you to feel obligated to be involved on a full-time basis."

"We've talked about it."

"You have? Why haven't you said anything?" My face must illustrate my confusion because Piper laughs at me.

"Cams, I know we weren't hurt by this the way you were, but we were all affected. I would love to take this on full-time, and I can continue to take on contract work at night or in my free time if I want to, although I don't anticipate that being a big desire. Rachel has busted her tail bringing in contributors in an effort to show you how much she wants to stand beside you. So yes, we have talked about it, and yes, we both want to be involved full-time if you will let us."

Shelly takes the lead from me. "Cam, you have a team of people working tirelessly for nothing, bringing them on staff only solidifies Healing Wings' foundation. I'd say let's take a vote, but since you, me, and Piper are in agreement, even if Dax and Fisher aren't, they lose by default." She smiles that smile a woman does when she's in a win-win situation. I quit keeping score a long time ago, but there's another point for Shelly.

"Just so everyone knows, I think having Piper and Rachel on staff is an awesome idea. They both bring skills to the table we need, but they've also been a part of Cam's recovery, which will be an asset to anyone they encounter whether in the center or working with people outside." I love Dax. I just look at him knowing he sees in my eyes everything I want to say but can't in front of the people around.

"If it's okay with you, Cam, I'll reach out to Rachel tomorrow to talk about employment. And Piper, you and I can get together, too." Shelly looks at me for approval.

"That would be great. The less I'm involved in their hiring the better." I look over at Piper and beam. I never in a million years thought I would have two of my best friends working with me. I wish I thought I could find places for Charlie and Sutton. "So the last order of business is opening and a ribbon cutting ceremony. What are everyone's thoughts?"

Matthew and Hope have been relatively quiet throughout the meeting, but both agree the sooner the better. The group mulls over ideas while I sit and listen to the banter. Leave it to practical Pete, better known as

Dax, to bring me down from my high with his need to present a realistic picture.

"I'm sure Cameron hasn't bothered to mention to anyone she received a phone call from her lawyer yesterday." The room goes silent as all heads turn in his direction.

"Dax, really, this isn't the time to discuss this." I plead with him not to out me, as I'm not ready to acknowledge, even to my friends, that I'm about to go before the firing squad.

"Cam, they have to know in order to make an educated decision about opening." I drop my head on to the table, slowly shaking it back and forth to silently protest knowing I won't win.

"So what did her lawyer say?" Piper is all ears and reaches her hand under the table finding mine, squeezing me for support.

"Her attacker refused to plea, so Cam will be going to trial. She is going to have to testify against him. It will be public, there will be media attention, and the question becomes, do we think it's best to open before or after the trial?"

"I'm not a PR guru or hell much of anything in the business world, but in my opinion, you open beforehand. Try to establish the center on what you designed it to be, a refuge. You want to have your staff firmly in place, your machine working like it's just been oiled, and when the media starts looking into what's going on here, they don't find something thrown together for a trial and a jury. Instead, they find hard work, hours of dedication, and a team of professionals on a mission. Then let the media work as an advertising firm until the trial is over." For being a fitness buff, Moby has a lot on the ball. I don't know what it is about the Cooper men presenting this dumb, bad boy appearance, but they are all seriously smart.

There's really no discussion. His reasoning is sound, the board agrees, we vote, and the decision is to open September 1st, two weeks away. We opt not to do a ribbon cutting ceremony because the idea isn't to attract attention to our facility but for people to feel safe here.

As everyone starts to disperse, Moby takes Piper home. I wink at her as she's leaving, but the only response I get is a head shake. Shelly, Hope, and Matthew take off leaving me with Dax and Fisher. I move around the house turning off lights, locking doors, and making sure everything is secure before rejoining them in the lobby. When I come in, they both stop talking.

"What's up? Am I the topic of conversation? Would you like me to wait in the car, Dax?" I elbow him in the ribs to let him know I'm kidding.

"No, you are not the topic of conversation, but have you talked to Sutton recently?" Fisher questions.

"Umm, now that you mention it no, I haven't – not in the last couple of days. I think she had training or drill this past weekend. Why?" The real question is why the hell are Dax's friends starting to scope out my Fish.

"I haven't heard from her and just wanted to make sure she's okay," he tries to act nonchalant.

"Gah, you too? What is up with you boys? I'm sure she's fine Fisher, but I'll call her when we get in the car to make sure. If she's not, should I call the station or you directly?"

"Ha, Ha, Cam. She's a nice person. Just wondering. Please don't make a big deal out of it."

"Gotcha." Turning to Dax, "Are you ready to go baby? I'm beat and ready to head home." I turn on the alarm and open the door for them to exit. Dax gives Fisher some weird guy handshake hug thing, and Fisher kisses me on the top of my head in parting.

CHAPTER THIRTY

I had preconceived notions about what Healing Wings would be once we opened the doors; it was nothing like the reality of what hit. I expected people to slowly start to drift in and have plenty of time to work with each person. I never anticipated being bombarded by calls from physicians and psychiatrists all over Greenville the day we opened trying to place their patients. The phones ring off the hook daily, and we are all answering calls, trying to work in appointments, and sadly, we still have people on a waiting list. I'm appalled this need exists, and no one knows about it. This should be a need our community meets with arms wide open, but the people we see and talk to daily are hurting and scared, they're afraid to tell anyone their secret, and many have lived with the shame and guilt they feel for years. We offer anonymity, we don't request social security numbers, and giving us contact information is completely optional. We do issue all patients an identification number for us to reference their file and do our bookkeeping, but if they want to go by a random name that's who they become the moment they walk in our door.

All of the staff are putting in ten plus hour days on rotating schedules so we can keep the center open seven days a week, and we always have a physician on call for after hours needs. It breaks my heart knowing this on call doctor gets as many calls as we do during the day. I want to say it's easy to keep patients at an impersonal distance, but the fact is it isn't. I see the hurt in their eyes when they walk in the door, and I hear it in their voice when I answer the phone. Since I have no medical training, I'm truly acting as an office manager at this point.

Dax is in and out a lot. He's here a good bit during the day but has also been working on other projects at the house. I've yet to find out what he's been doing in the building behind the main house, but he assures me today is the day he and Shelly will fill me in on what they've been working on.

Today is also the day I go meet with Douglas Drake to give my deposition. Dax goes tomorrow, and the list of people before and after me is a mile long. He isn't leaving any stone unturned, which I appreciate, but

I feel guilty everyone I know and even more that I don't are being forced to break away from their every day lives to give my lawyer a statement before we go to court in four weeks. I thought it would take longer to get a date, but somehow it's now right around the corner.

Dax wants to go with me, but I insist this is something I have to do myself. The fact is I will have to get on a witness stand and answer questions from two attorneys, and only one of those will have my best interests at heart. It will not be a cakewalk, and I will not have anyone sitting next to me holding my hand or coddling me. If I want to come off as a credible witness, I will need to be able to get through this without having a mental breakdown. Today is the day we find out if that's possible or not.

Strolling in around lunchtime, Dax brings us both salads. I roll my eyes at him wishing he'd brought a pizza or hot dogs or maybe just a bucket of ice cream and two spoons. I do not need healthy shit when I'm stressing. It proves to be a moot issue when I don't eat anything and simply push the food around on the plate.

"Cameron, you need to eat." He doesn't look up from his food – just gives me the command I know he expects me to follow simply because he issues the decree.

I try to bore holes in his head glaring at him, but my super powers seem to be failing me.

"Seriously, it isn't going to be any easier on an empty stomach. Eat." Gah, I just want to pop him in the mouth.

When I don't comply, he raises his eyes to meet mine. I have no idea what he sees because I can't decide myself what I'm feeling – rage, frustration, humiliation, embarrassment, self-pity...and any other synonym you want to throw in there. Setting his fork down, he turns the seat to open his lap while simultaneously extending his hand to me across the desk. I take it as he leads me around to my safe spot. I crawl into his lap as though I'm a small child instead of a five-foot, nine-inch tall grown woman. The need for my mama today is overwhelming, and I'm just trying to hold my shit together. That must be the emotion he picked out of the whirlwind he had to choose from.

"Talk to me, Kitten," he says into my scalp as he presses a firm kiss in my hair.

"I'm scared." It's the plain and simple truth.

"Do you want me to take you?" I shake my head in response. We have been over this a hundred times and he knows my position. "You're being stubborn for no valid reason. I don't have to go in with you. I can wait in the truck so I'm there when you're done." Again I shake my head no. "Okay, but the offer is on the table."

"I miss my mama, Dax," I fight the tears that want to come with the mention of her name. She's plagued my mind for weeks. What I wouldn't give to see her just one more time, to have her hug me, to tell me she loves me. There's nothing he can say or do to heal this wound or even any salve he can put on it to temporarily ease the pain. It's raw and it's savage. The fact is I didn't grieve for any of them when they died. Now there are so many open wounds, there are days I feel like all I do is grieve. The more stress I'm under, the more that hole gapes open. I've tried to push the rape back into the recesses of my mind, but with the trial getting closer, I'm unable to escape it.

He holds me silently until I'm forced to get up to leave. I wish I could buy myself a little more time in the safety of his embrace, but the sooner I get this over with the sooner I can get back to him. I pry myself from his arms. I see the desire to protect me in his eyes, but he doesn't verbalize it. He kisses my fingers before walking me to the front door. I give him a peck on the lips then make my way to my attorney's office.

This is the first time I've been here alone, and it suddenly seems a much more daunting task than I realized. Everything seems to dwarf me in size – the enormity of the building, the lobby, the receptionist's desk. The span of time from announcing my arrival to the moment when Douglas comes to fetch me from the holding chamber seems to be on a much grander scale than I remember.

Taking the same seat I did when Dax and I were here before, Douglas goes through the formalities before asking me if I'm ready to begin. I am surprised by the additional person in the room. He must have caught me staring, "Cameron, this is Leslie; she will dictate your deposition so I can focus on our conversation." I give her a mute wave of the hand acknowledging the introduction but say nothing to her. She must have been prepped before I arrived because I see the sad look on her face as if she doesn't want to be here anymore than I do.

"Basically, what I'd like for you to do is take me through the night of the incident starting with you and your friends at the bar. I need you to go into as much detail as possible. Remember, the more information I have, the easier it will be for me to fend off unwanted advances from the defense team. There can't be any holes for them to climb in and break you apart."

I retell the story in agonizing detail, putting me back in the night, reliving every detail of the assault on my body. It's threatening to overtake my mind. I wish I had brought Shelly with me to help talk me through the parts that my mind wants to gloss over. Each time I reach one, I force myself to take deep breaths, count to myself, and wait for the blackness to clear for me to recall the memory. Douglas is patient, never rushing me through anything, never losing focus. He waits for me to deliver my story in my time with all of the ugly pieces put together. We break for a bathroom visit and to get a bottle of water before resuming. We focus on what I remember of being in the coma, waking up to Dax, what the doctors at the hospital told me, the officers coming to the hospital, identifying Josh in the lineup, and finally, my journey to Healing Wings.

When I think I'm done, I glance at the clock, completely exhausted both emotionally and physically, and realize it's almost seven o'clock. In a frenzy, I start to gather my things, realizing my phone is in my car and Dax has no idea where I am. When Douglas releases the do not disturb on the phone, his receptionist chimes in, "Mr. Drake, there is a Mr. Cooper here waiting for Ms. Pierce."

"Thank you. I'll let her know." He looks to me to confirm I heard the message. I give him a weak smile before rushing out the door to go meet Dax.

Meeting him in the reception area, he captures me in a warm embrace. "I'm sorry. I had no idea what time it was. I hope you weren't worried. I didn't think to bring my phone in."

"It's okay, Kitten. I called around five, and the receptionist told me that she was told it would be a late appointment. She said I could come wait for you. I didn't want you to have to drive home alone, so I had Shelly drop me off." Taking my hand, we walk out into the cool evening air. "How'd it go?" he asks.

I just look at him scrunching my face up, raising my shoulders, telling him without words that it went as well as could be expected. The fact is it absolutely sucked, but I made it through it with only minor pauses, and the truth is that I would never have to sit that long in court without a recess. The only difference is I had two witnesses to my turmoil in Douglas's office. There will be at least eight times that number in a courthouse and likely more unless Douglas can get a closed trial.

CHAPTER THIRTY-ONE

"Cameron, wake up!" His voice has that authoritative tone, but I can't quite seem to reach it. The nightmare I'm trapped in won't let me go to him. I feel him shaking my shoulders, but I can't retreat from the hell I'm caught in.

Then there's light; it is blinding it is so bright. "Cameron." Silence. "Cameron."

My eyes squint trying to evade the light seeping in through the cracks. As I adjust to the room, I realize I'm freezing before it dawns on me I'm covered in sweat, my clothes sticking to every inch of my body they touch, my hair matted to the sides of my face. Searching frantically, I find his face, then his eyes. They ground me. My pulse slows with each moment that passes, staring into those sage green orbs searching my face. His hand touches my cheek, and I lean into it, giving him a weak smile.

"Nightmare," I confirm for him.

"You haven't had one in a long time, but, Cam, this was by far the worst. I've been trying to wake you up for nearly ten minutes."

I get up to go to the closet; I need to change my clothes before I shiver to death. "I'm okay. I'm sorry I woke you up."

"I'm not worried about you waking me up; I'm concerned about what happened today at your attorney's office that triggered this."

Sliding back into bed in dry clothes, I tie my hair in a knot before lying back down. "I'm sure it's just from dredging up memories I've been trying to let go of."

He accepts that simple explanation, and that in and of itself completely shocks me. He turns me over so my back is to him, pulling me against his chest. I rest my head on his bent arm while his other arm secures me to him by my waist. Any other night, it might have been suffocating, but tonight, it is reassuring, comforting, and safe. I wish I could say I sleep soundly through the rest of the night, but Dax wakes me several more times before the alarm goes off signaling the start of a new day.

I'm restless. I'm cranky. I'm a borderline raging bitch. I don't do well without sleep, and the nightmares are getting progressively worse each night. Poor Dax is there every step of the way, never complains, just holds me until I fall back asleep and the next episode starts again. He keeps asking what the dreams are about. While he knows they are about that night, he doesn't know more and more details are making their way to the forefront of my mind. These are details I don't want to remember. Intimacy is such a personal word, and before now, it only held warm feelings for me. Now, that word brings so many ugly thoughts to my mind. It's a word that should be reserved for Dax only but I seem to be stripping him of that privilege in favor of letting Josh Fitz steal it.

He's patient; he never wavers. My comfort is his only concern. As we get closer to the trial, I wonder how long it's been since either of us has actually slept. I question whether Dax is sneaking off during the day to catch power naps, but even if he is, I certainly couldn't deny him that. I would do the same except Josh Fitz comes to my dreams regardless of where I am, and I can't keep visiting him.

"Baby, have you told Shelly about the nightmares?" He's sitting across my desk, looking yummy enough to eat, if only I had the energy.

I shake my head in response. Shelly is working crazy hours as she's slowly shutting down her practice and taking up full-time residence at Healing Wings. I've been meeting with her for my regular visits, but I feel like this is regression, so I don't ever mention it. I keep hoping I can make it through the trial and the nightmares will stop once this is no longer such a pressing issue.

"You need to talk to her, Cam. She can't help you if she doesn't know what's going on." I nod in agreement; he's right, but I'm still not telling her. "I know what you're doing. You're nodding with zero intention of doing what I'm suggesting." I smile at him and keep nodding. "We will deal with that issue tonight at home. Maybe a spanking would do you some good." He's playful, and I love the banter, I love how he tries to keep me alive, and I love how he won't allow me to wallow in self-deprecation.

"Promises, promises," he knows I'm playing, but the truth is it's been a minute since we've had sex, and I know he has to be frustrated.

"I'll show you promises tonight, but first, we got side tracked the other day, and I haven't been able to show you what Shelly and I have been working on."

"Oh my gosh, Dax, I'm so sorry. I have been so consumed by my own drama."

"Kitten, it's not a big deal. No need to apologize. But I do want you to come see it."

"Eeepp. Right now?" I'm giddy. He has been working on whatever is in the back building since we signed the lease, and it has been hush-hush since day one. To my knowledge, the only other people who know what's going on out there are Shelly and Moby. Moby only has the knowledge because he has helped Dax with the physical labor.

"Yep. I want to warn you though, while the space itself is completed, the project is a work in progress Shelly and I will continually modify on a case by case basis, but we want to start with the kids. Come on, she's out back waiting."

I can't help it; I'm dancing around like a little girl who needs to go to the bathroom. Seeing his eyes twinkle as he talks about this project elates me. I love his passion, and the fact it has something to do with Healing Wings just makes me want to soar on the wings of eagles.

Right before we get to the door, he steps in behind me, placing a hand over my eyes. "I want you to get the full effect when I uncover your eyes." He leads me through the door, and I hear it close behind me, and I assume it's Shelly who steps up beside me. Before removing his hand, he lowers his lips to my ear and whispers, "I love you beautiful," kisses my neck, then removes his hand.

I see a baby grand piano, several guitars – acoustic and electric, and what appear to be workstations of some sort with individual amplifiers in each one. As I wander around the room, running my fingertips over the edge of every surface, I come to a wall filled with books of sheet music, organized by genre. There's something here for every taste from classical to hard rock.

I'm blown away by what I see, and while I don't fully understand it yet, I'm trying to take in the beauty of the room. I hadn't noticed the walls when we first came in, but someone had spent painstaking hours painting this room. The wall directly in front of me is covered in what I can only classify as street art, some might say graffiti, but that has a negative connotation to me. This is beyond words. At first it seems like an abstract work of art, but the longer I stare at it, the bright pinks and reds take on the wings of a butterfly filled with blues and greens and purples. There are tags on top of the butterfly giving it more of an authentic street feel. Every inch of the wall is covered in color, bright colors that make my heart sing.

My eyes fill with tears as I turn to him. The only words I manage to choke out, "It's breathtaking." I close in on him, pulling him to me, hugging him tightly. "The butterfly..." he doesn't respond, but he doesn't need to. I know the butterfly is for me. "I'm sorry, I'm such a mess. I just wasn't expecting this. Tell me about it – what are you guys up to?"

Shelly starts to explain allowing me to hang on to Dax, "Dax came to me when we first started talking about Healing Wings and wanted to contribute but didn't know how he would fit in to the big picture. He wants to be here with you, helping you and anyone that walks through that door, but obviously his expertise in this arena is limited. We started talking, and the idea of music therapy was born. When you found this location, it provided the perfect space for it – it's separate from the rest of the house so it won't disturb people in counseling, with Matthew, or anything else. As the idea came to fruition, we wanted to make the space inviting, a place people would want to come and submerge themselves in, hence the bright colors. The butterfly is something even I didn't know about; that is all Dax, and it is absolutely for you."

"So how will the music therapy work? I'm blown away by this entire endeavor. What you guys have done in here is amazing. I have no idea how you got a piano in without me seeing it."

"The initial thought is that I will start with a couple of kids who want to explore learning an instrument. Their options are limited to piano or guitar for now. Each kid will have a lesson time just like they would anywhere else, except here it's free and will correspond with their counseling. Shelly will oversee the lessons more from an observation stance, but the idea is to allow them to find an escape that's safe, something that takes them out of the darkness and into a new light. I can't tell you the countless hours I have spent at a piano processing my emotions whether they were happy, sad, painful, angry – the whole gamut."

"You guys, this is phenomenal. When are you going to introduce it?"

"We were waiting to show you, so hopefully in the next week. Shelly will talk with the kids to see who has an interest and then their parents to make sure they are okay with it. We felt that Shelly needed to be in the room since I'm the only male running around the facility, and most of our patients are females."

I tug Shelly into our hug. "I just can't tell you both how excited I am about this." I look to Shelly, "Thank you for helping him find his place here." She smiles and excuses herself saying she's going back to her office leaving Dax and me alone.

"Baby, you blow me away everyday." I lift up on my tippy toes to kiss his jawline. He captures my neck tugging my face to meet his. The kiss is passionate, so full of emotion, our tongues dancing to a tune only our souls can hear. He pulls back leaving me panting, wanting more from him.

"I glad you like it. I can't wait to get started. I never thought twenty years ago when I was making decisions about Juilliard and coming home, then Furman, then Jeremy, and everything that has led me to you, that I would ever be using the gift God gave me to serve people like this. You make me a better person, Cam."

"Ditto." I mutter against his lips with my forehead pressed to his. Tangling my fingers in his hair,

I attempt to entice him back into a make out session with me in the studio. He indulges me briefly before pulling back.

"We need to go home before I take you against that wall. God, I've missed the feel of you against me." He's breathless and apparently as desperate for a physical connection as I am.

CHAPTER THIRTY-TWO

Driving like a bat out of hell, we arrive safely home roughly fifteen minutes later. Making our way in the front door, he calls over his shoulder to me, "Cameron, go upstairs, take off your clothes and wait for me on the bed facing away from the door."

"K," I call back.

"Try again, Kitten," his voice is stern and it dawns on me he doesn't just want me waiting on the bed, he wants me submitting on the bed and my response should have been, "Yes, Sir," I say correcting myself.

While Dax and I know each other intimately, he has been very reserved in our *playtime*. Many of our physical connections are still vanilla in nature and have been non-existent since the nightmares started again.

He holds me all night long, but we've both been so tired there's been no hanky-panky. I love when he gives me the opportunity to serve him this way. Even if he thinks I'm not ready for a full-blown Dom/sub relationship, I want him to know I will keep working to get there as long as he works with me. I think I want it to happen faster than he does, but it's important to me I embrace who he is. He doesn't seem to understand I want him to be rough with me, I need him to treat me as though I can handle anything, conquer the world as long as he's leading me.

Dax has refused to take our sexual relationship to a more forceful level for fear it will cause irreparable damage to my psyche or sever our bond.

He needs this, sure, but I need it more. I need to face the horror of what Josh Fitz did to me, face it in safety, with love. I trust him enough to be my guide, and he trusts me enough to allow him. Turned away from the door as requested, I can't see him approach but listen to the sounds of his footsteps on the hardwood floors. Their cadence steadies my breathing. The breeze coming through the open window brings the scent of him to me, that sweet woodsy musk that I imagine only I can detect.

"You can do this, Cam...." The mental pep talk doesn't bring the reassurance I hope for. The tremor in my voice gives away my vulnerability. Luckily he doesn't hear me muttering to myself.

He deserves this happiness just as I deserve peace. I truly believe this is the only way, but he won't cross this imaginary line he has set, and I will have to force him over it. I'm sure mere minutes pass as I hear his shoes hitting the floor, the sound of his belt coming through the loops, his shirt hitting the floor with a whoosh through the air, and his pants falling to his ankles as I imagine him stepping out of them. It seems like eons as I wait for him, poised and kneeling facing the wall, my head dropped and my eyes cast downward.

Unconsciously, I have closed my eyes, but when I open them, he is standing behind me, completely bare, his cock standing at attention, a narrow beam of sunlight from a shuttered window silhouetting him. His face is shadowed, but I can still see the outline of his jaw. And those eyes – I tell myself eyes can't really glow, yet his do. Even shadowed, I can see them piercing and green, narrow with intent. I never fail to find stability in those orbs; they ground me, stabilizing my otherwise chaotic mind.

"You okay?"

I don't answer. I can't. I didn't set out with this intention. When we got home, I figured we would play around, cuddle, and go to sleep until the demons set in. While this has been brewing in the back of my mind, I know this is going to take courage, and I figured I would have bravery to spare, but for the moment it has left me.

"Cam, what's wrong?" he asks, his bare feet carrying him across the hardwood floor silently like a dancer moving gracefully for his size.

Dax is unsettled, my silence confusing him, but I am paralyzed until the distance closes between us and his hands come to rest on the backs of my arms.

"Say something, sweetheart," he whispers, his concern almost heartbreaking, "You're scaring me."

"I want to do something for you..." I clear my throat and steel my resolve. "I'm nervous."

Those gorgeous green eyes widen – part in relief, part in humor – and then he smiles.

"So, I see," he chuckles, taking in my quivering hands and white knuckles. "And what's the occasion?"

"Fuck me, Dax."

My words don't register immediately. Certainly he wants me. He craves me. My naked body is the only aphrodisiac he's ever required. But he senses this time is different and takes a step back.

"Talk to me," he pleads softly. "Tell me what's wrong."

"No. Nothing's wrong," I reply, and then I am on him, attacking him. I rise from my kneeling position, nipping at his skin with my teeth and my nails, desperate for this raw experience. There is a moment of resistance, a moment where Dax is actually fighting me, attempting to restrain me, hesitating, before he relents. He returns the kiss, engaging in the intimacy, enfolding me in his arms, then helping my hands do as they wish. He pulls me off the bed, and we stand, ravishing each other's flesh, writhing together.

He picks me up, I feel my back slam against the wall as I lift my thighs up around his hips. Then I feel that sudden, brutal penetration, which I have come to both loathe and love so much. His cock is pounding into me, his tongue taking control of mine, one hand clutching my cheek, the other sustaining my weight.

I kiss him, bite him, and buck against him. We are animals in a savage garden together, and there is no law. No right or wrong. No crime or justice. No pride or shame. There is only need, a shared and desperate desire neither of us wants to restrain. He needs to know I trust him completely with my body and my heart. I will let him take me as far as he wants to go, but he has to get passed the barrier he has put in place. I need him to take me further than he thinks I'm ready for. I need him to claim my body brutally.

I push against him, forcefully, literally using all my strength to pull the length of him from inside me. He relents, allowing my freedom, as I turn around, my hands splaying against the wall.

Looking at him over my shoulder, panting out the words, "Like this..." I gasp. "Take me rough, Dax! Don't hold back." I need him to forget his own limits, taking from him what he won't freely give. I need to replace the anguish and fear imparted by Josh Fitz with the animalistic, ravaging love from Dax.

He is inside me again, thrusting and thrusting and thrusting from behind until there is nothing beyond the building ecstasy. I feel it coming, but I feel something else as well. The fear I had felt a year ago, the utter helplessness as my body was violated again and again against that brick wall in the parking lot behind that bar. I am strong enough to feel it. I have the courage. There is only one last piece of the puzzle.

"Choke me."

"What?" I hear him pant.

"Choke me!" I demand and plead simultaneously.

There is a moment when he slows, a moment where I fear he will stop, but then those strong hands come to my throat, his weight pressing me against the wall, and I feel them close and constrict like bands of steel. There is steel from behind, but this is different, this is constant, this is increasingly tight.

"Do it! Choke me, Dax!"

His hands continue to tighten, and my breath is shallow, but it's the blood flow he's cutting off with increasing pressure.

I can't find any terror in what I'm experiencing. I want to, and I feel I need to, so I can finally move beyond what happened to me that night in the parking lot, but fear just isn't a part of it. Instead, I feel lightheaded, I am drifting away from the world around me, darkness taking over my peripheral vision, all while his powerful organ is driving into me with euphoric repetition.

"This is what being dead must feel like," I try to say, but there is no breath for my words.

There is warmth instead, soothing and dark, and I feel like I am sinking further and further down into a comforting abyss. Am I really dying? If I am, I can't imagine a better fate. This is peace, this is bliss, even as my body convulses with the orgasm we are sharing.

"I love you..." I try to whisper, but the universe collapses and becomes nothing as our souls become one.

I wake for a lack of a better term in his arms, concern brewing in his green eyes when mine meet his. His brow furrowed with worry. I reach up to stroke his cheek, the corners of lips turning up to show my appreciation. "What's wrong, Dax?"

He shakes his head as if to say he's not answering, blinking hard several times slowly. "Dax, did something happen?"

"You scared me. I was completely shocked by your request, or should I say demand. I shouldn't have allowed it to happen, but Jesus you looked so beautiful calling out to me, taunting me. It was so fucking intense, and then you were limp. I've been sitting here holding you waiting for you to wake up. This wasn't like coming out of subspace, Cam, baby; you were unconscious."

My body is fatigued, but watching him speak, listening to the words flowing from his mouth, I can't help but feel the need to claim him. I want him in me, me wrapped around him, as close as our bodies can be. Crawling from his embrace, I straddle him, grinding slow rhythmic circles with my wet pussy on his semi-hard shaft. "Cam, what are you doing? Are you listening to me?"

Stealing a kiss, talking into his mouth, my lips pressed to his, "I'm trying not to, but you're making it difficult since you won't stop talking," my grin shapes my face against him.

"You're not going to distract me. We need to talk about this. What came over you? Why on earth did you want me to choke you?"

I ignore his pleas for answers and continue searching his body for pleasure dragging my nails down his arms, up his back, catching my fingers in his hair. Continuing little figure eights on his crotch. He can try to ignore me, but his friend sitting beneath me is turned on and ready to play. "I don't want to talk, Dax. I want you to make love to me, slowly." Lifting myself just slightly, the head of his dick pops into place. I pull on his hair breaking away from his face, watching his eyes as I impale myself on his cock. They go from stormy jade to a crystalline green almost instantly. Never breaking eye contact, he rolls me over, nestles himself between my legs, and strums my pussy like a guitar. For the first night in a couple of weeks, I slept soundly.

CHAPTER THIRTY-THREE

One week from today the trial will start. I'm having a hard time focusing and an even harder time not allowing myself to be consumed with worry. Shelly has been hovering; I'm sure it's at Dax's suggestion. I appreciate the way she gets me to talk without asking me directly to do so, and if I'm being completely honest, having her around is comforting. She's not my mama, but she's coming in a close second.

Most of the staff is out to lunch when the front door opens. The staff uses the back entrance, so I know it's someone that needs attention. I hop up from my desk, excusing myself from Shelly's story time to go see who it is. When I enter the front room, I'm paralyzed. Standing in the doorway with an envelope in hand is Josh Fitz. There are no words; fear and panic set in simultaneously, drowning out reality. Stepping away from his forward motion, I run into the wall, my hands splayed against it for support as the images from that night flood my memory. I watch him intensely as he proceeds toward me, and I scream out, "Nooo, please stop. Please don't touch me." My wails echo against the walls reverberating off the ceiling. The hollow sound of my voice is deafening as I sink back into the recesses of my mind. As he clutches my blouse, I try to keep if from being ripped from my body; his hands are everywhere. I look up to see the same man, clutching at my arms, shaking me, screaming something, but the words are incoherent.

"Please leave me alone…please…." The words fall on deaf ears. "Daxxx," I wail his name hoping this time he can stop the intruder, but he doesn't come. As I kick, scream, pound against the hands that forcibly took me once before, the same smell permeates my nose; it's putrid, making me want to vomit. He has my clothes off, and I'm standing in that same parking lot, my tattered thong the only shred of clothing still clinging to me. The pain in my head is excruciating as he pummels me against the brick. He undoes his pants, releasing his weapon; he's hard, armed, and ready to violate. I hear myself sobbing the word no over and over, but he's relentless in his pursuit. He penetrates me, poisoning me with his intimacy, ripping apart my insides, finishing inside of me. I pray he's done, but the nightmare continues. Still holding on to consciousness, I try to let go, but he pulls the metal rod from his pocket, hitting me repeatedly before he penetrates my essence in a bloody massacre of my womb. The hands are everywhere, so many of them touching me, grabbing at me, invading my space. They're like snakes crawling over my skin.

I hear screaming around me and am no longer sure if the words are mine or belong to someone else. I just need to escape the nightmare, and I give in to the darkness.

"Jesus Christ, what the fuck happened? Cameron, baby, wake up!" Dax is finally here, but he is too late to stop it from happening again. I want to go to him, but he let him get to me. "Cameron," he calls, but it's futile. I can't go back to that place, I can't go back to a realm where an attacker can still reach me. "Shelly, what the hell happened?" He's looking for answers, but no one is providing them. Why isn't he going after Josh? He has to know he's here. Anger spills over the shame.

"Cameron, can you hear me sweetheart?" Shelly calls to me. If they are here, why did they let him hurt me again. They're supposed to love me, to protect me; this is my safe haven. My frustration, the need to scream at them, to confront them, surpasses my need to hide as I follow the sounds of their voices back out of the darkness.

"Kitten, please talk to me. Baby, I'm here. Fuck! Shelly do something!" he wails, but I can't understand his frustration.

I open my eyes to blinding light, people crowded around me so thick I can't see through them. My head is pounding, the pain debilitating. Holy fuck, he's still here, standing above the rest, looking down at me with concern on his face. I push further away, scrambling, trying to get to my feet, bumping into a hard wall of arms. "Let me go, please." I don't know if anyone can make out the garbled words.

"Cameron, baby, I've got you. Look at me." I feel his breath on my neck as he utters the words, darting my head to meet his face. As I lock in on his beautiful green eyes, he says, "Focus on me, Cam." The world around me falls away as I hone in on his eyes, calming my savage spirit. "Don't take your eyes off me. Just listen to the sound of my voice. I've got you. You're safe." I nod in understanding as he continues to sooth me with his smooth baritone voice, like velvet caressing my emotional wounds. He strokes my cheek as he pulls me into his lap and leans against the wall; I am lost in him. Time had ceased to exist; we could have been sitting here for five minutes or five hours, although I'm guessing it's closer to the first.

"Can you talk to me, sweetheart?" I start to look around to see who my audience is, but he stops my chin with his hand. "Look at me – nothing else matters.

What happened?" I shake my head. "Cameron, baby, it's just me. Stay with me and talk to me."

"He's here," I croak, unable to control the tears falling from my eyes, tears of fear, frustration, loss of control, pain, heartache – uncontrollable tears.

"Who's here?" Confusion mars his face.

"Josh," my breathing is erratic, my words broken. I keep trying to look around, but Dax has control of my face forcing me to meet his eyes.

"Baby, Josh isn't here."

"He. Is." He just doesn't get it; he can't see him because he's focused on me. I'm exasperated by his unwillingness to acknowledge what I'm telling him. Jerking my face from his grasp, I find him in the audience, singling him out. "There! Dax."

"Cameron. Look at me." His voice is firm, so authoritative it almost scares me. I turn to him. "That is not Josh Fitz. That is Roman Williams. I worked with him at Furman. He came out to tune the piano."

"Please ask him to leave, Dax. Please…" I whisper. He doesn't understand. If that's not Josh Fitz, the similarity is so uncanny that it's literally making me crazy.

Shelly hears me and instantly flanks Roman escorting him out the front door. Having discarded him, she makes to break up the audience surrounding my performance on the floor. Dax continues searching my eyes for clearing, but it's not coming. There's an emotional storm raging that I can't calm.

"Dax, son, get her upstairs to my office. I'll be there in a minute." Shelly's voice is melodic, almost hypnotic. If I could crawl into sound, it would be a tie for where I'd rest my troubled head, her voice or Dax's.

"Put your arms around my neck, love. I've got you." I do as I'm told as he lifts me from the floor carrying me up the stairs before settling us on the couch in Shelly's office.

He holds me, silently comforting me, tucking me into his chest and shoulder. He doesn't say anything when she enters the room, closing the door behind her. Making her way to her chair, she gives me a weak smile.

"I'm so sorry," I mumble. I'm embarrassed by the scene which took place with a stranger, but even worse many of the staff witnessed some portion of whatever just happened because they were hovering around me.

"No, baby, don't apologize." Dax will forever be my protector, my valiant knight.

"Cam, you were fine when you walked out of the office. What happened when you went to the door?"

"I walked up there and saw him standing there. I swear to you I thought it was Josh. The smell was there; he looked just like him only cleaned up. He touched me. He puts his hands on me, grabbing my arms. He ripped at my clothes. He stuck his dick in me, Shelly!" The irrational words pour from my mouth.

"Dax, why don't you step outside?" He tries to release me, but I cling to him like a lifeline. If he's with me, the outside world can't touch me. "Cameron, it's okay, let him go. He'll be right outside." I comply unwillingly watching the door close behind him.

She looks at me with a motherly concern crossing her face, as if she's waiting for me to begin, but I don't know what she wants me to tell her.

"You relived the incident downstairs, didn't you?" She finally breaks the silence.

I nod my affirmation as the tears begin to flow again.

"You remembered more than you ever have?" It's a question she already knows the answer to, so I just nod. "Can you tell me about it?"

I just stare off into space weighing my options. Do I want to verbally acknowledge the details that came to the forefront of my mind, or do I want to push them back into the box they've been stored in?

"You're at an impasse, Cam. This is the point where you will choose the road your life takes. The choice is yours. I won't try to force you to go one way or the other, but know that your mind is telling you it needs release. To continue to repress these thoughts will not benefit you in any way."

I stutter as I try to formulate sentences to express what I feel, what I saw, what I remember from that night. Straightening my shoulders, I mentally slap myself into relenting.

"Before today, I couldn't remember past my head being slammed into the brick wall. Now there's the sound of his zipper. That sound echoes through my mind as though it is being amplified it is so loud." I take a deep breath, pushing through my brain trying to regress. "Today, there was more than just new sounds; I saw his penis, and I felt him push into me. He emptied himself into me right before he brutalized my vagina and womb with a steel rod." My voice sounds distant and monotone, as though it is coming from someone else, carrying a monotone note. It's distant, hollow.

I talk with Shelly for the rest of the afternoon. Someone must have rescheduled her appointments, but no one ever interrupts us. I tell her about the nightmares that have been plaguing me for weeks and how little sleep I've been getting for fear of reliving the scene every time I close my eyes. She prescribes a mild sleeping medication and anti-anxiety medication suggesting we can revisit their necessity after the trial. As much as I don't want to accept chemical assistance, I realize I need a reprieve. If I'm going to face this demon head on in a week, I need to be doing so well rested with the ability to function without flipping out. I will be face to face with him in less than seven days for an extended amount of time.

CHAPTER THIRTY-FOUR

Dax is handling me with kid gloves when we finally arrive home. He's allowed me to sit in silence, mulling over the events of today and what I'm facing next week. His patience never ceases to amaze me, and the fact he doesn't feel the need to fill the silence is one of the things I love most about him. Physically, he's distant, which is driving me insane. I need the familiarity of his touch, not sexually, but as a reminder of the protection he gives me.

I go to the family room when we get home, while he goes to the kitchen to start dinner. Sitting on the couch, I grab my journal from the coffee table and start scribbling like a mad woman. Anything that comes to mind, most of which doesn't make sense, but it's become the way I process. Mr. Whiskers and Sassy hop up beside me, making themselves comfortable in the fold of my knees. Even the cats anticipate this being a long night.

When my hand refuses to write anything else, I close the journal and push twenty-five pounds of fur from my legs to go see what Dax is up to. I stop at the entry to the kitchen; his back is turned to me, as I admire him. Love doesn't describe the importance of this man in my life; it's simply a four-letter word associated with hearts and flowers. Dax is *breath* to me. Every ounce of him exudes life, without that breathe, I would flounder, whither. I step up behind him, wrapping my arms around his waist, pressing my body to his back, squeezing my feelings into him. He turns lifting one arm over my head to pull me to him, kissing me on top of the head.

"I need to tell everyone at the center what happened to me, Dax but I'm scared." I pull away from his chest enough to see his face.

"Baby, you don't have to justify what happened today. While people may not know the details, just about everyone who was there knows you have a story. Don't feel like you need to do that for them."

"I know, but I need to do it for me. I need to express my pain and my continued struggle, my anguish. I'm sure that it will be all over the center tomorrow for those who didn't witness it, and Dax, I can't pretend patients won't find out about it. I would rather them hear the truth on my terms."

"I'll support whatever decision you think is best, just don't do it out of obligation, do it for their growth and your own," he smiles at me, touching his forehead to mine before lightly brushing our lips together. "I love you, Cameron."

"I know, baby. I love you too. I'm sorry you're having to deal with all of this."

"I'm sorry you're going through it, but I'm not sorry I'm with you through the process."

The next morning when we arrive at the center, I gather all of the staff together for our usual morning meeting. I also asked the Fish to come, the Coopers, and the Wrights. I'm not sure I can do this more than once, so I need them all here at the same time. We meet out in the back building because it's the largest space. As people enter I see the looks of pity, which I hate, but just give a soft smile in return.

Thirty minutes later, the room is silent. I don't give out graphic details, but I share my story from the moment that door closed at the bar to where I am today. I asked all of the staff members to be honest with any of the patients who might inquire about what happened yesterday but to keep it at an age-appropriate level. I also tell them I am more than happy to discuss my story with any other victim in their counseling sessions. I admit as much as I hate what has happened to me, hiding it makes me a victim. Today I made the choice to be a survivor.

CHAPTER THIRTY-FIVE

Arriving at the courthouse, I am flanked by Dax on my left side, clutching my hand, and Douglas Drake on my right, leading me with a hand to the small of my back as they push through the crowd. There are news crews outside, a ton of people Douglas later tells me want to get in the actual court room to witness the trial, and even some people brandishing signs in support of me. I try not to acknowledge any of it.

When I got dressed this morning, I put on a suit I haven't worn since leaving the bank and a kickass pair of heels. When I looked in the mirror, I saw the strength which had left me over a year ago that night at the bar. I'm not the same person, but the determination that carried me through my parents' death will carry me through this as well. I straighten my spine and hold my head high. Donning my inner boardroom bitch, I brave the day ahead of me.

My friends are all here in support; they meet us inside and follow Douglas's instructions about where to sit. Shelly is here with Moby as well and tells Dax all of the Coopers and Wrights wanted to come, but she insisted they stay home. It warms my heart to know I have so much support.

Trials in reality are nothing like they are on television. Yes, the media is here, but the judge rules they are not allowed in the courtroom and closes the trial to anyone outside of family for the prosecution and defense. I panic thinking my support team is about to be ousted, but Douglas waltzes off, returning to tell me they are clear to stay. I notice the group of people behind Josh and his attorney is even larger than mine. Suddenly, I empathize with his family. He is someone's son and someone's friend. Whatever his motivation, there are people who love him whom this will destroy. Instantly, Dax's hand hits my shoulder, squeezing it reassuringly. I look over my shoulder to him as he quietly shakes his head. He knows where my mind went looking at Josh's family.

The opening statements aren't dramatic; no one is screaming, "You can't handle the truth." It's simply statements of intent for what each attorney will attempt to prove to the jury who is made up ten females and two males. I watch their faces as each lawyer speaks, noting at some point, every one of the women looks to me with sorrow-filled eyes. They were selected last week, but Douglas never told me anything about the process, but from the looks of them, he has faired far better than the defense.

The first day is long, breaking for lunch and two recesses; the only witnesses that have been called to the stand were Fisher and Jackson. They both present their recollection of that night giving what I assume is an accurate depiction before cross-examination. Josh's attorney, Rex Parlin, digs in to what the officers remember about Josh's mental state that night. Fisher clearly states there was no mental state to be observed since the bartender had beaten him to a pulp when he pried him off of me. He was borderline unconscious and had lost a lot of blood. Jackson affirms Fisher's testimony, and no amount of questioning changes their stance on how they found Josh Fitz before he was taken away.

The second day is more of the same. This time it's the paramedics and the physicians who were involved in both of our immediate medical care. Again, sterile responses, although one of the paramedics does give me props for taking a chunk of his flesh in one last ditch effort to fight Josh off. He gives me a wink as he says it, as if he is proud of me. Of course, Rex objects.

Day three brings my medical team from the hospital, and I try my best to block out most of what they are saying when Dr. Johnson begins to describe the brutal wounds left behind by my attacker, the broken bones, the coma. I don't remember much about those details; my memory of that time is filled by the voice of an angel who sang me to safety. I don't want to taint the rainbows of colors he played for me, so I refuse to listen. The undeniable proof that Josh was the perpetrator is presented - the bartender testifies that he pulled him off of me with his penis still hanging out of his pants, although his verbiage is much more verbose. The doctors testify to the accuracy of the DNA testing done on the semen recovered from me.

The hardest day I have had to endure in this trial is today, day four. Today, Josh's team of psychiatrists and specialists are spilling their theories on his mental stability. My frustration level is through the roof. Of course he's insane, he raped someone, but does that mean he should get off with a slap on the wrist and therapy for the rest of his life? It's hard for me to listen to these doctors dismiss his actions as though he didn't violate another human being. He showed no signs of mental instability prior to that night and had never received any type of counseling. For the most part, he hadn't even taken anything more than a damn aspirin his entire life, but these asshats are willing to sit on the witness stand to try to convince twelve citizens something snapped in his mind that night causing him to brutally attack me in a dark parking lot. I hope he is certifiably insane since then. God knows he's made me that way at times, but to try to portray him as the victim here is simply pissing me off. Douglas senses it and asks for a recess.

"Cameron, you are wearing your feelings on your sleeve," Douglas says after taking me to a private chamber to calm me down.

"This is absurd, Douglas. There was no temporary insanity. Or hell, maybe there was. Maybe that's what happens in the mind of every criminal. They just lose it and do something stupid. By all means, let's give them all a second chance," the sarcasm is dripping from my lips.

"Get it out. Say whatever you need to say in order to go sit back in that courtroom looking poised."

My mouth drops, "Fuck!" I don't know why but it feels good to cuss, so I just let out a long string of them, the vilest that come to mind. I stomp my feet with each explicative as if that emphasizes them even more, makes them more powerful. When I have stomped out my final cuss word, Douglas turns to open the door leading me back to our seats.

The day wears me down more so than the other three put together. When we finally leave the courthouse, I don't utter a single word to Dax. He knows just looking at me that the pain is at the forefront today, and this is exactly what I didn't want when he pushed me a year ago to press charges. I don't hold him responsible; I'm not angry with him. I'm just worn down. Taking me home, he tugs my hand up the stairs to our bedroom, into our bathroom. Dropping my hand, he turns the water on in the tub, plugging the drain, and then pours bubble bath in. Turning his attention back to me, he looks me in the eyes as he works his fingers through the buttons on my blouse, untucking it as he goes. Reaching the hem, he pulls me closer to him, gently unzipping my skirt from behind. When it drops to the floor, he holds his hands out for me to take, silently encouraging me. Doing so, I step out of my high heels, suddenly dwarfing me next to him. Standing there in my bra and panties, he raises his hands to pull the clip from my hair, allowing it to cascade down my back. I undo the clasp of my bra; dropping it to the floor, then shimmy out of my panties. There is hunger in his eyes, but this is for me. With the tub full, he takes me by the neck, dropping his forehead to mine, looking me in the eyes, "Love you, baby. I couldn't be more proud of you."

Smiling back at him, I kiss his pouty lips. "I know." He helps me into the tub as I sink into the bubble filled bliss he stops.

"Don't get out until I come back. Do you want me to turn some music on for you?"

"Mmmm, yes…please."

He flips on the sound dock, filling the air with Rachael Yamagata. I love her throaty voice and her haunting lyrics; the music is beautiful. It's soothing, and if I allow, it will completely consume me. I love the things he has introduced me to over the last year but admit the music is captivating. He always knows what suits the mood or what to play to put me where he wants me to be.

When he returns, the only clothing he's sporting is low slung sweat pants, accentuating the V that drives me insane and instantly brings a smile to my face. Admittedly, it's a tired smile, but it still makes me want to drool. My ascent from the tub is met with a warm towel he must have gotten from the dryer to wrap around me. He lovingly dries my weary limbs before dressing me in his t-shirt and a pair of panties. Sitting on top of the bed, is a platter of fruits, cheeses, crackers, and two glasses of wine. He picks up the tray, setting it on my nightstand before turning down the covers. As he props up the pillows, he encourages me to climb in bed. We spend the rest of the evening eating the meal he made for us, coupled with several glasses of wine, before cuddling until I fall asleep on his forearm with the rest of his body wrapped tightly around mine.

CHAPTER THIRTY-SIX

Today is the last day of testimonies and closing arguments. This is the pinnacle of my hell. I listen to the testimony of witnesses Josh's attorney has called, but in all honesty, I hear them talking but don't hear the actual words as I am so consumed by my own fear of the stand that I'm mindlessly staring. I'm shaken from my trance when Douglas calls me to the stand. My eyes meet his, and they're encouraging, strong. I take my seat in the chair, the bailiff swears me in, and then the questioning begins.

I knew what to expect from my attorney. We had gone through the questions multiple times to make sure my answers were consistent and that I avoided information leading to openings for the defense to attack me. No matter how many times Douglas tried to warn me, I wasn't prepared for cross-examination.

The defense's attorney goes after both my frame of mind that night and my overall character.

"Is it possible, Ms. Pierce, that you were too intoxicated to remember encouraging the defendant?"

"No, it's not. I only had a couple of drinks that night."

"Yet, you were too intoxicated to drive?"

"Sir, I believe there is a legal limit for a reason. Both of my parents were killed by a drunk driver, and I do not now, nor will I ever drive with the slightest bit of alcohol in my system."

"Is it true, Ms. Pierce, that you are currently a willing participant in a Dominant/submissive relationship?"

"Objection," Douglas hollers out.

The judge holds up his hand to silence my attorney, looking at Rex, "Make your point quickly, Counselor."

"Ms. Pierce? It's no secret that your partner was a member of prominent BDSM clubs in his youth. Is that the lifestyle the two of you practice?"

I hesitate, looking to Dax for approval; his face gives me nothing to go on. Clearing my throat, I'm embarrassed to admit any of this with my friends sitting feet away.

"Somewhat, yes."

"Somewhat? Either you are or you aren't."

I sigh, "Then, yes, but most likely not in the manner you are assuming or insinuating."

"Then you admit you like rough sex?"

"Objection!" My attorney's face is beet red.

The judge allows him to continue.

"I would say that my appetite for sex in a committed relationship doesn't come before you or the court."

"You met Mr. Cooper after the incident, correct?"

"No, I met Mr. Cooper several weeks before when he made multiple deliveries to my office on different occasions."

"But you entered into a sexual relationship with him upon being released from the hospital after the incident. It was indeed a rather quick turn around for a rape victim, was it not?"

"I did no such thing. As I mentioned earlier, both of my parents are deceased. When I was released from the hospital, Dax had been with me for days. He was the only person I trusted, felt safe with. He never left my side."

"Where were your friends, Ms. Pierce?

"Unaware of my situation for the most part. My phone was demolished that night, so no one knew who to call and quite honestly, sir," I lace that last word with eager sarcasm, "even when I regained consciousness, I didn't know any of their phone numbers to call them myself. The police department had to get in touch with one of them for me."

"Have you been living with Mr. Cooper since that night?"

I know my body language is critical, but I can't help but feel the defeat. Never in my life have I felt so belittled, so small, degraded. He hasn't come right out and called me a whore, but he's certainly insinuating my lifestyle is less than pristine.

"I've been living with him since I was released from the hospital," I concede.

"Ms. Pierce, it seems as though your sexual lifestyle might make you susceptible to advances such as these."

I stand up, angered by the accusation, raging over my lawyer's objections and the judge yelling order, "Let me tell you something. Prior to that night, I was the head of Regional Bank. I busted my ass getting to the top of that ladder at age thirty-five, and I didn't sleep my way there. Prior to that night, I had never so much as had a rough encounter in the bedroom or out. I wasn't a prime target, not that I believe such thing exists; I was a woman out with my friends. I didn't encourage him; hell, he blindsided me in a dark parking lot, and I sure as hell didn't ask him for rough sex. Regardless of your client's mental state that night or any other, he robbed me. He stole something from me far more valuable than money. He violated the most intimate place on my body – he brutalized it. For you, or anyone else, to insinuate I might have some how brought that on myself because I chose to take a cab home instead of driving after having consumed a few drinks with my girlfriends is asinine.

"As for my relationship with Dax, if I allow him to whip me or paddle me until my ass is as red as a tomato – that is my business because it is consensual. I freely give him my body. Josh Fitz took what didn't belong to him." My hands are balled into fists at my side, shaking from the adrenaline coursing through my veins, my jaw clenching in anger.

"Order! Ms. Pierce, if you don't sit down, I will find you in contempt. Counselor, do you have any further questions for the witness?"

"No, your Honor." The smug look on his face says he received the outcome he hoped to get from me. I knew he was goading me, and I knew he wanted me to crack. He pushed for the scene I just gave him.

I take my place with my attorney, who reaches over and pats my leg. I expected Josh to take the stand, but when the judge asks if there are any additional witnesses, both counsels say no. With closing arguments complete, we sit and wait.

Douglas takes Dax and me to lunch at a little hole in the wall restaurant a couple of blocks. I'm disappointed in myself and simply sit, picking at my food. Dax hasn't said much either, just held my hand or put his arm around me, somehow always touching me. It's reassuring, not sexual.

"Cameron, I know you're beating yourself up for losing your control, but the fact is the jury saw the real you. Women find empowerment in each other, and those women sitting on that jury saw you taking back what is yours, not allowing another man to try to strip you of your dignity. My honest opinion is you won votes just because Rex pissed them off."

I nod my head but don't say anything else.

Arriving back at the courthouse, we avoid the media, or should I say we ignore the media, climbing the steps into the building. My Fish are waiting inside. Moby is all hugged up on Piper, who appears to have been crying, and the others are talking amongst themselves. Shelly is sitting nearby on a bench alone. Starting to pull away to go to her, Dax stops me as Douglas informs him the jury is returning. It's been less than four hours, and they have already made a decision.

"Baby, go with Douglas. I'll get Shelly." I don't let go of his hand as he tries to pull away. He turns back to see why I'm holding him there.

With tear-filled eyes, "I'm scared, Dax. I don't want to go back in alone."

He comes back to me, taking both cheeks in his hands, "It's over sweetheart. No matter what the outcome is, this is done, today. Go with Douglas. I'll be right behind you." He kisses me sweetly before letting my face go. I do as I'm told and follow my attorney back into the courtroom to await the verdict.

When the juror stands to read the verdict, I hold my breath, "We the jury, do hereby find the defendant, guilty of criminal sexual conduct in the first degree."

I let out the breath I've been holding; my shoulders slump as I collapse in the chair. My head finds my hands as I bury my tears in them. People mull all around me, words of congratulations are piled on Douglas as he effortlessly fends off well-wishers, including my friends. The shoulder shaking silent sobs take over. Then he's there. His arms engulf my weary frame, kissing my temple.

CHAPTER THIRTY-SEVEN

The sentencing didn't take place the day Josh was convicted. The hearing for that is today. It's been a couple of weeks since we were last in court. I don't know what to expect today, but as usual, I have my entourage by my side and know I can take on anything life throws at me. There was no stopping the rest of the crew from showing up today. All of Dax's brothers are in attendance; the Wrights are all here as well.

The judge gives Josh the opportunity to say anything he'd like to the court which he refuses. I'm not surprised. He looks rough. When we were in court before, it was obvious someone had gone to painstaking lengths to dress him up. Today, it looks as though the almost thirteen months has taken its toll on him.

I leave knowing Josh Fitz will serve the next twenty years behind bars without the possibility of parole. For the first time in over a year, the weight of that night isn't pressing on my shoulders. I know I will deal with it for the rest of my life, and I will probably be in counseling for years to come. I hope to continue using my nightmare, to help other women and abuse victims, but for today, my load is a little lighter.

CHAPTER THIRTY-EIGHT

Climbing out of the bathtub, I dry myself off. Taking the time to put lotion all over my body, before wrapping up in a big terry cloth robe. Making my way to the closet, I start to change into one of Dax's shirts and put on a pair of panties. It's faint, but I hear the notes from the piano downstairs through the closed bedroom door. He hasn't played since the night months ago when his story stopped. I'm sure he's played at the center but if he has, I haven't heard him.

I creep to the top of the stairs to steal a seat to his concert. "Kitten…" Damn his sixth sense.

"Yeah, baby?" I call back trying to pretend I'm not engrossed in the music.

"Come down here."

I creep down the stairs as quietly as possible. I don't want to disturb the playing but more importantly, I don't want to miss a note. As I round the corner, there is a sea of color, every color calla lilly imaginable covers every surface of the front room. He doesn't make eye contact with me, just continues to play. I wander in the room, listening to the familiar tune, the same life song he played for me before, never missing a note. I make my way through the room, stopping at every stem to admire each flower's unique beauty.

About halfway through the room, the darkness falls in his life, I pause, inhaling the scent of the flower, taking in the power of the notes. I wait for his storm to pass. I listen through the seasons we have shared; completing a circle through the room, looking back at the flowers, it dawns on me. The flowers are my rainbow; the colors he played for me in the hospital, drawing me back to life. I don't know if he knows what he's doing but he's drawing me out of the darkness again, his playing enveloping me a myriad of hues. I'm overcome with emotion – the realization this man has brought so much color into my world and continues to be my angel is more than I can handle. I love listening to every note he taps out but I can't take it. With tears streaming down my face, I cry out, "Butterfly."

Instantly he stops. I'm not even sure I can use a safe word outside of play. Standing he comes to me but before he can reach me, I hold out my hand halting him, whispering, "butterfly…"

He stops, taking my hand in his, smiling. His other hand reaches to my face, wiping away the endless flow of tears. "Baby, stop crying," he coos. For whatever reason, he anticipated my reaction to this, but hell; Dax Cooper anticipates my reaction to everything.

He waits patiently for the tears to stop. With my face puffy red, staring him in the eyes, I watch him lower himself down on one knee. My brain doesn't register what he's doing until he kisses the fingers on my left hand.

"Baby, I loved you before I knew your name but the woman who I loved was just a prelude to the most beautiful version of you that could ever exist. I would be honored if you would be my wife. Let me watch you fill the world with color and spread your wings to fly. Will you marry me?"

Somehow I end up on my knees in front of him. I don't respond verbally, instead I kiss him with a thousand yeses. Pulling back, he slides a beautiful diamond ring on my finger.

The End

ABOUT THE AUTHOR

Stephie currently resides in Greenville, South Carolina with her daughter and two cats.

Made in the USA
Charleston, SC
16 April 2015